PROTECTED BY THE SHADOWS

Also by Helene Tursten

The Inspector Irene Huss Investigations

The Detective Inspector Embla Nyström Investigations

Other titles

PROTECTED BY THE SHADOWS

HELENE TURSTEN

Translation by Marlaine Delargy

SOHO
CRIME

First published in Swedish under the title *I skydd av skuggorna*
Copyright © 2012 by Helene Tursten
Published in agreement with Copenhagen Literary Agency, Copenhagen

English translation copyright © 2017 by Marlaine Delargy

First English translation published in 2017 by
Soho Press
853 Broadway
New York, NY 10003

Library of Congress Cataloging-in-Publication Data
Tursten, Helene, author. | Delargy, Marlaine, translator.
Protected by the shadows / Helene Tursten ; translated by Marlaine Delargy.
Other titles: I skydd av skuggorna. English.
An Irene Huss investigation; 10

ISBN 978-1-61695-973-9
eISBN 978-1-61695-846-6

1. Policewomen—Fiction. 2. Murder—Investigation—Fiction.
3. Gangs—Sweden—Ghoteborg—Fiction. I. Title.
PT9876.3.U55 I313 2017 839.73'8—dc23 2017021389

Printed in the United States of America

10 9 8 7 6 5 4 3 2 1

For Karin A. and Ola C.
because you've been with me all the way

THE DELIVERY CAR moved slowly along Ringövägen as the driver spoke agitatedly on his cell phone.

He ended the call abruptly and tossed the phone onto the passenger seat. The boss had bawled him out because he couldn't find the address, and then the stupid jerk couldn't remember the number. "It's on the piece of paper, Adem! Just read it!" he had yelled. But the scrawled figure could have been two, seven or nine. Where the hell was Kolgruvegatan anyway? And was it too much to expect the boss to install a GPS system in the car? Unfortunately his old cell didn't have one. That was the first thing he planned to buy when he got paid: a new cell. An iPhone.

It was Adem Guzel's third night delivering pizzas, and right now he bitterly regretted taking the job. He had only just acquired his driver's license, and in two weeks he would be starting his final year of high school. He had spent the summer in Turkey; it had been good to catch up with family and friends, but there had been no opportunity to work. At least this gave him the chance to earn some money before he went back to school, plus he got to drive. The owner of the pizzeria was an old friend of his uncle's, and it was this uncle who had brokered the deal. Unfortunately the pizzeria was in Brunnsbo, a part of the city Adem had never even visited.

He tried to cheer himself up with the thought that this was his last delivery of the night. The pizzeria stayed open until 11:00, which meant he would get back more or less at closing time. If he could find the goddamn address, of course.

He peered at the street signs, but it was too dark to see properly. In several places the signs were missing, or were twisted so that he couldn't read the names. Some were covered in black spray paint. And it had started raining again, which didn't exactly help.

An old VW pickup behind him signaled, wanting to pass. The driver looked like an old hippie, with a floppy hat and a long grey beard. He gave Adem the finger as he shot past. Adem swore and was about to put his foot on the gas, but he changed his mind when he spotted a street sign that seemed legible. He stopped the car and leaned over toward the passenger window. Kolgruveg-atan—*yes!* He might manage to make the delivery after all. He made a ninety-degree turn onto the street. He loved the sound of screeching tires and the smell of burning rubber. Car chases. *No one's going to catch me*, he thought, laughing to himself. Then he slowed down and checked out the low buildings, trying to see the numbers.

The dark, desolate area seemed to consist mainly of run-down blocks and storage depots. Most of the street lamps had been smashed, but a few faded signs informed him that he was passing a car shop, some kind of import company, and a paint shop. Everything was derelict; no commercial activity seemed to have taken place here for several years. Adem felt like he was driving through a ghost town. A chill made the hairs on the back of his neck stand on end, and the sense of being in a horror film was steadily growing. He let out a yell, his heart pounding like crazy, as something swept by in the beam of his headlights. But it was only a large black bird, probably a crow.

A street lamp that was actually working illuminated the hull of an old boat propped up on bricks ahead of him. It was probably *The Flying Dutchman*, Adem thought in an attempt to dispel his fear with humor. Beyond the boat he could just make out the black surface of Göta River. This was the old docks; no one lived out here. Who would call and order a kebab pizza with extra sauce late on a Saturday night? No one, no one at all. He tried to breathe calmly, but panic was making his stomach contract into an ice-cold lump. What if he were driving straight into a trap? The place was deserted! Best get out of there right away.

Adem stopped the car to turn around, but realized the street was too narrow, so he started backing up. On one side was a high fence topped with barbed wire; the iron gates were almost nine feet tall, with a faded, illegible yellow sign on one of them. The asphalt in front of a single-story wooden building was strewn with trash. Suddenly Adem thought he saw a flicker of light at one of the filthy windows; there must be people around after all. He slowed down, searching for a number. Had he found the right address at last?

All at once a heavy door was flung wide open, crashing back against the wall. Adem braked instinctively, wondering what the hell was going on.

A blinding light streamed from the doorway, then he heard a loud roar. The roar turned into a heart-rending scream, and a man staggered out into the yard, arms flailing as he tried to run toward the gates. He dropped onto all fours, his cries growing weaker by the second.

Adem sat in the car, frozen to the spot as he watched the burning man's death struggle. He couldn't tear his eyes away from the horrific sight. When the man finally fell silent and collapsed on the ground, there was an eerie calm. Adem could hear the crackle of flames, and the acrid smell of burned flesh filled the air.

The car jolted and shot backward as Adem released the brake pedal and reversed toward the main road at full speed. Two motorbikes were traveling slowly along Ringövägen, and Adem avoided a collision by a hair's breadth. The bike he almost hit was on the wrong side of the road; it was sheer luck that he didn't crash into it.

His heart was pounding so hard he felt as if it was trying to hammer its way out of his chest. Waves of panic flooded his body, and all he wanted to do was floor the accelerator and get away. He didn't care where he ended up, as long as he was as far from Ringön as possible. He managed to suppress his flight impulse and pulled over. With shaking fingers he picked up his cell phone and called the emergency number. Almost immediately a professional female voice asked how she could help him.

"He's . . . he's on fire! He's . . . on fire!" Adem managed to sob.

THE HUSS FAMILY was celebrating. As one might expect, given their connections to the restaurant business, the table was adorned with artistically folded linen napkins and flickering candles, along with a range of glasses and cutlery to go with each course. Needless to say the menu was pretty special too, thanks to the two chefs in the family.

Krister raised his glass and cleared his throat. "Right now we have plenty to celebrate. Jenny, your mom and I are so pleased that you've completed your training to become a chef, and found an apartment and a job. Congratulations!"

Everyone joined in the toast, sipping vintage Champagne, while Jenny stuck to alcohol-free cider. When she was a teenager she had followed a strict vegan diet. Her training in vegetarian cuisine had softened her approach somewhat, but she still refused to touch alcohol.

Krister allowed the delicious sparkling wine to linger on his palate for a moment.

"And of course we want to congratulate Katarina and Felipe, even though it's been a month since you got engaged. We wish you every happiness!"

Once again the glasses were raised.

"And on Wednesday Irene and I celebrated our silver wedding anniversary. Twenty-five years. And you've been with us for twenty-four of those years," Krister went on, winking at his daughters.

That wasn't quite true; the twins had been there throughout their marriage. Irene recalled the wedding photo with a shudder; she had been seven months pregnant, and had looked like the battleship *Potemkin* in the full-length shot. She hadn't framed it, but had chosen a close-up where she and Krister were both smiling into the camera. We were so young, she often thought when she glanced at the picture. She had been almost a year younger than the twins were now when she became a mother. Somehow they had managed to steer their little family through a quarter of a century; it hadn't always been easy, but now it seemed as if things were beginning to fall into place for all of them—not least Krister.

"My turn, I think," Irene said, smiling at her husband. He rolled his eyes, but couldn't hide his pleasure.

"We all want to congratulate you, my darling, on becoming the owner of Glady's. You've run the place for many years, so I have no doubt that it will be a success. Here's to you, my love!"

With that she kissed Krister on the lips as the others whistled and cheered.

"Why did Månsson suddenly decided to sell the place to you?" Jenny asked when things calmed down.

Krister's expression immediately grew serious.

"He didn't have a choice. I had no idea, but apparently he gambled, and he was heavily in debt. That was the reason behind the divorce, and that was also why he moved here just under two years ago. He must have gotten a good price for the restaurants he owned in Stockholm, because he was able to pay off his debts and buy both Glady's and Sjökrogen. Or maybe he borrowed some of the money . . . I don't know."

"So now he's sold both restaurants here in Göteborg in order to pay off new debts?" Katarina said.

"Presumably. He had some counseling to help him beat his addiction back in the spring, and he seems to have sorted out his finances; he and his new girlfriend . . . what was her name . . . Jeanette Stenberg, that's it. She worked as head waitress at Glady's for a while before she took over at Sjökrogen, that's how I know her. Nice girl."

Krister took a sip of Champagne before going on:

"Anyway, Janne and Jeanette are moving to Majorca on Monday. He called me yesterday to say goodbye. He was still packing and I was working, so we didn't even manage to get together for a beer."

"What are they going to do over there?" Irene was curious.

She didn't know Jan-Erik Månsson very well; he was an old friend of Krister's. They had worked well together in Stockholm, and had become friends. Irene and Krister had met while she was doing her police training in Stockholm, and she had seen Janne a few times. He was a friendly, likeable, outgoing guy. When Irene completed her training she wanted to move back to Göteborg, and Krister joined her. Janne worked overseas for a few years, then returned to the capital where he had a brilliant career. A lot of people were surprised when he suddenly sold his two-star restaurants and relocated to Göteborg, his hometown, following his divorce.

"They're going to run a restaurant in an upmarket

hotel in a small town called Puerto Pollensa. Apparently the owner is an old friend of Janne's," Krister said.

It was time to serve the starter. Krister headed for the kitchen to grill Jenny's herb and tofu stuffed tomatoes and the omnivores' lobster, almost tripping over Egon, who suddenly appeared, moving at top speed.

"Egon!" Krister exclaimed, saving himself by grabbing hold of the doorpost.

The little dachshund stopped dead. In his mouth he was carrying his beloved blue ball, which he had inherited from Sammie, the family's first dog. He sat down and tilted his head to one side, his tail swishing to and fro as he kept his eyes expectantly fixed on his master. Naturally Krister melted as usual. He bent down and picked up the dog.

"Not now, little man. Later. Let's find you some food first," he said, burying his nose in Egon's soft coat.

The word "later" wasn't part of Egon's vocabulary, but he heard "food" very clearly and started yapping. It was one of his favorite words.

"I'll come and feed Egon so you can concentrate on dinner," Irene said, getting to her feet.

THROUGH THE HALF-OPEN bedroom door, Irene watched as Egon scrambled up onto the bed. He belched a couple of times, then rolled over on his back with his paws in the air. His meal of dog biscuits mixed with morsels of tender saddle of venison had obviously been delicious; he had eaten every scrap and licked the bowl clean.

Egon fell asleep on the bed as the conversation and laughter continued in the living room.

THE INSISTENT SOUND of the telephone woke Irene early on Sunday morning.

"Leave it," Krister murmured, trying to pull her close.

"I can't. It might be important," Irene said, fumbling for the receiver. Her head felt heavy, and she knew she had drunk more than usual the previous evening. But it had been a family party; they didn't get together very often now that the girls were grown up and living their own lives. It was hard to find an opportunity when everyone was available at the same time.

A glance at the alarm clock told her she had slept for less than four hours, so it was hardly surprising she wasn't firing on all cylinders.

"Irene Huss," she said, trying to sound brighter than she felt.

"Morning—it's Fredrik. I'm really sorry, but you're going to have to come in today," said Detective Inspector Fredrik Stridh, as full of life as ever.

"But it's my day off. Krister and I celebrated our silver wedding anniversary yesterday." Irene didn't even try to hide the yawn that made her jawbone crack.

"So you're a little the worse for wear? I do understand, but there's no one else. Hannu, Sara and Jonny are still on vacation. I've checked the roster; Jonny and Sara are due back tomorrow, but I can't get hold of either of them. I'm afraid you're the only member of the team who's available."

Krister had been right; she shouldn't have answered the phone.

"Okay. What's it about?" she said with an audible sigh.

"There was a barbecue at Gothia MC's old place out at Ringön late last night," Fredrik replied.

"A barbecue?"

"They decided to flame-grill some guy."

AFTER A HOT shower, three large cups of coffee and a cheese roll, Irene got into the car and set off for Hisingen and Ringön. There was hardly any traffic at eight o'clock on a Sunday morning, so the trip into Nordstan and over the Göta Bridge was fast. The light drizzle enveloping the city was unlikely to inspire the residents to leap out of bed at this hour.

The air was still warm in spite of the fact that it was the middle of August. In just a few weeks the first real autumn winds would sweep in across the west coast. The thought of fall made Irene sigh, but it was a sigh of contentment; she really liked that time of year.

She and Krister had been back at work for only a week following a fantastic summer vacation. They had taken the car and traveled around northern France, staying in charming hotels in small towns and villages. They had celebrated their silver wedding anniversary in advance by booking a night in a top hotel right in the center of Paris, where they had eaten a lavish dinner in a ridiculously expensive restaurant; she couldn't even remember the name of the place. They had drunk fine wines and more than one glass of Champagne during the course of the evening, and the next day she had felt more or less the same as she did right now. Perhaps slightly worse, in fact. But it had been worth it.

It suddenly occurred to Irene that she could be stopped and breathalyzed by uniformed colleagues. There was no guarantee that she was under the limit. What had she been thinking of, getting in the car? She slowed down and tried to focus. Kolgruvegatan wasn't the easiest street to find, even though she had been out there several times in the past.

It had been a while since she'd seen Fredrik Stridh. The two of them had been co-workers in the Violent Crimes Unit back in the day, but he had been transferred to the Organized Crimes Unit. They worked on long-term projects and monitored criminal gangs in the city but were not involved in homicide inquiries. When incidents of that kind came up, they contacted the unit where Irene had worked for almost twenty years.

"WE HAVEN'T IDENTIFIED the victim yet; there's no wallet, no ID card, no cell phone. However, we don't think it's a straightforward mugging. No one saw or heard anything, apart from the pizza delivery kid, and he only saw the guy stagger out of the building in flames. He didn't see who was responsible for setting fire to the poor schmuck," Fredrik said. "Even if we assume the dead man is a gang member, it's a hell of a way to die."

Irene and Fredrik were standing in the yard outside the dilapidated building that had once been Gothia MC's base in Hisingen. The CSIs were busy packing up

the tent that had sheltered the scene of the crime from last
night's rain. The body had just been removed; the fire had
burned the outline of the dead man into the asphalt. The
stench of charred flesh still pervaded the whole area,
making Irene's stomach turn over. In an attempt to dis-
tract herself, she gazed around the yard. A faded yellow
sign with red writing hung on the tall gates: TRESPASSERS
WILL BE SHOT! SURVIVORS WILL BE SHOT AGAIN! BANDIDOS.
The motorbike gang known as Bandidos had used this
place for a few years before handing it over to Gothia MC,
another gang.

The yard was around two thousand square feet, covered in old, cracked asphalt, with weeds sprouting
through the gaps. Mysterious piles hidden beneath tarps
lay here and there; it was difficult to work out what they
might be, but the odd protruding piece looked like scaf-
folding. Maybe a building firm used the yard for storage,
Irene thought. The building itself was a run-down
wooden structure with a rusty corrugated metal roof, but
as they walked in Irene realized it was pretty spacious.

While they were checking the place out, Fredrik gave
her a heads up on how the serious crime scene was
looking in Göteborg.

Apparently Gothia MC had suffered serious problems
both during and after the major gang war of 2008–2009.
The conflict had raged between a number of notorious
biker clubs and two substantial gangs, one of which was
the Gangster Lions, who had tried to move in. Gothia
MC and the Gangster Lions had been bitter enemies for
a long time when it came to drug dealing territory, which
meant that both were drawn into the war. Several members had been injured or killed. Things had improved a

little when Gothia MC's internal organization started to splinter and members began to leave. The decimated group had withdrawn to a small place outside Gråbo to lick their wounds. They erected high fences all around the plot and set up CCTV cameras. Over the past few years they had kept a low profile as they tried to build up their reputation and expand membership. They were slowly beginning to regain their share of the drugs market. According to rumors, they were also active within the protection racket, which Bandidos and above all their subchapter X-team had run in the past. However, as X-team had virtually been eradicated in the Göteborg area, Gothia MC had taken over. Fredrik had also heard a whisper that their new leader, Per "The Champ" Lindström, had tentacles inside the construction business.

When Irene asked what he knew about Per Lindström, Fredrik told her that he was a thirty-eight-year-old ex-amateur boxer with a rap sheet as long as the distance between Gothia MC's old base and the new one outside Gråbo. He was a fearless, ruthless, habitual criminal who had done time for everything from narcotics dealing to grievous bodily harm. Irene remembered that he had been accused of homicide, or at least of having been an accessory in a homicide, but the main witness had vanished without a trace; four years on, there was still no sign of him. The other witnesses had suddenly been struck by a total loss of memory, and the prosecutor had been left with no choice but to drop the whole case.

Irene and Fredrik were standing in what used to be the club's main room. The small windows were thick with dirt, hardly letting in any light. The place was damp, and the smell of rat droppings mingled with the stench of gasoline and burned flesh. A large dark stain on the cement floor showed where the killers had poured gasoline over the victim and set him on fire. A hunting knife had been found next to the stain; the horn handle boasted a grinning skull, and on the razor-sharp steel blade the letter *P* had been engraved in a Gothic style. Both Irene and Fredrik knew this kind of knife was popular among bikers and probably belonged to the victim. The CSIs had also secured several bloodstains, suggesting that the man had been beaten up before the torching.

A rough bar counter made of ordinary planks of wood ran along one wall; not the most sophisticated carpentry, Irene thought, but it had served its purpose. Countless bottles and glasses had left marks on the untreated surface.

Behind the bar CSI Matti Berggren found an empty plastic container, which stank of gasoline. It looked brand new. The discovery brought a blissful smile to his lips. "Yes!" he rejoiced, carefully placing the container in a large bag. Fredrik shook his head and expressed some concerns regarding the mental health of his colleague, but Irene had no such reservations. If Matti thought the container was important, then it was. He was probably hoping to find the killer's fingerprints. Irene had great confidence in the young technician who had replaced Svante Malm, their oracle for so many years. Matti had also been living with Irene's colleague Sara Persson for the past six months, thus providing further evidence of his sound judgment.

There was no other furniture in the room, apart from the bar. The place looked totally abandoned. However, the floor was littered with cigarette stubs, empty beer cans, broken glass, pizza boxes and all kinds of crap. *It's not going to be easy to find any trace of the killer or killers in this garbage dump*, Irene thought wearily. Apart from the brand-new gasoline container, of course.

"So Gothia MC is flourishing; how about the Gangster Lions?" Irene asked.

"They're doing even better. The Gangster Lions and their subchapter the Pumas are growing very fast, but recently there have been several run-ins with other gangs wanting to muscle in on the market. They're all trying to mark their territory," Fredrik said.

An officer appeared at a small back door.

"We've found something interesting," he said.

Irene and Fredrik followed him into a yard that was similar to the one at the front, although this was an inner courtyard, surrounded by dilapidated wooden buildings. Once again piles of what looked like construction materials were covered by tarps. The officer went over to one of these piles and folded back the tarp to reveal a spotless, gleaming Harley-Davidson. Fredrik let out a low whistle.

"Hells Angels, I presume," Irene said.

"Possibly, but not necessarily; there are other biker gangs that ride Harleys."

"Have you managed to find out who the owner is?" Irene asked the colleague who had made the discovery.

"It's registered to a Patrik Karlsson, aged twenty-one. That's all we know about him so far, but I've got something else to show you." He led the way to one of the buildings surrounding the courtyard; when he pushed down the handle, the door swung open on well-oiled hinges.

"Someone didn't want anyone else to hear when they went through this door," he said.

They walked into a room that stank of mold. There was a good half inch of water on the floor because the rain was coming in through holes in the roof. On the opposite side was a larger doorway. The uniformed officer opened the door—once again without a sound. He pointed to the street beyond.

"Manufakturgatan."

"Were these doors locked when you got here?" Irene asked.

"No. The key was in this one; the same key fits both locks, and they're pretty new."

"So someone has gone to the trouble of fixing up a smart emergency exit through the back door. Or a discreet entrance. I'm guessing that's how our killer or killers made their escape," Fredrik said.

"Could it have been Gothia MC who fitted the new locks?" Irene wondered.

"Possibly; we'll have to ask them. And find out if they're missing a member by the name of Patrik Karlsson," Fredrik replied.

It turned out to be much easier than they had expected to get ahold of Gothia MC's leader, Per "The Champ" Lindström, since he was actually in custody in a police cell. With a broad grin, the duty officer confirmed that Lindström had been sitting there since 10:25 the previous night. At 9:55 he and his second-in-command Jorma Kinnunen had been stopped by a routine traffic patrol on Gråbovägen, just to the southwest of Olofstorp. The brand new BMW was striking as it came zooming along at around 25 mph over the speed limit, and when the cops saw who was in the car, they suddenly became even more interested in taking a closer look.

Per Lindström was driving. The cops drew their guns and ordered the two men to get out of the car and put their hands in the air. They had reluctantly complied, with Lindström loudly protesting that they were being subjected to police harassment. When the cops patted the two men down, they discovered they were both wearing bulletproof vests, and a search of the car revealed a small semi-automatic gun that resembled a homemade Uzi, which turned out to be fully loaded. The magazine held twenty-five bullets instead of thirty-two, but the caliber was a 9 x 19mm Parabellum, just like the standard weapon. It was hidden under the front passenger seat. Needless to say, both men denied all knowledge of the gun; they had absolutely no idea how it came to be there. Someone must have planted it in order to frame them. They also claimed that neither of them owned the BMW, which turned out to be true; it had false plates. When a check was run on the vehicle identification number, it transpired that the car had been stolen from the Kungshöjd area of central Göteborg the previous night.

When Lindström was asked to blow into the breathalyzer, he refused. He and Kinnunen were taken to the custody suite, where he was forced to provide a blood sample. The officers who had picked him up could smell booze, and hoped that he would be charged not only with speeding, but with driving under the influence. Needless to say, illegal possession of a firearm would also be added to the charge sheet.

• • •

"ACCORDING TO THE record, Patrik Karlsson is missing two fingers on his left hand as a result of an accident with a firework ten years ago. I've spoken to the pathologist, and they've confirmed that the victim is also missing two fingers. So we can be pretty sure it's Karlsson," Fredrik said.

"That's strange. So he was a member of Gothia MC, and he was murdered in their old HQ. If this is an internal matter, wouldn't Gothia MC have made sure the killing took place as far from their territory as possible?" Irene said.

They were waiting for 1:00 P.M., when they would be allowed to interview Per Lindström. Meanwhile Fredrik told her that Lindström and Kinnunen had met when they were in the same jail. When Kinnunen was released a few months after Lindström, the newly elected biker gang leader brought his associate into the inner circle. Kinnunen enjoyed the status of second-in-command from the start. He didn't come from a biker gang; his background was as part of an immigrant gang involved in serious crime. His old "friends" were all locked up for narcotics offenses, and several of them would be deported when they had served their time, which meant the gang would be dispersed. If there was anyone who knew the narcotics scene inside out, it was Kinnunen, which was why he hadn't needed to go through a subchapter to gain access to Gothia MC. He had had the perfect qualifications and the expertise that the gang and its leader required. Fredrik smiled meaningfully.

"To be honest, the Uzi surprises me. The bosses don't usually carry guns. It's the subordinates' job to protect the leaders. That's one of the things they do in order to be accepted into the club, and to be allowed to put on the much longed-for vest," he added pensively.

"Speaking of which, both Lindström and Kinnunen were wearing bulletproof vests, which suggests they thought they were at risk of being shot. Could Kinnunen have been armed in order to protect Lindström?"

"That's not impossible. The gun was underneath the passenger seat; he probably didn't have time to throw it out of the window when the patrol car appeared. They were driving too fast."

PER LINDSTRÖM LOOKED anything but happy. In fact he looked distinctly pissed off, with good reason. If he was convicted on all counts, he would be looking at a long jail sentence. Fredrik and Irene had agreed in advance that she would lead the interview; he would take over at a later stage if necessary.

The gangster reeked of sweat and stale booze. He was wearing a T-shirt with Gothia MC's emblem on the chest; the same emblem was tattooed on his right forearm, and more or less every inch that Irene could see of his massive body was covered in tattoos. A colorful snake wound its way around his neck, ending up by his left ear. It showed up clearly on his shaven head. The snake was a skillful piece of work, but the rest of the tattoos were of varying quality.

The trend for inking was one of the best things that had happened as far as police were concerned, Irene thought. It didn't take much to identify a perp with the help of tattoos; a decent photograph was enough. Besides they were pretty difficult to hide. Per Lindström would need to wear a burka if he didn't want anyone to see his artwork.

Irene introduced herself; Lindström's expression barely changed. He glanced at her, then fixed his gaze on the wall behind her.

"I have to inform you right away that I will not be asking you any questions relating to the incident yesterday evening, when you and Jorma Kinnunen were picked up. Other colleagues will be handling that interview," Irene began.

Something flickered in the gangster's expression, but he remained motionless, arms folded across his chest. His bulging biceps were impressive, which of course was the point of the pose.

"We are dealing with a far more serious matter," Irene went on calmly.

Lindström snorted and gave her a supercilious look, making it clear that she might as well give up on her pathetic attempts to get him to talk. Irene ignored him.

"Homicide," she said quietly.

The man opposite blinked involuntarily. Irene didn't say another word; she simply stared at the gang leader. He didn't say anything either for a while, but eventually he turned his pale blue eyes on her.

"I don't know anything about fucking homicide," he spat.

"Okay, but right now we're only interested in hearing what you know about a man who was killed last night. After you and Jorma had been picked up by the police, please note, so neither of you is a suspect."

At those words Lindström relaxed a fraction. He realized there was something behind this conversation; he just couldn't work out what it was. His hangover probably contributed to his carelessness. Under normal circumstances he would have remained tight-lipped. Or perhaps his curiosity had been aroused.

"Who's been killed?" he asked.

"I'll tell you in a minute, but first of all I'd like to know whether Gothia MC still owns the property on Kolgruvegatan?"

"No—we've had a new base for a couple of years."

"Do you have any idea who uses the old place nowadays?"

"Nope."

"Was it Gothia MC who changed the lock on the door leading to Manufakturgatan?"

Lindström snorted again and did his best to look totally uninterested, but after a brief silence he couldn't help himself.

"So who's the dead guy?"

"A member of your gang: Patrik Karlsson."

The gang leader raised his eyebrows and seemed genuinely surprised.

"Patte? Are you kidding me?"

"Absolutely not. If Patte is Patrik Karlsson, who was a full member of Gothia MC, then he's the homicide victim."

Lindström nodded. Irene could see the cogs turning as his brain tried to deal with the news of Patrik Karlsson's death."

"Who shot him?" he asked.

"He wasn't shot." The eyebrows were raised again, and this time he didn't even try to pretend he wasn't interested.

"So how the fuck did he die?"

"He was beaten up and then set on fire while he was

still alive," Irene replied, keeping her tone neutral as she tried to suppress the memory of the nauseating stench in the air, the outline of the body burned into the asphalt.

"Jesus Christ!"

"Yes, it was a terrible sight."

Per Lindström sat in silence for a while, staring at a point above Irene's head. Eventually he spoke. "This has nothing to do with us. It must have been some personal crap."

"Possibly, but it happened at Gothia MC's former base on Kolgruvegatan. He met his killers inside the building, but staggered outside after they'd set fire to him. He burned to death in the yard."

"Fucking hell."

Once again the cogs in Lindström's hungover brain began to turn, very slowly. Irene sensed a change in him; the account of how Karlsson had died had told him something.

"Have you any idea who might have murdered Patrik Karlsson?" she asked.

Lindström merely shook his head, a distant look in his eyes. Whatever had occurred to him, he had no intention of sharing it with the police.

IN SUBSEQUENT INTERVIEWS, Per Lindström claimed that he and Jorma Kinnunen had been test driving the BMW. A young guy had offered him the chance to buy it, saying that he couldn't afford such an expensive car. No, he had no reason to doubt what the guy said. No, he couldn't remember his name. As for how the gun came to be in the car—that was a complete mystery. Presumably the owner of the BMW had hidden it under the seat. The level of alcohol in his blood was easily explained; he had misjudged the strength of a drink his wife had served him before dinner. Combined with the speeding, it would cost him his license for a few months, but nothing more.

Kinnunen refused to speak, maintaining a sullen silence throughout all attempts to question him.

Irene sighed as she closed down her computer after reading through the transcripts of the interviews with both men. Even if they knew or suspected the reason behind the murder of Patrik Karlsson, there was no way they would ever say a word about it to the cops.

"So I come back from my well-earned vacation, and I walk straight into a case involving the worst criminal elements in Göteborg!" Detective Inspector Jonny Blom exclaimed, pretending to shudder in horror.

He was sitting with the others around the table looking tanned and pretty happy because there were freshly baked cinnamon buns on offer. However, he couldn't resist commenting on Irene's account of the weekend's macabre homicide on Kolgruvegatan.

"Welcome back," Superintendent Tommy Persson said, raising his coffee cup in a mock toast.

"Thanks a bunch—it's my first day, and already the mafia are in a killing mood. Makes me feel insecure— who's our health and safety officer?" Jonny said, looking around the table.

DI Sara Persson was sitting next to him. Ever since she joined the team there had been jokes about the fact that she and Tommy had the same surname, and Jonny liked to mention nepotism at every opportunity.

The latest reorganization of the police in Västra Göta-land had produced two positive changes, in addition to the name change: the Organized Crimes Unit had moved up one floor in police HQ, and Tommy was made super-intendent on a permanent basis. His predecessor, Efva Thylqvist, had resigned after the attack on her the pre-vious year. She had been left with long-term repercussions; among other issues, her voice was hoarse and rasping following the violent attempt to strangle her. Her secret affair with Tommy Persson had also come to an end. He had been devastated to learn that she had been sleeping with another colleague, and the fact that the man in question was a superior officer made it so much worse. Irene couldn't suppress a sigh of relief when she heard that Thylqvist wasn't coming back. Apparently she had transferred to the National Crime Unit in Stockholm; Irene had no idea what she was doing there.

Tommy had asked Irene if she wanted to take over his role as deputy, but after careful consideration she had turned down his offer—mainly because she didn't enjoy admin, but also because she was very happy in her present post. She preferred action and variety to being stuck behind a desk. She also struggled with spelling and written communication. These days it was called dyslexia. When she was in school she had been dismissed as stupid and lazy.

Hannu Rauhala had taken over as Tommy's deputy, which turned out to be an excellent move. Hannu was a master when it came to combing the archives and producing information that no one else could find. How he did it had remained a mystery over the years. He would be back from his vacation the following week, and Irene knew that he was much missed.

"We're conducting this investigation in collaboration with the Organized Crimes Unit, and in particular with our old friend and former colleague Fredrik, of course," Irene said.

"Excellent. He has detailed knowledge of what goes on among Göteborg's gangs," Tommy said, topping up his coffee.

"He can take over the whole thing if you ask me," Jonny muttered, grabbing the last bun.

Tommy smiled, then grew serious as he began to go through each person's tasks for the day. As usual it was a matter of gathering all available facts about the victim and the crime as quickly as possible.

• • •

DURING THE COURSE of Monday morning, a young wannabe tough guy walked into the police station and demanded to "talk to the fuckers who've pulled in the boss." It was some time before the duty officer understood that the fat teenager in the hoodie wanted to speak to the police officers who were investigating the Per Lindström case.

The boy was doing his best to look as arrogant as he sounded, but his eyes were darting all over the place, and his forehead was shiny with perspiration. No teenage criminal feels comfortable in a building crawling with cops. He also realized that this visit was going to cost him a year or two in the care of the state, but it was part of his duties; the reward made it worthwhile.

He was taken to an interview room and left to sweat for an hour or so. His name was Kevin Berg. He was seventeen years old, and a member of the Desperados, as the black and white emblem on the back of his hoodie confirmed. It was around sixteen inches in diameter, with a smoking gun in the center. The Desperados were a suburban gang made up of teenage boys who aspired to gain entry into Gothia MC. Kevin already had a record for stealing cars and mopeds, possession of cannabis for personal use and helping to break into a tobacconist's shop.

He confessed that he was the one who had stolen the BMW on Friday night. The following day he had contacted Per Lindström, offering to sell him a top car. Needless to say, he didn't mention that the car was stolen. At first Kevin stated that the two Gothia MC bosses had come over to his place to inspect and test drive the car, but when he was asked where exactly Per Lindström's own car was parked right now, he couldn't come up with an answer. After a while he changed his story. In the new version two older associates had helped Kevin, driving the BMW over to Gothia MC's base outside Gråbo. No, he didn't know their names, but he was sure they both had a driver's license. One had driven his own car, the other the BMW. When they arrived, Kevin had handed the BMW over to the prospective buyer; they agreed that Lindström would call him on Sunday to settle the deal. That didn't happen, of course, because Per Lindström and Jorma Kinnunen were picked up by the police.

He knew nothing about the gun; the owner must have hidden it. Since the legal owner of the car was a seventy-one-year-old retired female dentist who had never featured in any criminal investigation, this seemed unlikely.

Disappointingly there were no fingerprints on the gun; it had been meticulously wiped clean. Jorma Kinnunen didn't even bother trying to explain why he had been wearing thin leather gloves when the car was pulled over. He simply gave the officer who asked a blood-chilling look.

Since Kevin was under eighteen, he would be given a reduced sentence if he was convicted, meaning that he would serve only half. When he came out he would either become a full member of Gothia MC, or at least be among the first of those eligible to be admitted. The Desperados were all between thirteen and eighteen years old, and carried out the riskiest enterprises, particularly any activity that could carry a jail term, such as drug dealing. Gothia MC distributed narcotics to the Desperados, who were then responsible for selling to addicts on the streets, which was where the greatest danger of being arrested lay. The teenagers were prepared to take their chances in order to win the greatest prize of all: entry into Gothia MC.

On Monday evening Per Lindström and Jorma Kinnunen were able to walk out as free men, although Lindström had had his driver's license revoked, and had been charged with driving under the influence. Everyone involved in the case was asking one question: Where had the two men been going in the stolen car, wearing bulletproof vests and carrying a fully loaded semi-automatic gun? They would probably never know.

KRISTER HUSS HAD increased his hours when he became the owner of Glady's. The time he devoted to admin was still sufficient, but an extra pair of hands was needed in the kitchen, so he worked every Monday evening and every fourth weekend to give the other chefs a decent amount of time off. When Krister was in the office, Egon accompanied him to the restaurant and settled down in his basket. When the little dog got bored, he reminded his master of his existence, and Krister would take a break. They usually went for a walk in Lorensberg Park, or around Heden center. It suited both of them, and Krister thought it was good he had a reason to get some exercise at regular intervals. Egon didn't have to be alone for long on Monday evenings when Krister was in the kitchen, because Irene would make an effort to get home early.

Both Irene and Krister were fitter since moving to the city center. This was particularly true in Krister's case. They had sold the old Volvo and now had only one car, a Renault Megane that was in pretty good condition. They took the tram or the bus only if it was pouring rain; the car spent most of its time in their private parking space, but when Krister was working in the kitchen he

always drove because he rarely got home before midnight. It took him around fifteen minutes to walk to the
restaurant, while the police station was about half an
hour away for Irene. Sometimes she cycled and was at her
desk twenty minutes after leaving home. The return
journey was significantly more taxing, as she had to
climb a long, steep hill up to Guldheden. She usually
went straight to the bathroom and took a hot shower,
followed by a blast of cold water to wake her up. Cycling
was the perfect form of exercise; it didn't require any
extra time, and it cost nothing. Together with two jiujitsu classes a week, it kept her fit. The disadvantage was
that as a cyclist in Göteborg during rush hour, she felt
like a living air filter. In spite of the fact that she had
never smoked, she had a suspicion that her lungs would
eventually become completely blocked up by filth and
exhaust fumes.

Krister drove to Glady's on Monday; it was normally the quietest evening of the week, but tonight they
were fully booked. A large party was celebrating with a
six-course tasting menu and a selection of wines to
accompany each course. Jenny had helped him to come
up with vegetarian alternatives to each dish. He was so
proud of his daughter and her choice of profession. No
doubt in the future all restaurants would have chefs who
could prepare gourmet vegetarian food, but right now
Glady's was on the forefront.

He began to sing, loudly and out of tune, but it didn't
matter because the kitchen was buzzing with activity,
drowning out his efforts. His colleague Ingrid grabbed a
bottle of Pernod and headed for a table where the diners

who had ordered flambéed fillet of beef were waiting expectantly. A tap on Krister's shoulder interrupted his warbling. It was Anton Fritzell, who had recently joined the team. He was a hard worker and a phenomenal fish chef. Right now he looked terribly embarrassed.

"I'm so sorry Krister, but I have a problem."

"Anything I can do to help?"

"Linda called; she's locked herself out of the apartment, and the car keys are inside. She's got the kids with her. Could I possibly borrow your car and nip home? I cycled in today, so—"

"No problem. We're busy, so it's in my interest to have you back as quickly as possible," Krister said with a smile.

He asked Anton to stir the sauce while he went to the changing room to fetch his car key. When Krister returned, Anton looked relieved and thanked him profusely before dashing out of the door without bothering to change.

Krister hummed to himself as he reached for a pot of fresh thyme. Before he touched it the building was rocked by a deafening explosion. The large windows overlooking the yard shattered, and the kitchen was showered in fragments of glass. For a fraction of a second no one moved as they froze in shock; when someone started screaming the others regained the power of movement. Krister raced toward the reinforced back door.

"Anton!" he yelled.

He ran outside; his own car was ablaze, and the flames had spread to the car parked beside it. Thick, billowing smoke made his eyes and airway sting. A few yards from the burning cars, he saw a body lying motionless on the ground.

His voice thick with tears, Krister mumbled, "Oh my God! This is my fault . . . My . . ."

He tried to hold his breath as he rushed over to Anton. The heat was almost unbearable, but he forced himself to keep going. Tears were pouring down his face now, and the pain in his lungs was agonizing. Several of the staff joined him, and together they managed to move Anton away from the cars. They were all coughing and gasping for air. Anton was bleeding from two deep wounds in his head. His eyelids were twitching, but he didn't respond when they spoke to him.

After a few minutes the small backyard was illuminated by the flashing blue lights of the emergency services. The ambulance was first on the scene. The paramedics confirmed that Anton was alive but unconscious. They informed his horrified colleagues that he had a broken arm and trauma to the head, then sped away to Sahlgrenska Hospital.

JONNY BLOM AND Irene stood side by side in the pale light of dawn, contemplating the blackened vehicles. The nauseating stench of burning at the scene of the crime was starting to become routine, Irene thought gloomily. She was deeply shaken by what had happened, but at the same time she couldn't really process the fact that something like this had affected her family. *Why? Why?* The question went around and around in her head, but she resolutely pushed it aside and tried to concentrate on what was in front of her. A glimmer of light in the darkness was that Anton's injuries weren't life-threatening. He had a concussion, but the doctor Irene had spoken to had assured her it wasn't serious. They would operate on his arm later that day; the break was complex, but the doctor promised he would make a full recovery. It would be several weeks before he was able to work, however, so Krister had lost a full-time chef. Not a good start for a new owner.

Jonny wandered around the wreckage, yawning widely. He nodded to himself several times before turning back to Irene.

"This is going to take more than one cup of coffee. By the way, does Krister have life insurance?"

"No," she replied; his question had surprised her to say the least.

"Good. In that case it probably wasn't you who planted the bomb under his car," he said with a broad grin.

"Very funny!" Irene snapped. This really wasn't the moment for humor. She was worn out after a sleepless night, and her emotions were all over the place. And Jonny was making jokes! With great self-control she quashed the impulse to kick his fat ass.

Jonny didn't appear to have noticed Irene's fury. He gazed at the depressing sight of the cars and said, "You have no idea who could have done this?"

"No."

"In that case we'd better ask your husband."

Krister was at home, so Irene suggested they drive over to Guldheden.

"Katarina is with him at the moment; Jenny is coming over this afternoon, and I'll be there this evening. We don't want him to be alone—at least not today," Irene explained.

"And what does he think?"

"He says he's fine, but I can see how shocked he is. Last night he kept saying it was all his fault, but he doesn't have to feel guilty just because Anton was borrowing his car. It could just as easily have been . . . him."

The word stuck in her throat. The very thought of it was unbearable.

IT WAS OBVIOUS that Krister hadn't slept a wink. The morning sun shining in through the kitchen window emphasized the deep lines in his face and the bags under his eyes. Admittedly he was ten years older than Irene, but for the first time in their twenty-five years of marriage, it suddenly struck her that he looked his age. Her heart filled with love and sympathy. Poor Krister; this was more than anyone could handle.

Katarina made a pot of strong coffee, took some rolls out of the freezer and defrosted them in the microwave.

Jonny asked the first question: "Did anyone know Anton was going to borrow your car?"

"No . . . it just came up. His wife called to say she'd locked herself out. She had the kids with her, and it was late. Anton always cycles to work, so he asked if he could borrow my car to speed things up."

Krister rubbed his eyes as if to try and keep himself awake, but Irene knew the real aim was to improve his concentration. He was bone weary, and he couldn't relax. He had barely touched the roll on his plate.

"So we have to assume the bomb was meant for you," Jonny said.

Krister was already pale, but now his face turned almost grey. *What if he faints?* Irene thought. Jonny may have been an insensitive jerk, but it was probably

best if he led the interview so she could focus on listening to Krister's answers.

Krister swallowed several times before he spoke.

"It . . . looks that way. Or maybe they got the wrong car?"

"The wrong car? Does anyone else have the same
model?" Jonny said with a frown.

"Well . . . Janne also has a red Renault Megane,
although it's newer than ours. I guess one Megane looks
much like another in the dark."

"Who's Janne?"

"My former colleague, Jan-Erik Månsson. He bought
Glady's just under two years ago, and now I've bought it
from him."

"When did you take over?"

"The sale went through three weeks ago."

"And does this Janne still park in the yard? I mean,
you're the owner now, right?" Jonny looked searchingly
at Krister, who seemed to wilt under his scrutiny.

"Well no, he doesn't . . . No, not really," Krister
mumbled, shifting uncomfortably on his chair.

Jonny allowed the silence to grow. The sunshine
flooding in was reflected in the shiny new cupboard
doors, bathing the small kitchen in light. Neither Irene
nor Krister noticed; Irene felt as if darkness was slowly
filling her mind. *This has nothing to do with us!* she
thought, over and over again.

Krister took a deep breath. "There are four parking
spaces in the yard. Janne doesn't live far away, so if he
can't park close to his apartment block, he sometimes
borrows one of our spaces," he said with a certain amount
of desperation.

"And does he do this on particular evenings?"

"No . . . No, not really," Krister said quietly.

Jonny leaned back, and his chair creaked loudly.

"So this Janne doesn't work at Glady's anymore. But you do. Sometimes Janne uses one of the parking spaces in the yard, but no one knows when he's going to be there. But everyone knows that your car is always there on Monday evenings. Janne might have an almost identical vehicle, but I think we can rule him out as the target of this attack," Jonny concluded.

Something occurred to Irene. "Krister, do you remember when Janne sold the Merc? Was it March or April?"

Krister rubbed his forehead.

"I'm not sure. The end of March, I think. Why—is it important?"

Irene didn't know, but she had a feeling it could be significant. "Maybe not, but he was driving around in one hell of a smart Mercedes—one of the largest models, and it was almost new. And then suddenly he turned up in the Megane, which is much smaller and cheaper."

Krister nodded and said thoughtfully, "You mean the change of car could have something to do with his gambling debts? You might be right. He probably sold the Merc to pay off at least part of what he owed. And then he sold the restaurants and—"

"Hold on. Are you telling me this Janne has gambling debts?" Jonny interrupted.

Krister nodded wearily. "Yes, but he said he'd paid them off. And last spring he went to counseling to help with his addiction."

"Hmm. I'd like to speak to this guy. Where do I find him?" Jonny asked.

"Majorca. He left yesterday. He and his girlfriend are

going to stay over there for a few months; they've already sorted out work and somewhere to live."

Jonny took a deep breath. He drummed his fingers impatiently on the table, then suddenly leaned forward and stared at Krister. "Have you been threatened?"

"Threatened? No . . . no," Krister said, sounding bewildered. He looked down at his hands, resting on the kitchen table. Jonny's eyes narrowed, but he kept them fixed on Krister. Irene realized he didn't believe her husband; she was filled with a sense of impotence. Strange—surely she should be angry? With Jonny? Or with Krister? Right now she felt tired and confused. She ought to try to get some rest, but on the other hand she didn't want to stay home. She had to find out what had actually happened, and why.

WHEN IRENE AND Jonny got back to the department, Fredrik Stridh was waiting for them.

"Morning. Nice to see the Organized Crimes Unit up and about," Jonny said with a grin.

"Always at the ready!" Fredrik replied with a perfect salute.

"Is this about our flambéed friend on Kolgruvegatan?" Jonny went on.

"No—the car bomb outside Glady's. Forensics called us a little while ago; it's exactly the same type of bomb that killed Soran Siljac last year."

Irene gave a start. Soran Siljac and Krister had known each other. The hardworking refugee from the former Yugoslavia had spent a year or so in the kitchen at Glady's before moving on to other restaurants in Göteborg. Two years ago he had bought his own place in Vasastan;

less than a year later he was blown up in his brand new Volvo V70.

The only motive that had come up during the investigation was the possibility that Siljac had been under pressure to pay for protection, "so that nothing unpleasant would happen to him or his restaurant." According to an anonymous witness, Siljac had told the person who conveyed the threat to take himself off to considerably warmer climes, and had respectfully declined to pay. The police knew that one of the criminal gangs lay behind the attempt at extortion, but they had been unable to establish which one; both the Gangster Lions and Gothia MC believed that Siljac's restaurant was in their territory.

"The same type of bomb . . . Interesting," Jonny said, glancing at Irene.

She didn't say a word; she simply tried to look as if the information about the bomb wasn't particularly striking. Meanwhile, her head was spinning: Why had a gang planted a bomb under Krister's car? Did he know the answer to that question? Or did the incident really have nothing to do with the Huss family? Was it a mistake? Were they actually after Janne?

"So that means we'll be collaborating on this case too," Fredrik explained. "Have you spoken to Krister yet?"

Jonny nodded and gave him a brief rundown on their conversation. Fredrik remained silent for a moment as he absorbed what he had heard.

"So you had the feeling that Krister knew more than he was telling you?" he said eventually.

The question was addressed to Jonny, but Fredrik was looking straight at Irene. Her mouth went completely dry when Jonny focused his attention on her as well.

"I don't think Krister knows anything. He's just in shock. I'll talk to him again . . . later," she replied lamely.

"It might be better if someone else does that," Fredrik said with a frown.

"No, it's easier if I do it, then you two can concentrate on all our other ongoing investigations," she insisted, attempting a confident smile.

"Okay," Fredrik agreed. He turned back to Jonny. "We need to speak to this Jan-Erik Månsson."

"He and his girlfriend left for Majorca yesterday, but I'm sure I can get ahold of the address of the place where they're staying," Irene offered, relieved that the spotlight had shifted from Krister to the former owner of Glady's. She should have no problem finding Janne's new address; Krister would remember the surname of the English hotel owner. And there couldn't be that many hotels in Puerto Pollensa, could there?

IT TURNED OUT there were lots and lots of hotels in the small town on the north coast of Majorca. One of them was owned by a Steven Williams. When Irene finally managed to speak to him and asked how she could get in touch with Jan-Erik Månsson, he had no idea what she was talking about. He hadn't seen his old friend and colleague since summer the previous year, when Jan-Erik had come over for a week in June. Since then they had exchanged Christmas cards and the odd email, but nothing more. Williams had no idea that Jan-Erik and his girlfriend were supposed to be moving to Majorca; he was even more surprised to hear that they would be living in Puerto Pollensa and working at his hotel. According to him, he and Jan-Erik had never even discussed such an idea.

When Irene had ended the call, her tired brain tried to process this new information. If Janne and his girl-friend weren't in Majorca, then where the hell were they?

IRENE CONTACTED EVERY airport in the vicinity of Göteborg. She checked the passenger lists for all departures the previous day, and established that neither Jan-Erik Månsson nor Jeanette Stenberg had been booked on a flight to Majorca. She did, however, find a flight to Miami in Jan-Erik's name. He had bought a single ticket that departed early Monday morning. Things got really interesting when it transpired that he had never checked in. If everything had gone according to plan, he would have been in the US by now, but something must have happened. Where was he? And why had he lied to Krister?

Irene called the numbers she had for Jan-Erik; no one picked up on the landline, and the cell phone went straight to voice mail. She managed to find Jeanette's home number, but no one answered there either. She decided to try the Sjökrogen restaurant; maybe someone would know where Jeanette was.

She was taken aback to say the least when a warm female voice said,

"Good morning, Sjökrogen. Jeanette here. How can I help you?"

"Good . . . good morning. My name is Irene Huss, Krister's wife. I'm a detective inspector and . . ."

"Oh hi, I know who you are. We met once when I was working at Glady's. What can I do for you?"

Irene remembered Jeanette as a curvaceous blonde in

her early forties. Her black suit had been a perfect fit, and the collar of her blouse had been dazzlingly white. She had no recollection whatsoever of the woman's face.

"I'm trying to contact Janne. Do you know where he is?" she asked, keeping her tone casual.

There was a brief pause.

"Does this have to do with your job?" Jeanette asked.

"Yes. I need to speak to him."

"Has something happened to him?"

"No, we just need to ask him a few questions about the car that was blown up in the backyard at Glady's last night. I'm sure you heard about it on the news."

"Yes of course—it's terrible. But what does that have to do with Janne?"

"We don't know; that's why we need to contact him, to clear up one or two points. Do you know where he is?"

"I'm afraid not. I tried to get ahold of him last night, but I didn't have any luck."

"When did you last speak to him?"

"On Sunday evening. We had dinner at my place."

"What time did he leave?"

"Just after eleven. He didn't want to stay over because he had to get up early to clean his apartment. He's in the process of selling it, and the realtor was due in the morning with a prospective buyer."

No, Janne was not going to clean his apartment, Irene thought. He was heading off to Florida without you.

"Do you have any idea where he might be?" she asked.

"No." Jeanette took a deep breath, then continued: "Unless of course he's playing poker somewhere. He loses track of time. That hasn't happened all summer, but maybe we're back there again."

The bitterness in her voice was unmistakable.

"Is there anything in particular that makes you think that?" Irene asked tentatively.

"Well . . . He seemed very distracted on Sunday. He wasn't listening to what I said, hardly spoke. I got mad, but now it strikes me that he could have given in to the urge to gamble again. It makes him kind of . . . distant."

Jeanette's voice broke, and Irene could hear her struggling to hold back the tears.

"Has he ever been gone for this long before?"

"Yes."

Was it really so simple? Was Janne sitting in some gambling den having lost track of time?

"What does he gamble on?"

"Anything and everything, as long as it involves money. But he promised me he'd stop. He's been going to counseling for his addiction . . . look how well that worked!"

Jeanette started to cry, then she asked Irene to hang on a moment. Irene heard her blow her nose, then clear her throat a couple of times.

"Try Casino Cosmopol, or Åby. There are also several poker clubs where he used to play. I don't know their names or where they are; they're probably illegal," she said calmly.

Nothing in her voice revealed that she had just been crying.

Irene thanked Jeanette and promised to get back to her when she had found out where Janne was.

In the afternoon the team gathered in the bright conference room to share what they had come up with so far. They knew that Jan-Erik Månsson had booked a single ticket with SAS to Frankfurt, then onward to Miami with Lufthansa. He hadn't booked an internal flight in America, nor had he reserved a hotel room or rented a car. There were no leads with regard to what he had intended to do after arriving. Everyone agreed that it looked as if he were running away and doing his best not to leave a trail.

Irene had discovered that he had withdrawn a total of 30,000 kronor from various bank accounts, which he had then changed into dollars at Forex on the Avenue.

"That's not a great deal of money for someone who's intending to go underground in the US. There's around 200 kronor left in his accounts now," Irene said.

"Except he never went to the US. So where is he?" Fredrik Stridh looked at his colleagues around the table.

"Maybe the temptation of having so much ready cash was too much for him, and he started gambling again," Irene suggested.

"Okay, but in that case why would he have changed the whole lot into dollars?" Tommy Persson asked.

Suddenly Jonny's face lit up. "What if he was mugged?"

To be fair, it wasn't a bad idea. Someone could have watched Janne making the transaction at Forex and followed him, waiting for the right moment to strike. Or he could have been robbed in some obscure gambling den. He had been carrying a significant amount of cash, after all. But there had been no reports of a victim matching his description over the past few days.

"Could Månsson have realized that someone had sussed out his escape plan, and decided to lie low for a while?" Tommy wondered.

Irene looked at her old friend. They had known each

other for over a quarter of a century. *The years are beginning to show*, she thought. Tommy's hair, peppered with grey, was thinning, and the furrows in his brow had deepened. He had gained more than a few pounds around his waistline, but he didn't seem to care anymore. The episode with Efva Thylqvist had taken its toll. As far as Irene was aware, there was no new woman in his life.

She realized she had tuned out of the discussion; tiredness was affecting her concentration. She made an effort to pull herself together.

"He could be playing poker in some illegal club, or he might be hiding from someone. In fact he could be absolutely anywhere," Jonny concluded.

"We'll put out a call for him," Tommy decided.

"But he hasn't committed a crime," Irene objected.

The superintendent hesitated before responding. "Not as far as we know, but he could well have important information with regard to the car bomb. He could also be at risk. Plus he's technically a missing person," he said.

True, Irene thought. Putting out a call seemed like the only sensible course of action right now.

"Should we check if his apartment has been sold?" Sara said. "If so it might have provided him with a little pocket money."

She started tapping on the keyboard of her laptop; after a couple of minutes she broke into a smile.

"There you go!"

She turned the screen around so everyone could see. The property was listed on a site used by multiple realtors. "Lorensberg, historical three-room apartment in beautiful condition, wonderful high ceilings, a thousand square feet, fourth floor with elevator. Service charge

5,280 kronor per month. Asking price: 4,250,000 SEK or highest offer." This was followed by a lyrical description of newly polished floors, rich stucco detailing on the ceiling, a brand new kitchen and bathroom, plus two working tiled stoves. The pictures showed light, airy rooms decorated in white, a brushed steel and oak kitchen, plus a fully tiled bathroom with a washing machine and tumble dryer, plus a combined shower and sauna. The bed was adorned with a mass of small silk cushions in a range of pastel colors, with matching throws.

Sara tapped the shot of the bed with her fingernail. "Professionally styled."

"How do you know?" Fredrik asked.

"Matti and I have been to a few viewings; you kind of get an eye for it," she replied with a smile.

"It hasn't been sold yet," Irene said.

"So all he has is the thirty thousand, which he might have gambled away by now. Or he might have won more, of course. I think we're going to have to forget about our friend Jan-Erik Månsson for the time being," Tommy decided. He turned to Fredrik. "Anything new on the Patrik Karlsson homicide?"

Fredrik nodded. "Some interesting information has come to light. First of all, the pizza was ordered on Patrik Karlsson's cell phone at 10:02. We don't have the cell, but we got the number and the time from the pizzeria's phone records."

"Who took the call?" Tommy asked.

"The owner. He said the man spoke Swedish without an accent. It was probably Patrik himself. It could have been his killer of course, but that seems a little far-fetched."

Tommy nodded in agreement. "Who spoke to the pizza delivery guy who witnessed the murder?"

Fredrik raised his hand like an obedient schoolboy. "I interviewed him yesterday afternoon. He was starting to get over the shock, and he suddenly remembered something. When he was reversing away from the scene of the crime toward Ringövagen, he almost collided with a motorbike. There were two of them heading straight for him, and one was on the wrong side of the road. Adem managed to swerve, but apparently it was a close call."

"Bikers close to Bandidos' old HQ, which is also Gothia MC's old HQ . . ." Sara said.

"Okay, let's just slow down here. I think we should leave this whole thing to our highly respected colleagues in the Organized Crimes Unit. Biker gangs are their specialty," Jonny said, smiling at Fredrik.

Even if he was joking, Irene detected a serious undertone.

"Thanks for that, dear friend and colleague," Fredrik answered, mirroring Jonny's smile.

Sara pursed her lips and exchanged a glance with Irene. She made no comment, but started doodling irritably on the pad in front of her. Irene knew from past experience that she would fill the page with a variety of psychedelic figures.

"Was Adem able to provide a description of these guys?" Sara asked without looking up.

"No, all he recalls was that they didn't seem to be in a hurry, which is why he didn't connect them with the murder. However, when he'd calmed down a little and had time to think, the incident came back to him."

"He didn't notice whether they were wearing jackets or vests with a logo or emblem?" Irene interjected.

"I asked him, but he had no idea."

"He might remember later," Sara said with a hint of optimism in her voice. She gave Jonny a long, searching look, then went back to her drawing. The figure appearing on her pad bore an undeniable resemblance to him. When she drew flower petals around the face as a finishing touch, there was no doubt that their colleague was the model. Irene couldn't help smiling.

"Let's hope so. Otherwise we have nothing to go on. Matti searched for fingerprints on the gasoline container, but either it had been wiped clean, or they wore gloves," Fredrik said.

"So the murder was planned," Tommy concluded. He turned to Jonny: "Any luck with the door-to-door inquiries around Glady's?"

"No. Which is surprising since it was just before nine o'clock in the evening. Even though it was a Monday, there were plenty of people out, mainly kids because the school year hasn't started yet. But no one has contacted us, and we've had no luck knocking on doors. The only interesting piece of information came from an old woman who lives directly opposite the restaurant; she says she saw a 'shady character' slipping in through the gate to the backyard where the car was parked," Jonny said, making quotation marks in the air.

"Shady character? What does that mean?" Tommy demanded, raising his eyebrows. Jonny started scrabbling among his notes, and fished out a piece of paper.

"Here we go: this witness was put through to me on the phone just before we came in here."

He put on his reading glasses, cleared his throat and began:

"'I was walking along the street toward the 7-Eleven on the corner. I guess it was around a quarter to nine. As I came around the corner I glanced along the street and saw a car slowing down by the entrance to the backyard. No, I have no idea what make of car it was, but it was a dark color—maybe black or dark blue? A shady character got out of the car and went toward the gate, which was open. He was kind of fat, with long greasy hair tied back in a ponytail. He was wearing dark clothes: a long-sleeved top with a hood. I think it was black. No logos, as far as I could see. Scruffy blue jeans. He was carrying something that looked like a small toolbox. And he was wearing heavy boots. I only saw his face in profile, but I got the impression that he had some kind of tattoo on the side of his neck and face. I'd say he was between twenty-five and thirty-five.'"

By the time Jonny had finished, Irene was feeling dizzy, almost seasick, as if her chair was bobbing up and down in a heavy swell. She needed food and sleep. Her legs were far from steady as she got up and made her apologies.

EGON WAS BARKING and scratching at the inside of the door. Irene had no idea how he could distinguish her footsteps and Krister's from those of everyone else who lived on their staircase. Dogs have excellent hearing, of course. When she walked in, Egon was so happy he didn't know what to do with himself. Every fiber of his little body radiated joy because his mistress was home, in spite of the fact that he hadn't been alone for a second all day. Jenny came into the hallway and gave her mother a big hug. The top she was wearing revealed her tattooed arms; it was cut low at the back, and in the mirror Irene could see the design on the back of her neck that spread across her shoulders. Jenny had gotten the tattoos when she was a teenager, singing in various punk bands. A few days ago she had mentioned that she was thinking of having the inking on her upper arm removed with laser treatment: a skeletal hand clutched a heart, in the middle of which was the name of a long-dumped boyfriend. She had abandoned the piercings on her face when she started working in kitchens.

To Irene's disappointment her daughter couldn't stay for dinner even though Glady's was closed. Her former employer at the Grodden restaurant had asked if she could fill in there for a few hours, and she had said yes.

"Dad managed to get some sleep this afternoon; he's feeling a little better," she whispered before she left.

"I'm glad one of us has slept," Irene said with a sigh.

Krister was preparing dinner: fishcakes and new potatoes cooked with dill. He planned to serve a cold sauce made of crème fraîche with chopped chives, which he grew on the balcony. A seductive aroma emanating from the oven told Irene that there would be apple cake for dessert. She was drenched in sweat after cycling home, and jumped in the shower. Alternating between a stream of hot and cold water brought her tired body to life, and she began to feel human again. She used a perfumed lotion that she had bought in France; it was ridiculously expensive, but a little luxury now and again is no bad thing. It was lovely to slip into her velour robe and pad barefoot across the smooth new wooden floor. She crept up behind Krister and wrapped her arms around his waist.

She kissed the back of his neck, burying her nose in his T-shirt and inhaling the smell of him. A warm wave of happiness and gratitude flooded her body. Thank God Krister hadn't been in the car when it exploded!

He turned and kissed the top of her head. He still looked tired, but his warm smile lit up his eyes. He put down the fish slice and pulled her close. They stood there holding each other for a long time.

"How are you feeling?" Irene asked, gently extricating herself.

"Better. I've spoken to the glazier; he's boarded up the windows, and he'll replace them tomorrow. Once that's done, the whole team will come in and clean the kitchen. Fortunately there was no other damage. Anton has been discharged from the hospital, but he'll be out sick for at least a month. We're closed until Friday."

Krister smiled at the thought of Anton going home. The pan was bubbling away, and the tempting smell of fresh fennel filled the air. He turned around and lowered the heat just as the timer pinged; he bent down and took the apple cake out of the oven. Irene's mouth was watering, and she realized how hungry she was.

"I called the insurance company and they said we can have a replacement vehicle until everything has gone through," Krister said, snipping chives into the crème fraîche.

"That was quick. Hopefully they'll give us the same one. I like the Megane; it suits us. Then again, sometimes I think we don't need a car now that we're living in town."

"We do need one occasionally—when we're buying something bulky, or when we're going up to the cottage."

Irene's stomach turned over when Krister mentioned

the cottage. As far as she was concerned, the place was linked to a terrifying experience that she was finding difficult to deal with.

The previous year, a serial killer had followed her as she drove up to their special retreat in Värmland, and low on gas and without a working cell phone, she had been forced to carry out a terrible plan down by the bog in order to escape with her life. The events that frosty night in October still haunted her today. Only one of them had survived.

Irene had been totally exonerated in the subsequent inquiry, but that didn't help. In her nightmares she was still standing there listening to the man's death throes.

She had forced herself to spend time at the cottage, but that horrible feeling wouldn't go away. She refused to go and pick cloudberries. The very thought of going any-where near the bog gave her palpitations.

Tentatively she had suggested selling the cottage and buying something a little closer to Göteborg, but Krister wouldn't hear of it. He had been born and raised in Säffle, but he and his siblings had spent the summers at the cottage outside Sunne, as had their own twin girls. Spending the winter mid-semester break up there was almost better than the summers. No, there was no way they would get rid of such a wonderful place. Irene's ter-rifying memories would fade with time, he said. And that was the end of the discussion.

Irene made a salad of radishes, baby spinach, tomatoes and cucumber. The crispy fishcakes were garnished with a slice of lemon and a few sprigs of dill. Krister drained the potatoes and tossed the fennel in salted butter. The afternoon sun was still warm, so he had set everything out on the small table on the balcony. The fact that it faced west was a major bonus; it was in the afternoons and evenings that they had time to sit out there.

THE ICE CUBES clinked in Irene's glass of water as she absent-mindedly swirled it around. Dinner was over, and it was high time she tried to talk to Krister about the car bomb. She had promised to find out if he knew more than he had admitted to her colleagues. On a personal level she also felt it was important; she just didn't quite know how to start.

"I was wondering . . . Has Janne ever said anything about being threatened?" she asked.

Krister didn't answer right away, and she avoided looking at him. Which was why she didn't realize that he was about to explode.

"No he fucking hasn't! What the hell are you and that idiot Jonny talking about?!"

Irene was totally taken aback by his reaction, and for a moment she was lost for words. Eventually she stammered, "But sweetheart, what's . . . what—"

"Nobody has threatened anybody, okay?"

Krister leapt to his feet with such force that he banged the table. The jug of water crashed onto the cement floor and shattered. Ice-cold water splashed over Irene's bare feet, but she hardly noticed. All she could see was the furious expression on her husband's face. She had never seen a reaction like that in all the years they had been together.

"Fuck! I'll clear it up," he said, disappearing into the apartment.

While he was gone, Irene tried to gather her thoughts.

He returned with a dustpan and brush and a cloth, and quickly cleared away all trace of the incident. Without a word he went back inside. Irene could hear the tinkle of glass as he emptied the dustpan into the recycling bin. It seemed to her that even the sound was angry. Had he lost it because he was still in shock? She would like to think so, but her instinct as a cop told her it was something else. This was a sensitive issue, and it had to be sorted out.

After a while Krister reappeared with a fresh jug of water; this one was made of plastic, to be on the safe side. He slumped down on his chair and put on his sunglasses. Was it because of the evening sun, or because he didn't want to look her in the eye? Irene suppressed a sigh.

"I know I overreacted. I'm sorry. I just can't talk about that fucking bomb anymore," he said, turning to face her with a wan smile. But he didn't take off his shades, so Irene couldn't see if he meant what he said.

Enough pussyfooting around, she thought. "You have to talk to me, otherwise you'll be called into the station for a formal interview, which will be conducted by someone else. I've requested the opportunity to deal with this on an informal basis so you don't have to go through that."

Krister took a deep breath and focused his attention on the setting sun.

"I don't know what you want me to say!"

"Just tell me. Tell me what you know. We can help."

"There's nothing to tell! And I don't need your help."

The last vestiges of Irene's patience were rapidly ebbing away.

"So someone put a bomb under our car for fun?"

"How the fuck should I know?!"

She reached across the table for his hand, but he

pulled away. Trying to hang on to her self-control, she said, "You have to understand that we're taking this extremely seriously. We recognize the signs. A car bomb is a signature move for criminal gangs around here. You knew Soran Siljac. Who was killed by a *car bomb*. Which was exactly like the one that blew up our car."

Krister didn't reply; his jaw tightened even more. Irene decided to try a different tack.

"Krister, talk to me. I love you, and I'm just trying to help you. There have been plenty of car bombs in this city in recent years; all the victims were threatened before the bombs were planted. Every single one of them, without exception. But you maintain you haven't been threatened, and you have no idea why someone put a bomb under our car."

"Got it in one."

Before Irene could think of anything else to say, Krister stood up.

"I'm taking Egon for a walk."

A couple of minutes later Irene heard the front door slam.

IRENE MANAGED ONLY a few hours of restless sleep that night, but she was grateful all the same. Every time she woke up, she could hear Krister tossing and turning. She spoke to him or reached out to caress him, but he simply rolled over and pretended to be asleep.

When the alarm clock went off, Krister's side of the bed was empty. The aroma of freshly brewed coffee filled the apartment; she pulled on her robe and got up. The sun was shining straight into the kitchen, but to her surprise there was no one around. A quick check revealed that neither the dog nor his master were home. *Little Egon is going to get a lot of extra walks over the next few days*, she thought wearily.

AT THEIR DAILY meeting, affectionately referred to as "morning prayer," the team had two additional members—or three, to be more accurate, because Fredrik Stridh was there too.

When everyone had a cup of coffee and a cookie, Tommy Persson smiled and introduced his inspectors to the newcomers. "We're joined today by Superintendent Stefan Bratt and DI Ann Wennberg, both of whom work for the Organized Crimes Unit, and are colleagues of our old friend Fredrik. Perhaps you'd like to say a few words?"

Irene noticed that Ann Wennberg had a particularly friendly smile. She was in her thirties, slim and fit. Her chestnut hair was cut short, with a long, thick fringe. She wore discreet makeup that brought out her blue eyes. She reminded Irene of a highly efficient personal assistant, possibly thanks to her dark blue linen suit and white blouse.

The man beside Ann Wennberg cleared his throat. "Stefan Bratt. I've been with the Organized Crimes Unit since it was set up, and became a superintendent six months ago. We work on various projects. Fredrik, for example, has been analyzing the development of violent crime within the gang culture in Västra Göta-land, focusing especially on assault and homicide."

Bratt was in his early forties. He had alert grey-blue eyes, thin dark grey hair with the beginning of a bald patch on the top of his head, and he was slim, almost skinny in fact. Irene thought he looked more like an amiable bank clerk than a senior police officer. Maybe it was what he was wearing: beige chinos, white shirt, sand-colored linen jacket. *Okay, so we'll be collaborating with a bank clerk and a PA,* she thought, suppressing a giggle. Not that she doubted her colleagues' competence for a second.

"Ann Wennberg. My specialty is biker gangs. I've been with the unit for six months."

Her voice was warm and inspired trust. Irene was surprised; the biker gangs were a tough assignment for a woman. *I guess I have my preconceptions,* she thought; *if she'd said financial irregularities I wouldn't have reacted.*

"Okay, let's see what we have so far," Tommy Persson said energetically.

"So there's no doubt that the car bomb and the murder of Patrik Karlsson are linked to the biker gangs?" Jonny broke in.

"Yes, we're pretty much one hundred percent convinced on that score."

"I knew it," Jonny muttered.

Stefan looked amused, while Jonny glared into his almost empty coffee cup.

Tommy continued: "Let's start with Patrik Karlsson. We're in the process of going through the footage from CCTV cameras in the area. We are mainly interested in the Ringön and Frihamn intersections; everyone has to pass through one or the other in order to get to Ringön. The motorbikes the pizza delivery guy saw should be on film; we know the time frame."

"Did you find any prints or anything else at the scene of the crime?" Stefan asked.

Tommy nodded to Sara, who took over.

"Plenty inside the building; most were already in our records. They belong to the older members of Gothia MC, and there were even a few from the dear old Bandidos. Unfortunately the plastic container was clean."

Tommy turned to Ann Wennberg.

"So what do you think? Is this an inside job?"

"You mean did Gothia MC kill one of their own?" She considered the question. "It's unusual for a gang to do that. It could happen if the victim had betrayed someone, or tried to swindle the club out of a large sum of money. Occasionally a gang member dies after being beaten up because of some perceived transgression, but such a brutal murder? No, I don't think so."

"So what is going on here?" Tommy asked.

Once again Ann took her time before answering. "The most-likely scenario is we're looking at a revenge attack by another gang. Or it could be a private matter that has nothing to do with the gangs."

"If it is another gang, who would you go for?" Irene asked.

This time there was no hesitation.

"The Gangster Lions. Revenge could well be a motive. According to our informants, the member of the Gangster Lions who was shot outside McDonald's on the Avenue back in March was killed by bikers, but no one knows which gang was responsible."

"I don't know anything about that incident, apart from what was in the press; could you refresh my memory?" Jonny said.

"No problem. Caesar Roijas was shot from a car at two-thirty in the morning. Classic drive-by; the killer simply put the window down and fired, then the car disappeared down the Avenue and across the bridge. It was found burned out on an industrial estate not far from Säve Airport the following day; presumably the perpetrators got in a waiting car. According to the guy who witnessed the shooting, there were two people in the car. Unfortunately he wasn't close enough to see their faces," Fredrik explained.

"That doesn't sound too promising. If you're right, it looks as if we have a new gang war on our hands," Tommy said.

• • •

Irene had been given the task of contacting the witness who had seen a man enter the backyard at Glady's. Her name was Ritva Ekholm. Jonny had referred to her as an old woman, but in fact she was a year younger than Irene. She was a lecturer in organic chemistry. Irene managed to get ahold of her at Chalmers University of Technology, and discovered that she spoke with a soft Finland-Swedish accent. There was a hoarse quality to her voice, as if it had been strained for some reason. They arranged to have Irene visit Ritva Ekholm's apartment just after five, which suited Irene perfectly; she wouldn't need to divert from her normal cycle route home.

During the afternoon they had both a positive result and a setback. The two guys on motorbikes were spotted on the CCTV footage from the Ringön intersection, and the emblems on their vests indicated that they belonged to the Red Devils, a Hells Angels subchapter. Unfortunately the time was 10:36 p.m., which meant they couldn't possibly have had anything to do with the murder of Patrik Karlsson; by then he had already staggered out into the yard and burned to death in front of a horrified Adem Guzel. No, the two bikers had nothing to do with the murder, but the question remained: What were they doing nearby? The police had no answer yet, but the information was added to the file as a detail worth pursuing.

Ritva Ekholm lived in an apartment block directly opposite Glady's; the entrance leading to her staircase was on Södra vägen. A small brass plaque on the carved oak door with small, beautifully polished panes of glass informed Irene that the building dated back to

1892. Ritva had given her the entry code, and she tapped in the numbers. The door opened with a low hum. Inside time had stood still. There was a wealth of stucco on the ceilings, attractive floral frescoes, and an impressive, sparkling chandelier. Irene felt as if she had stepped back a hundred years, but at least there was a modern elevator to whisk her up to the fifth floor. Ritva had told her to walk up another flight of stairs; the elevator didn't go all the way to the top.

The heavy front door looked brand new; Irene noticed that it was equipped with three locks, two of which appeared to be seven-pin cylinders. From inside she could hear the sound of classical music: a string quartet, perhaps. She had to ring the bell several times before she heard footsteps in the hallway. Keys were turned, and the door opened on a security chain. The music was deafening; Irene could just see a pair of large glasses and bushy blonde hair.

"Detective Inspector Irene Huss," she said, showing her ID.

"Come on in!"

There was a rattle as the security chain was released and the door flew open. Ritva Ekholm was a small, neat woman. Her fair hair, peppered with grey, was caught up in a messy bun on top of her head. She was wearing a man's shirt in thin, pale blue cotton, and black harem pants. The shirt was several sizes too big. Her feet were bare, her toenails painted bright red. Behind the round-rimmed glasses her sparkling eyes were heavily made up with kohl. Her smile was warm and welcoming, though her teeth were badly stained with nicotine; the smell of cigarette smoke in the apartment was overwhelming.

There was nothing about Ritva that fit with Irene's pre-conceived notion of a female university lecturer.

"Sorry. I guess I didn't hear the first time you rang the bell," Ritva said as she turned and walked away.

"No prob—" Irene broke off when she realized Ritva wasn't listening. She stepped into the airy hallway and closed the door behind her. She also turned the key in one of the locks; something told her Ritva valued her security.

As she moved further inside she realized she was in a two-story apartment. The lower floor was completely open-plan, with a combined living room and kitchen. An elegant wooden staircase presumably led up to a bedroom and bathroom.

The décor was an eclectic mixture of different styles. Most of the furniture could well have come from a trunk sale, but some pieces appeared to be genuine antiques. There were also a couple of designer items that looked new. Irene thought it was a shame the room was so messy, because the overall effect was kind of cozy. Three of the walls were completely covered with over-stuffed book-shelves, while the fourth was made up of narrow windows reaching from floor to ceiling. Four large paintings hung between the windows; if they were genuine, they were extremely valuable. Irene recognized the style of Ivan Ivarson, the Göteborg artist. A few months earlier she had been caught in a shower while shopping in town, and had sought refuge in the art gallery, which was holding a major exhibition of Ivarson's work. She imme-diately fell for his colorful paintings of France and the west coast of Sweden. Before she left she bought a poster, which she intended to frame and hang in the hallway.

She also recognized Inge Schiöler's work. Most Swedes were familiar with them since they had appeared in a number of auction shows on TV. Irene was no expert, but she knew these two artists commanded sky-high prices. And Ritva Ekholm had two of each.

"I inherited them."

Irene gave a start; she hadn't noticed Ritva was standing beside her.

"My parents inherited an art collection from my maternal grandfather. Mom was from Göteborg, but moved to Åbo when she married my father. They were both teachers, and didn't exactly amass a fortune during their lives, but they did keep Grandpa's paintings. When they died I sold almost the entire collection and bought this apartment. But I held on to those four; they're my pension," she said with a smile.

"Is that why you have so many locks on the front door?"

"Yes; the insurance company insisted. I also have an alarm that's switched on whenever I go out, plus another alarm when I go to bed."

"You live in Fort Knox," Irene said, returning the smile.

"Indeed I do."

Ritva went over to a generous black leather sofa, which was next to a large, far-from-modern swivel chair. The coffee table was a solid combination of a white marble top on a cast-iron base. Irene thought it was beautiful, but probably impossible to move. An overflowing ashtray clumsily modeled from blue-painted clay was in the middle of the table. The woven rug in shades of green with orange spots clashed with everything else in the room.

"Please sit anywhere you'd like."

Irene chose the swivel chair, which turned out to be extremely comfortable.

"Would you like a cup of coffee? Or tea?"

"I'll have whatever you're having," Irene replied.

Ritva went over to the kitchen area and put the kettle on. She opened a cupboard and took out two mismatched mugs and a jar of instant coffee. She placed them on a tray and added two spoons, a carton of milk and a box of sugar lumps. She carried the tray over, then shook the milk carton and pulled a face.

"Not much left. I haven't had time to go shopping . . . even though I'm home unusually early today. I'm a regular customer at the 7-Eleven," she said.

"That's where you were going on Monday evening?" Irene asked.

"Exactly. I'd run out of cigarettes and bread."

The kettle switched itself off with a loud click. While Ritva went to fetch it, Irene put a spoonful of coffee into her chipped pink mug. Her hostess returned and poured hot water into the mug. This didn't qualify as coffee in Irene's book; if she'd known it was instant, she would have chosen tea.

"Milk? Sugar?"

"No thanks."

Ritva added four sugar lumps and what was left of the milk to her lime green mug. She leaned back on the sofa and fished a packet of cigarettes out of her breast pocket. She offered them to Irene, who shook her head. With a shrug she lit up and greedily inhaled, before allowing the smoke to filter out slowly through her nostrils.

"Monday evening. That's why you're here," she said, taking another drag.

"Yes. We're investigating the car bomb, and we're very interested in what you saw."

Ritva nodded pensively, narrowing her eyes at Irene through the haze.

"I understand. As usual I had nothing edible in the refrigerator; I'm not great when it comes to planning. I normally shop on the weekends, but during the week I'm hopeless. I work long hours, so my go-to place is the 7-Eleven, unless I pick up a takeaway. Or sometimes I just don't bother to eat."

She smiled and blew smoke rings up toward the heavy beams before going on:

"On Monday I got home just after eight. I had some food left from the weekend, so I didn't think I needed to go shopping. Then I realized I was almost out of cigarettes. I can manage without most things, but not those. So I went out again."

"What time was this?"

"I'm not sure, but I'd say shortly after eight-thirty. I didn't look at the clock when I left."

Ritva sat up and stubbed out her cigarette in the ashtray, causing several of the old butts to spill over onto the table. She picked them up and added them to the pile once more, then pointed at the ashtray. "I made that in fifth grade and gave it to my dad for Christmas. He didn't want to upset me, so he always kept it on display."

Her hoarse laugh turned into a rattling cough.

"So you went out for cigarettes," Irene said, keen to get back on track.

"Yes. The rain had stopped, and it was a lovely evening. I walked slowly, enjoying myself. When I was about to cross over Lorensbergsgatan, I made sure to look both ways, and I saw a car that had stopped down the street. A man got out; I know I said he looked like a shady character when I called the police, which might sound a little odd, but I stand by my choice of words."

She was interrupted by another coughing fit and took a large swig of her coffee.

"Could you describe him in as much detail as possible?" Irene asked.

"I'll do my best. He wasn't very tall, but he was powerfully built. Fat, actually. Short neck. Long, lanky hair in a ponytail. Dirty, ripped jeans with his gut hanging over the waistband. Black T-shirt, black hoodie. That's it! The other guy in the car said something to him, and he stopped and pulled up his hood. Then he waved and went into the backyard where the bomb went off later. He was carrying a small toolbox in his left hand."

Ritva reached for her cigarette packet. It was less than a minute since she had finished the first one, but clearly it was time for another. She shook out a cigarette and began to roll it between her fingers.

"What did the driver do?" Irene asked.

"He waved through the sunroof and moved the car forward a little. Then—"

"The sunroof? The car had a sunroof?" Irene broke in.

"Didn't I say that? Maybe I forgot when I called in, but yes, it did. He stuck his hand through the gap and waved. I noticed that the hand was completely black. At first I thought he was dark-skinned, but then I realized the color came from tattoos—all the way down to his fingertips."

"Did you see any more of him?"

"Nothing—the car had tinted windows."

"Did you notice if the other guy had any tattoos?"

Irene knew Ritva had mentioned this in her initial statement, but wanted to double-check.

"Yes. I only saw him in profile, but he had a tattoo up the side of his neck and cheek."

"Could you make out what it was?"

"No. I can see pretty well with my fabulous new glasses, but they have their limitations, and I was at least fifty yards away."

"Okay . . . Would it be possible for you to come in to the station first thing tomorrow morning to meet our sketch artist—say seven-thirty? I say sketch artist, but of course they use a computer program these days," she corrected herself.

"I know how it works, but I'm afraid I couldn't be there before eleven. It's almost the beginning of the semester, and we have a meeting that I really can't miss. It's the most important meeting of the year," Ritva said firmly.

Irene thought fast; it was essential to get an image of the suspect as soon as possible.

"If I call the station and see if there's someone who could work with you this evening, would you come in now?"

Ritva smiled and shrugged. "Sure. I'm not doing anything special."

Irene made the call and asked to be put through to forensics. There was no answer, which was hardly surprising. It was almost six o'clock, and the chances of anyone still being around were small. She decided to try Fredrik Stridh.

"Hi, Fredrik. Ritva Ekholm is prepared to come in and

work on a composite of the guy she saw on Monday evening; her description could be very useful," she explained quickly.

"Great."

"There's no reply from forensics; do you have Göran's direct line? It would be good if Ritva could get this done tonight."

"Let me just check. Hang on."

Irene could hear him talking to someone else in the room. A female voice responded, and there was at least one male voice in the background.

Fredrik came back on the line: "Ann will find Göran's number and call him."

Göran Nilsson was the only one who was familiar with the computer program, so Irene had no choice but to wait, and hope that Ann Wennberg could get ahold of him.

"Tell her to give him my number and ask him to contact me."

"Okay."

Irene couldn't suppress an impatient sigh as she ended to call. It suddenly seemed very important to issue a wanted notice for Ritva's "shady character." She wasn't entirely sure why, but she had learned to trust her instincts.

She spent the next fifteen minutes trying to get Ritva to remember what the car had looked like, but it was a waste of time; Ritva didn't have a driver's license, so of course she didn't have a car; nor did she know anything about cars. They eventually decided that it was a medium-sized dark sedan with a sunroof and tinted windows. Irene also had to accept another cup of the almost undrinkable instant coffee. When her cell phone finally rang, she noticed that her hands were shaking—probably thanks to a combination of too much coffee and too little food.

"Hi. I'm afraid I haven't managed to speak to Göran," Ann said right away.

"Can't be helped. Could you please leave him a message saying that Ritva Ekholm will be in at eleven o'clock tomorrow morning?"

Irene could hear the disappointment in her voice, but there wasn't much more she could do at this stage. And it didn't really matter whether Ritva came in at seven-thirty or eleven the following day; they should still have the sketch by lunchtime.

"Will do," Ann promised.

I guess she doesn't do small talk, Irene thought.

"Unfortunately we'll have to wait until tomorrow, but if you can come in straight after your meeting, that would be great," she said to her hostess.

"No problem. At least that means I have time to go shopping this evening," Ritva replied with a smile, blithely showing her nicotine-stained teeth.

WHEN IRENE GOT home she was met by Egon, who told her a tale of woe as he tried to convince her that he had been by himself all day. Fortunately she knew better; Jenny had taken him for a long walk before she went off to work at Grodden, less than four hours ago.

Irene quickly fed him, then heated a leftover fishcake and some potatoes from yesterday's dinner for herself. She couldn't be bothered to make a salad. Egon was the only one who knew she was missing out on nutritious greens, and he was unlikely to tell. Even though she loved Egon, she felt a little lonely eating dinner with her canine companion, particularly as he finished a lot faster than her, and immediately started scratching at the door. Krister was still clearing up at Glady's, and probably wouldn't be home until late.

They went down to the wooded area behind the apartment block. It felt nothing like a city park; there were no flower beds, no neatly clipped shrubs. The trees were tall and dense, and if a tree came down it was left to rot. The air was filled with the smell of damp earth and decaying vegetation, and mushrooms were poking up through the ground here and there. Darkness was falling, but there were plenty of people around on the well-lit asphalt path—mainly dog owners out for an evening stroll.

As they headed toward Doktor Fries Square, it started to drizzle. Egon tugged at the leash, sniffing eagerly to pick up all the latest doggie news. Irene could hear the squeal of the trams down in Wavrinsky Square. Childhood memories. This whole area was full of them. She had grown up there, in the apartment where she and Krister now lived; she had inherited it from her mother, who had lived there for almost fifty years. Thanks to Katarina's fiancé, Felipe, the renovation had gone like clockwork. He was not only a student of architecture, but also a very handy guy. He had helped them to repaper the walls and to lay new floors. With the assistance of an electrician and a plumber, he had also fitted the new kitchen, and now the apartment was exactly the way Krister and Irene wanted it to be.

It had come as a total surprise when Jan-Erik asked if Krister was interested in buying Glady's. They had discussed the offer at length, and after due consideration decided to accept. Their lawyer prepared all the necessary paperwork to form a limited company; that alone cost 50,000 kronor. By the time everything was paid for, the money they had left from the sale of the house in Fiskebäck was gone, and Krister actually had to borrow several hundred thousand as a start-up fund. There was no getting away from the fact that his staff expected to be paid from day one. They were both relieved when the very last piece of paper had been signed, and Glady's was theirs.

And then the car bomb exploded. It wasn't only their car that had been wrecked, it was their entire existence. Every scrap of security had been blown away. Irene felt nothing but despair when she thought about how badly the conversation with Krister had gone exactly twenty-four hours earlier. They were facing disaster, and suddenly they couldn't talk to each other.

KRISTER WAS STILL sound asleep when Irene cycled off to work the following morning. He had come home around midnight and collapsed into bed. Before he fell asleep he had muttered: "All done."

AS USUAL THE day began with morning prayer and a cup of coffee. Fredrik Stridh and Ann Wennberg were also present. After a couple of minutes of small talk, Irene gave her report.

"I spoke to Ritva Ekholm yesterday. She's coming in at eleven to do a composite sketch with Göran Nilsson, but she did tell me one thing we didn't know before: the car had a sunroof. She saw the driver wave through the gap, and his hand was covered in tattoos, all the way to his fingertips. That was all she saw, because the windows were tinted. I'm wondering if we should take a look at the CCTV footage from the area around the Avenue to see if we can spot a dark-colored car with a sunroof? And maybe we ought to check the footage from the Ringön intersection again, in case the same car turns up there."

"Why would it do that?" Tommy said with a frown. He was in uniform today since he was due to hold a press conference on the murder of Patrik Karlsson. There was still a high level of public concern over the macabre homicide, which even overshadowed the car bomb.

"I'm not sure, but these are two bad guys. Then again, perhaps that's not the car we should be looking for out there; maybe there's another car with 'gangsters' written all over it," Irene said.

A thoughtful silence settled over the room; after a moment Fredrik spoke up. "We've already gone through the films; we didn't see anything suspicious."

"No, but we were focusing on two bikers," Irene persisted.

"I'm with Irene," Ann Wennberg said. "If we go through the footage with fresh eyes, we might find something we didn't see the first time."

"You could be right . . ." Tommy said, tugging at a long hair in one eyebrow.

Irene could see the calculator clicking away inside his head as he worked out how much it would cost to check the CCTV one more time.

"Okay," he said at last. "But you'll have to do it yourself, Irene."

RUNNING THROUGH SATURDAY evening's CCTV records from the Ringön and Frihamn intersections wasn't a major problem because they knew the killer or killers must have arrived before 10:30. To be on the safe side, Irene started at 9:00.

A black BMW appeared at the Ringön intersection at 10:03, and Irene's attention was caught by the passenger in the front seat. The side window was down, his left arm dangling outside the car. He was holding a cigarette and wearing a black T-shirt and one of the largest gold watches Irene had ever seen. If it was real gold, it must be incredibly heavy and extremely valuable. The same applied to the gold chain around his neck. She could see several tattoos on his arm, although it was impossible to make out what they were. She hoped the tech guys would be able to improve the definition.

The plate was clearly visible; a quick check revealed that the vehicle was registered to one Melek Ekici, forty-two years old, resident in Gunnared, married with four kids. He worked at a café in Linnéstaden, and it seemed he was also part-owner. One thing was certain: he wasn't the guy sitting in the car.

Irene had her prey in her sights now. Her brain was crystal clear, and she knew exactly what she was looking for. The car appeared again at 10:41, heading into town. It was traveling just below the speed limit. The side window wasn't open this time, but she could see a man in the front seat. The picture wasn't clear, but she thought it was the guy in the black T-shirt.

The dark-colored car with the sunroof was even easier to find. It was an Audi A4, far from new. She spotted it on footage from a camera on Södra vägen at 10:36 on Monday evening; it then turned off toward Engelbrektsgatan. Unfortunately there were no cameras on Lorensbergsgatan, but the time fit with Ritva Ekholm's statement. She checked the number, which belonged to a Saab 95 in Hedemora. As she had expected, the car had false plates. Thanks to the light falling in through the sunroof, she could clearly see two people in the front seat. There was nothing to suggest that there was anyone sitting in the back.

The man on the passenger side was probably the one

Ritva had described as fat. His head was turned toward the driver, and they seemed to be having an intense conversation. His thin hair was pulled back in a ponytail, and his face was round and flabby, like the rest of his upper body. He was wearing a black T-shirt and a black hoodie. What interested Irene the most was the tattoo running up his neck and cheek, across the cheekbone and around the eyes. Again, it was impossible to make out what it represented, but its presence was in no doubt.

"It won't take me long to identify you," Irene murmured to herself.

The driver was more of a problem. He was dressed in similar clothes, but also wore a baseball cap pulled well down over his forehead. The sleeves of his hoodie were pushed up, revealing his forearms. As Ritva had said, the number of tattoos gave the impression that he was dark-skinned. His neck was completely covered in images. Irene couldn't see his face, but she thought he was taller and considerably more muscular than his companion.

She felt pretty pleased with herself as she sent the pictures off to the technicians; within a few hours she should know who the four men were.

IRENE WAS ABOUT to go for lunch when the phone on her desk rang.

"Hi, Irene. Göran here. I had a message saying that you'd arranged for a witness to come in this morning to work on a composite sketch with me: Ritva Ekholm?"

"That's right."

"She hasn't turned up."

"What?" Irene was completely at a loss; a few seconds passed before she pulled herself together. "She's a chemistry lecturer at Chalmers. I interviewed her last night. She's a little different . . . slightly Bohemian, with something of the classic absentminded professor about her. She probably forgot she was supposed to come in."

She was making an effort to sound a lot less worried than she actually was.

"Okay. Call me when you've spoken to her."

"Will do. Thanks."

Irene quickly tried Ritva's work number; a young female voice answered.

"Ritva Ekholm's phone. Lina Johannesson here; can I help you?"

"Detective Inspector Irene Huss; I'm trying to get ahold of Ritva Ekholm."

The young woman inhaled sharply. "She's not here."

"Where can I reach her?"

"The thing is . . . she didn't come into work today. We had an important meeting this morning, and she didn't turn up. We called her landline and her cell phone, but there's no answer. We were just wondering whether one of us should go over to her apartment during the lunch break to see if anything's wrong."

Irene's head was spinning. Ritva had said she had a very important meeting that she definitely couldn't miss, but that was exactly what she had done. Why wasn't she answering either of her phones? This wasn't good. She made a quick decision.

"There's no need. I'll go."

"Oh good! She lives alone; if she's sick or something, she might not be able to get out of bed," Lina Johannesson said.

"I'll check it out," Irene said and ended the call.

• • •

As Irene hurried toward the elevator she passed Sara Persson's office.

"Sara, can you come with me? It's urgent."

Something in Irene's voice made Sara leap up and grab her coat. She didn't ask what was going on until they were in the car; Irene quickly filled her in.

Sara tried calling Ritva several times during the trip, but there was still no response. They parked in the only empty space, which happened to be a disabled bay, and Irene flipped down her police vehicle parking permit. Fortunately she still had the entry code for Ritva's apartment block in her cell phone. The door opened with a hum, and they stepped into the cool hallway. Sara glanced around appreciatively as she followed Irene to the tiny elevator, which was more than a little cramped with two of them inside. When they reached the top floor Irene yanked open the door and raced up the stairs to Ritva's apartment. She pressed her ear to the door; she could hear the faint sound of a string quartet. It was the same music Ritva had played the previous evening, which gave Irene a spark of hope. Her index finger was shaking as she rang the bell. They waited for quite a while, but nothing happened. After several more attempts Irene crouched down and pushed open the letter box.

"Ritva, it's Irene Huss. Could you open the door, please?"

She stayed there for some time; she could hear the music more clearly now, but nothing else.

"Ritva, you were supposed to come into the station today; I was worried when you didn't show up. Please open the door."

Sara took a closer look at the locks.

"I don't think the seven-cylinder locks have been activated; I can't see the catches. I think it's just the ordinary lock."

Irene straightened up; Sara was right.

"Ta-da!" With a triumphant smile Sara produced a small leather case from her pocket. "A present from Matti," she said.

Gently but firmly she pushed Irene aside and inserted a slender tool in the lock. After a few seconds there was a click, and she opened the door. They both stepped inside, and immediately saw the figure lying motionless on the sofa. Ritva's face was covered in blood, and her glasses lay smashed on the brightly colored rug. Irene rushed over and knelt down beside her. The relief when she heard Ritva's faint breathing was overwhelming.

"Call for an ambulance and backup! She's alive!"

If the injured woman was aware that there were people in the apartment, she gave no sign of it. She didn't move, and there were long intervals between the rattling breaths. There was a strong smell of urine and excrement, which didn't bother Irene; she had experienced far worse. The main thing was that Ritva was alive.

The blood had come from a deep gash at her left temple. The wound was quite large, around three to four inches, with jagged edges. Not a knife, Irene thought, but definitely a sharp object. She looked around; at first glance everything appeared to be the same as the previous day, but something wasn't right. Suddenly she realized what it was: one of the Ivan Ivarson paintings was missing.

• • •

"RITVA EKHOLM HAS a severe concussion, and she's unconscious. The wound has been stitched and she's still in Intensive Care. She's lost a considerable amount of blood. The hospital will contact us as soon as she comes around."

Superintendent Tommy Persson's expression was grim as he addressed his colleagues. Once again Fredrik Stridh and Ann Wennberg were present. The fate that had befallen their only witness in the case of Monday's car bomb was worrying, and Tommy made no attempt to hide his displeasure. When Irene and Sara told him that they had been able to get into Ritva's apartment because the door had been left unlocked, his skepticism was palpable. The truth was that they had found the keys to the cylinder locks under the hat shelf, but the key to the ordinary lock was missing. The perpetrator must have taken it with him after locking his badly injured victim inside the apartment, but they had chosen to keep that detail from the rest of the team.

If it had been the weekend no one would have missed Ritva at work, and she probably wouldn't have survived. The very thought made Irene break into a cold sweat; she somehow felt responsible for what had happened. It had never occurred to her that Ritva might be in danger. Should she have realized? No, there had been no reason for concern, because only a handful of police officers knew the identity of the witness. Which didn't make her feel any better.

As if he had read her mind, Tommy said, "How could whoever attacked Ritva Ekholm have known her name and where she lived? And how did they get into the apartment? From what you've told us, Irene, she had a whole battery of locks and felt as safe as if she were in a fortress."

"Fort Knox," Irene automatically corrected him.

"Whatever. She locked herself in, and she felt secure, yet she was badly hurt. By whom?"

Tommy looked around the room, challenging someone to come up with a response.

Fredrik cleared his throat. "Maybe she knew her attacker, so she let him in."

"Possibly. But it was hardly a friend, given the violence and the stolen painting. Would she have opened the door to someone she didn't know?" Sara said.

Irene remembered the security chain; there was no way Ritva would have let a stranger in.

"How much is the painting worth?" Ann asked.

"I'm not sure. A few hundred thousand?" Irene replied.

She had spoken to the insurance company, and they had put out a call for the painting so that it couldn't be sold on the open market.

"People have been murdered for less," Ann said dryly.

"But why now? She's had the paintings for years. She becomes a witness in a case involving a serious crime, and suddenly this happens. I don't think it has anything to do with the Ivarson. And if the intruders were art thieves, surely they would have taken all four paintings," Irene pointed out.

Ann Wennberg merely shrugged. It was a warm day, so she had taken off her jacket. Her short-sleeved blouse revealed toned arms, and a thin tattooed chain encircled one upper arm where the sleeve ended. *Not exactly what you'd expect from a PA*, Irene thought, *but it's neat and attractive.*

"There's no sign of a break-in, so Ritva Ekholm must have let her attacker—or attackers—into the apartment," Tommy said.

Irene remembered something from her conversation with Ritva.

"There is another possibility," she said.

The others waited in silence as she thought it through.

"Before I left yesterday evening, Ritva said she was going shopping. Someone could have been waiting for her, forced his way into the apartment where he beat her up then stole the painting. Although I still don't believe this is about the painting; that's just a red herring."

Several of her colleagues nodded in agreement.

"I guess we'll have to wait until she regains consciousness and see what she has to say," Tommy said before turning to Jonny Blom. "Any news on Jan-Erik Månsson?"

"Nothing. The guy has vanished off the face of the earth. And he's taken his car with him."

Tommy sighed. "Well, we've put out a call, so I guess he'll turn up sooner or later."

Irene felt her stomach contract. Something had prevented Janne from leaving the country. He was probably in hiding; if he feared for his life, it could take a while before they tracked him down. The pressure on Krister would increase; only Janne could tell the truth about what had gone on when he was the owner of Glady's. If this was just about gambling debts, then why should his successor's car be a target? She knew this was a key point, and gradually the picture became clear in her mind. This was about the restaurant. She was sure of it. It always had been. What did Krister really know? He seemed stressed and confused, but who wouldn't be in his situation?

"Hello! Earth calling Irene Huss!"

She gave a start as Fredrik's voice interrupted her train of thought. She mumbled apologetically, "I was just thinking about something . . ."

"Something that might help the rest of us?" Tommy asked.

"I just need to give it a little more thought." Irene forced a smile to convince the others that it wasn't anything important.

"So as I said, we've identified two of the guys you found on the CCTV footage—one from each car, luckily," Fredrik said.

He tapped the keyboard of his laptop and an enlarged photoshopped image was projected onto the wall: the man with the ponytail and the tattooed face, in profile. The man who had probably planted the bomb. Irene's pulse rate increased.

"The car is an Audi A4, an older model with a sunroof. Three have been reported stolen, but none with this registration number. I've checked it out. The plates belong to a Volvo, so it could well be one of the stolen cars with false plates," Fredrik went on.

"This is the passenger from the Audi: Andreas Brännström, known as 'Dragon' because of the tattoo. The dragon covers the whole of his back; what you can see there is its tail, curling around his neck and up his cheek. He's twenty-nine years old and a member of Gothia MC— one of their veterans, in fact, with a rap sheet as long as your arm. The interesting thing is he came up in the investigation into the car bomb that killed Soran Siljac last year, but there was no proof of his involvement."

"Why was he a suspect?" Sara asked.

"A witness saw Siljac arguing with two men late one night a few days before the bomb went off. They were standing next to Siljac's car outside the restaurant. According to the witness things turned nasty toward the end, but the men walked away and Siljac got into his car and drove off."

"Was the witness able to identify one of the men as Brännström?" Irene asked.

"No. All he could say for sure was that one of them was a big guy and had a tattoo on his face; the other was tall and looked like a body builder. I also have to point out that the witness was pretty drunk," Fredrik added.

"And what did Brännström say?"

"Nothing. He insisted he'd never even met Siljac. The witness became more and more uncertain, and in the end he decided he might not have seen a tattoo on the man's face after all. Which meant that any kind of case against Brännström collapsed, of course."

Fredrik brought up a second picture: a young man with fierce dark eyes. His hair was a rich brown with big curls, the kind of hair women want to run their fingers through. He was smiling, and his long eyelashes cast a shadow on his high cheekbones. If Irene hadn't known better, she would have thought he was advertising a new male fragrance, but this photograph had been taken following an arrest.

"The BMW at the Ringön intersection does indeed belong to Melek Ekici, but he wasn't driving it himself on Saturday evening; he says he lent it to his eldest son, who is this guy. Unfortunately we couldn't retrieve any decent pictures of the driver; he's wearing a wide bandana, pulled down over his forehead, plus sunglasses in spite of the fact that it was already dark. He looks young and slim, we're guessing eighteen to twenty years old. But the man in the passenger seat is Kazan 'Handsome' Ekici, age twenty-one. He's been a member of the Gangster Lions for a few years and took the usual route via their subchapter the Pumas. He's actually done some modeling work, and he had a minor role in a children's TV series that was made in Hammarkullen a few years ago. But his career was interrupted by his criminal activities. He's been in a juvenile detention center twice, once for selling narcotics and once for repeated instances of violent assault. Word has it he goes crazy when he's high," Fredrik said.

Irene recognized Kazan's face. He had figured on the periphery of a homicide investigation she had been involved in a few years earlier, when the leader of the Pumas had been stabbed to death at Göteborg's central train station by the leader of another gang that was trying to move in on their territory; as usual it was all about drug dealing. Back then Kazan had been a mouthy little fifteen-year-old who had just been picked up for bootlegging. He looked good even at that age; it was easy to see why he was known as Handsome.

Tommy Persson took over. "So we can probably assume we're dealing with the Gangster Lions as far as the murder of Patrik Karlsson is concerned. This is bad news, given that Karlsson was a member of Gothia MC; we could well be facing a new gang war. Then we have the bomb that was planted under the Huss family's car; the suspect has been identified as our old friend Andreas Brännström, who is a faithful servant of Gothia MC. What does this new information tell us?"

"That the two cases are probably unconnected," Sara suggested.

"What makes you say that?"

"We know that the Gangster Lions and Gothia MC are old enemies; they've locked horns before. But the murder of Patrik Karlsson seems so . . . personal. Gang members tend to stab or shoot each other; this business of setting someone on fire . . ." Sara fell silent, glancing over at the wall and the pictures of Karlsson's charred body.

"On the contrary, I'd say this is typical of the Gangster Lions," Ann said firmly. "They're extremely dangerous and unpredictable, and often under the influence of a whole range of drugs. I wouldn't be at all surprised if they set fire to Patrik Karlsson."

Tommy gave her his full attention. "But what about Gothia MC? Why would they blow up Krister and Irene's car?"

Ann thought for a moment before she answered. "I have no idea. If it was them. We only have Ritva Ekholm's assertion that Brännström went into the backyard at Glady's, and she also gave us the time. No other witnesses have contacted us."

Tommy frowned. "You think it's possible that neither Brännström nor Gothia MC were behind the car bomb?"

Ann moistened her lips and took a sip of cold coffee. "It could be them, but maybe we shouldn't focus on that angle to the exclusion of everything else. This could be the Gangster Lions too; they've insisted for a long time that this section of the Avenue is their territory."

They spent a little while discussing their next moves,

and were about to bring the meeting to a close when the intercom on the desk crackled into life.

"Hello? Lennart Lundstedt would like to speak to Tommy Persson. He says it's urgent," a female voice informed them.

Lennart Lundstedt was the head of the special operations team.

"Put him through." Tommy leaned forward, ready to hear what his old friend and colleague had to say.

Lundstedt got straight to the point: "Morning. We've found Jan-Erik Månsson."

"That's great news! Has he said anything?" Tommy asked.

There was a brief pause before Lundstedt responded. "This guy hasn't said anything for quite some time."

A GROUP OF people out picking mushrooms had found the burned-out car. It had been driven into a dense thicket behind a rocky outcrop. One or two of the closest trees were singed, but the fire hadn't spread. The foragers could see that the car was empty, but the stench from the trunk was overpowering. They had seen plenty of crime series on TV, and had a good idea what was in there. Instead of opening it up to take a closer look, they called the cops.

The scene of the discovery was at the end of a narrow forest track leading down to Lake Landvetter. The perpetrators had gone to considerable trouble to hide the vehicle, choosing an uninhabited and isolated area surrounded by thick vegetation.

The body in the trunk was largely unaffected by the flames, though it was still a horrific sight. The registration plate from the back of the car lay a short distance away; it belonged to Jan-Erik Månsson's missing Renault Megane, which made the identification of the deceased considerably easier.

Establishing the probable cause of death wasn't too difficult either: Jan-Erik Månsson had been shot in the head, at least twice.

"EXECUTED," JONNY STATED gloomily, staring down at the corpse.

Irene had seen a lot of dead bodies during her career, but not since the very first case had she felt as physically sick as she did now. Less than six weeks ago she and Krister had had dinner with the charred, rotting mass of flesh in the trunk of the burned-out car, when they got together to sort out the final details regarding Krister's takeover of Glady's. What made the situation worse was that Krister was clearly in danger too. These guys were serious. She couldn't put it off any longer; she had to get him to tell her everything he knew. Right now he was busy with final preparations for the reopening of the restaurant tomorrow, but she would tackle it this evening.

"How long has he been here?" Jonny asked.

The question was directed to Matti Berggren, who was gathering evidence from the scene of the crime. The photographer had gone, leaving Matti with the painstaking task of going over the area with a fine-tooth comb.

"Hard to say—at least a couple of days. The pathologist should be able to tell you more," Matti said without looking up from the dark patch next to the rear offside tire.

Irene's cell phone burst into a rendition of "Mercy." It was a nurse from Sahlgrenska Hospital, informing her that Ritva Ekholm had regained consciousness and been moved out of Intensive Care. The doctors had said she was well enough to answer questions, so Irene and Jonny decided to go straight over.

"ONLY ONE OF you can go in," the male nurse said firmly.

He was young and dark-skinned, and spoke Swedish with a very slight accent. He folded his arms and gazed implacably at the two police officers. Jonny started to protest, then changed his mind.

"You go, Irene. She knows you," he said.

Irene had to put on sterile clothing before she was allowed into the room. Ritva's thin body was barely visible beneath the yellow blanket. Her face was ashen, and the contrast with the livid purple bruise around her left eye and temple was shocking. The wound on the side of her head was bandaged. One eye was swollen shut, although according to the nurse it wasn't damaged; the heavy bleeding had caused the swelling. He quietly informed Irene that their experienced senior consultant thought the injury had been caused by a blunt object with a sharp edge—some kind of metal weapon, he had said. Bearing in mind who they were dealing with here, Irene favored a knuckle duster.

"Just a few minutes," the nurse reminded her before leaving the room.

Irene turned to the small figure in the bed.

"Ritva? It's Irene Huss from the police. Do you think you could manage to answer a couple of questions?"

Ritva opened her right eye and looked up at Irene. She moved her lips, but nothing came out.

"As I'm sure you understand, we'd like to know what happened," Irene went on.

Ritva's gaze darted to and fro, and eventually fixed on a point on the ceiling.

Irene tried again:

"Do you remember what happened last night?"

Slowly the eye focused on Irene once more; Ritva's expression was unreadable.

"No. Nothing," she whispered.

"Nothing at all?"

"No. No."

Had the trauma affected Ritva's memory, or was she too scared to talk?

"You really don't remember anything?"

Ritva moved her head slowly from side to side.

"During the course of this investigation we've come across a number of people who've been threatened. Has anyone threatened you?" Irene asked, feeling as if she was being unnecessarily brutal.

Ritva froze, then she gave an almost imperceptible sigh. "No."

Irene decided to try a new tactic. "Do you remember our conversation yesterday evening?"

"Yes."

Not a hint of hesitation, which was encouraging. "Do you remember me leaving your apartment?"

"Yes."

"Do you remember telling me you were going shopping later?"

"Yes."

"And did you do that? Did you go shopping?"

"Yes."

The answer was immediate and confident.

"What time did you go out?"

There was a lengthy silence.

"I don't . . . remember," Ritva said hesitantly.

"Where did you go? The 7-Eleven? Domus on the Avenue?"

"I don't remember." Ritva closed her eye.

"Did you see anyone when you got back to your apartment?"

"I don't remember. All . . . black."

"You don't recall anything that happened before the attack?"

"No."

Irene asked a few more questions, but it was a waste of time; Ritva just kept on repeating that she didn't remember a thing. When the nurse came in and informed Irene that her time was up, she couldn't help feeling disappointed. Their only witness in the car bomb case appeared to have lost her memory. She consoled herself with the thought that it might only be a temporary state of affairs.

LATE IN THE afternoon they received confirmation that the dead man was Jan-Erik Månsson; the charred corpse had been identified with the help of dental records. Due to a skiing accident in his teens, Jan-Erik had a small bridge in his upper jaw, and so did the victim. There was also a gold watch on the wrist with the inscription "Jan-Erik 2009. With all my love, Sissela." Jan-Erik and Sissela had divorced in 2010.

Professor Yvonne Stridner had personally called to give Irene the news, which was unusual.

"This is a repulsive crime, definitely on a par with the young man who was set on fire out in Ringön," she explained. Then she hung up before Irene had the chance to thank her.

Irene sat there for a while staring blankly at the faded print of Monet's *Impression, soleil levant*, which had adorned the wall during all the years she had been with the unit; it had even come with them when they moved upstairs. When she stood up, she had made her decision. It was definitely time to talk to Krister.

AT FIRST HE refused to go with her. He got annoyed and pointed out that he had his hands full getting the restaurant ready to reopen, and that took priority over her nagging.

That was the final straw as far as Irene was concerned. She grabbed his upper arm and looked him straight in the eye, making a huge effort to keep her voice under control.

"Listen to me. Janne has been found dead. Murdered. The boss has told me to question you, but if you'd prefer one of my colleagues to do it, we'll go to the station right now."

Krister stiffened and stared at her as every scrap of color drained from his face. Irene was genuinely afraid he might faint, and when his knees began to shake she forced him to sit down on a stool just inside the kitchen door.

"Put your head between your knees and take deep breaths. There you go. It's okay, honey."

After a while he began to look a little better, but it was obvious he was still deeply shocked.

"Would you prefer to talk at home or at the station?" Irene asked, fighting back the tears.

"At home," he mumbled.

"Fine. But remember I'm not taking any crap."

She immediately regretted her brusque tone, but at the same time she realized that if she was going to get anything out of him, she had to stick to her guns. Her compliant approach had achieved nothing.

During the drive home Krister sat beside her in the passenger seat without saying a word. Irene didn't feel like starting a conversation either; this wasn't the time for small talk, and the serious discussion could wait.

She parked the car and got out, but Krister didn't move. She walked around and opened his door.

"Come on, honey," she said gently.

He gave a start, but made no effort to get out. Staring straight ahead, he said in a voice that was far from steady:

"Is it . . . is it definitely Janne?"

Irene took a deep breath.

"Yes, I'm afraid so."

As IRENE AND Krister walked into the apartment, Egon came hurtling toward them like a little cyclone made of silky reddish-brown fur. He wound himself around their legs whimpering with joy until Krister picked him up. Overcome with delight he licked his master's face. Like all dogs he liked the taste of salty bodily fluids, but after a little while he realized that Krister was sad. He calmed down, but carried on licking away the tears. He scrabbled his way up Krister's chest and buried his nose under his master's ear, licking and rooting around until Krister couldn't help laughing.

"I know this is a formal interview, but is it okay if I have a whisky?" he asked with a wan smile.

"Sure," Irene said, kissing him softly.

The last week had been something of an ordeal; a drop of Scotch wouldn't do either of them any harm. She poured both of them a generous measure of the amber-colored liquid, using the crystal glasses they had inherited from her parents. On the way to the living room she stopped in the hallway and took a small tape recorder out of her jacket pocket.

Krister settled down in one of the armchairs with Egon contentedly curled up on his lap. Slowly he stroked the little dog's back as he gazed out of the large picture window. The sun was setting, and the clouds were lit from below with a beautiful pink glow.

Irene handed him his drink; they both took a sip, then she said, "I'm sorry I told you about Janne's death in such a brutal way, but ever since the car bomb I've had the feeling that you've been avoiding talking to me. This can't go on; you have to tell me everything you know. This is serious. And I have no choice but to record what you say."

She switched on the tape recorder and placed it on the coffee table. Krister still didn't meet her eyes; instead he looked down at Egon, who was snoring quietly. Irene gave the date and time, but before she could state their full names, Krister interrupted her.

"How . . . how did he die?"

"Janne was shot. Then they hid his body in the trunk of his car, drove out to an isolated spot near Lake Land-vetter, and set fire to the car."

Krister swallowed hard.

"When was this?"

"We don't know for sure, but probably at the beginning of the week."

They sat in silence for a long time. Irene really wanted to go over and put her arms around him, but she knew she had to remain as professional as possible, otherwise there was a significant risk that they would both break down. She decided to try something out, see if he took the bait.

"We know that Janne was contacted by the gang known as Gothia MC. Did he mention it to you?"

Krister stiffened and gave her a quick glance before returning his attention to Egon.

"No. Janne didn't say anything to me. Nothing at all," he muttered.

Irene refrained from asking him to repeat his answer a little more clearly. It would have to do; she could see how hard this was for him. There was a lump in her throat, and she had to swallow several times before she was able to continue.

"We know he sold both restaurants very quickly. We also know that he was in the process of selling his luxury apartment, but he couldn't wait until that sale went through; he tried to run."

She told Krister about Jan-Erik's desperate attempt to flee to the US without his girlfriend, and that he had failed to check in at the airport. The last person to see him alive, as far as they knew, was Jeanette Stenberg at around eleven o'clock on Sunday night. Irene paused as she considered her next move.

"We know that Janne had gambling debts, but we don't think this is about those debts. It's something to do with the restaurants. Or in the case of the car bomb, your restaurant. Am I right?"

Krister sighed and took a large swig of his whisky. He rubbed his face, as he were trying to wake himself from a bad dream.

"It started with the gambling debts. They're saying he didn't pay off everything he owed, so now they want me to pay!"

The last words were followed by a sob. Egon whimpered in confusion and pressed himself closer to his master's chest.

"When you say 'they,' who do you mean?"

Irene did her best to sound unmoved, but her throat was constricted by the effort of holding back her own tears. She knew her voice was shaking, but hoped it wouldn't come across on the tape.

"The gang . . . the biker gang."

"Gothia MC?"

"Yes. There were two of them. They wore vests . . . Oh God, I can't believe it's only been a week since this nightmare began!"

He put down a protesting Egon and got to his feet. He strode out of the room; Irene heard the bathroom door open, and sound of water running for a long time. When he came back he seemed more composed, although his hand was trembling as he raised the whisky glass to his lips. He put it down and looked her in the eye.

"They threatened to kill you and the girls. Then me."

Irene felt as if someone had punched her in the stomach, but she managed to maintain a neutral tone. "So why did they plant a bomb under our car?"

"I don't know. To show me they weren't messing around, I guess."

He could be right, Irene thought. The bomb had been a warning.

"Why did they threaten to kill us? What did they want you to do?"

Krister sighed, but at least he was facing up to the situation. "They said I'd inherited Janne's debts, insisted I had to pay."

"They said you'd inherited his debts?"

"Yes. As if . . . as if he was already dead. But he wasn't. Jeannette saw him on Sunday. But he must have been . . . condemned to death."

"When was this?"

"Last Friday."

Irene tried to think back. "We got home at almost the same time, around six," she said.

"Yes. They were waiting for me outside the restaurant when I left." He fell silent, clutching the crystal glass which was now empty.

"Can you remember their exact words?"

Krister got up and went over to the window, where the last rays of the setting sun caught the treetops down in the valley. He and Irene had stood there side by side enjoying the spectacle many times during the summer. When he turned around, his expression was grim. He went back to his armchair, picked up the empty glass and put it down again. It was a couple of moments before he felt he could trust his voice.

"The fat guy with the tattoo on his face informed me that because I was now the owner of Glady's, I had to pay four hundred thousand by Friday. Tomorrow. That's how much Janne owes them, and according to this guy, he used the restaurant as collateral."

"Four hundred . . . ! And what did you say?" She could hardly get the words out.

"I told them I don't have any money. That we've put everything we had into the restaurant, plus we've taken out a loan . . . Well, you know all that. I told them it was impossible." He slumped down in the chair, as if all the strength had left his body.

Irene knew exactly what their financial position was. Before she could ask a question, Krister continued. "If I don't come up with the money, they are going to consider themselves joint owners of Glady's."

She had been expecting something along those lines, but still her stomach contracted. A feeling of fury and impotence flooded her body. There had to be a solution, but what was it?

"So what did you say to that?"

"I told them to go to hell!"

For the first time during their conversation Krister looked angry, which pleased Irene. Any emotion was better than resigned acceptance.

"And how did they react?"

"They said I had to face up to my responsibilities, or something bad would happen to you and the girls. They knew our addresses—all of us. I was scared, of course, but I was furious too. So I told them to go to hell again."

Irene felt her pulse rate increase. It had been brave of Krister to stand up to those guys, but at the same time incredibly foolhardy. He had no idea who he was dealing with. Keeping her thoughts to herself, she asked, "And then?"

Krister rubbed his face before answering. "They said they'd show me they weren't messing around. Then they laughed and walked away."

"But you didn't say anything to me when you got home." Irene smiled so that her words wouldn't sound like an accusation.

"No . . . We were planning to have dinner with Felipe and the girls on the Saturday, and I didn't want to spoil things. Maybe I was trying to pretend it wasn't happening. It felt kind of unreal, as if it had nothing to do with me."

His voice was unsteady, and Irene could see the shimmer of tears in his eyes. She didn't want him to break down before he had told her everything. She didn't want him to break down at all.

"Did they contact you again before the bomb went off?"

"No, not until the day after. They called my cell phone. Withheld number. I recognized the fat guy's voice. He said next time no one would survive. I was the only person who could save . . . save you and the girls. If I paid up."

He cleared his throat and wiped the tears from his cheeks. After a couple of deep breaths he continued. "I repeated that the debt was Janne's, not mine, and he said that Janne was no longer in a position to pay. It was time for me to think about my own safety, taking care of myself and my family. I would be protected by the shadows, he said. I realized that 'shadows' meant him and his sidekick. Obviously I was going to have to pay for this protection somehow; if I didn't, then . . ."

He broke off, unable to suppress a sob. With great self-control he managed to pull himself together.

"If I didn't give them what they wanted, I would soon be meeting my friend Janne in hell."

"In hell . . . Were those his exact words?"

"Yes."

So the fat guy was well aware that Jan-Erik Månsson was already dead, Irene thought.

"And you have until tomorrow to come up with the money?"

"Yes."

Irene asked Krister to describe the two men who had threatened him; there was little doubt that he was talking about Andreas Brännström and his associate from the CCTV footage.

"Definitely Gothia MC," she said. "Cocky enough to show up in their vests."

"They were all in black apart from that—no, wait, the guy with the ponytail was wearing ripped blue jeans, I think."

Irene switched off the tape recorder. Her heart was pounding, but she knew exactly what she had to do. She took his hands and kissed them, and as gently as possible said, "Honey, you can't reopen Glady's tomorrow." He tried to interrupt her. "No, don't say anything. We have to think about the safety of the staff and the customers. There's a major risk of an attack tomorrow or in the very near future. You don't have any money, and if they don't get paid, we know what's going to happen."

Krister shook his head wearily.

Irene leaned closer. "You have to go undercover. You and the girls. You have to go into hiding."

"But . . . that's impossible! How long—"

Irene interrupted his objections. She couldn't hold

back the tears now, and her voice was trembling. "Janne is dead. Murdered. They've transferred their extortion racket to you. What if they kill you? Our whole family has been threatened, and they planted a bomb under your car. This is deadly serious, Krister!"

She dried her eyes and resolutely got to her feet. She fetched her cell phone and called Jenny and Katarina.

THE TWINS IMMEDIATELY understood that there was a crisis when their mom called and asked them to come straight over. By the time Jenny arrived, Katarina and Felipe had already been there for a while, but still didn't know why. Irene wanted everyone around her before she outlined her plan.

Two pots of tea and a pile of sandwiches later, they had all listened to the tape, and were in total agreement. They had to vanish without a trace.

IT WAS EXACTLY 5:00 when Irene rang the doorbell of Superintendent Tommy Persson's terraced house in Jonsered, keeping her finger on the button until he appeared, half-asleep and blinking in confusion. He was wearing a faded blue terrycloth robe, and with his early morning stubble and his hair standing on end, he wasn't exactly firing on all cylinders.

Irene got straight to the point. "Hi. Can I come in?"

"Sure . . . sure," Tommy said, looking even more bewildered. He stepped aside to let her pass. She could see how surprised he was when he noticed that she was carrying a small suitcase and two large paper bags containing bed linen. He closed the door and followed her into the kitchen, where she immediately set to work making coffee.

"I'm sorry to turn up like this, but it was absolutely essential that you didn't know I was coming," she said before he even had time to ask a question.

"Have you and Krister had a row?"

"Would I come to you if I'd fallen out with my husband?"

"No, I guess not. Listen, do you mind if I go and take a shower, see if I can wake myself up? I realize I'm not going to get any more beauty sleep."

When Tommy reappeared, fresh and clean-shaven, the kitchen was filled with the aroma of coffee and warm bread. Irene had brought bread and delicious jelly with her.

When they had finished eating and were both on their second cup of coffee, she said, "Okay, I'm going to play you the recording of my interview with Krister yesterday evening."

She went out into the hallway and fetched the little tape recorder. She switched it on without further comment, and they sat at Tommy's rustic pine table as his neighbors began to wake up to a new day.

NEITHER OF THEM spoke for a long time when the interview came to an end. Their coffee had gone cold.

After a while Irene said, "So today Krister is supposed to pay Gothia MC four hundred thousand kronor. If he can't come up with the money, he has to let the bad guys become joint owners of Glady's. Both options are unthinkable."

She got up and took the cups over to the sink. She threw away the cold coffee and refilled them from the pot, being careful not to spill a drop as she returned to the table. Tommy was still staring at her in silence.

"As you heard, all four of us have been threatened. We're supposed to live our lives under the protection of those shadows in the future. That makes me feel really safe! We had a family meeting last night, and we've come up with a plan. Gothia MC made it very clear that they know our address and Jenny and Katarina's addresses. So Krister, Felipe and the girls have gone undercover. I'll be staying here with you until further notice."

"What? I don't . . . Why?" Tommy said.

"Why? Because we, the police, can't guarantee the safety of my family!"

"Of course we can—" Tommy began, but Irene cut him off immediately.

"No. You know just as well as I do that's not true. We're crap when it comes to protecting anyone under threat; we have neither the time nor the resources. It takes weeks to set up a new identity, and in any case that's not an option as far as I'm concerned. We want our lives back! Without shadows and without their so-called protection!"

Tommy merely nodded.

"Besides which we—the police, that is—now have a major problem. Someone is leaking information to Gothia MC," Irene went on.

Tommy frowned; his colleague clearly meant what she said.

"I'm almost sure of it. There's this business with Ritva Ekholm; only a few members of our team and a couple of officers with the Organized Crimes Unit knew that she'd contacted us; that limits the number of people who had access to her name and address. We're looking at a maximum of ten cops—no one else."

"Hang on Irene. The perp could have seen Ritva Ekholm and—"

"I don't think so. Ritva crossed the street and turned her head in their direction. She saw a man on the side-walk and a tattooed hand waving through the sunroof. One of the guys might have seen her, but how could they know that she lived in the apartment block opposite Glady's? The door to her staircase is on Södra vägen, not

Lorensbergsgatan. There's no way they could have seen her leaving the building."

Irene paused to make sure Tommy was with her; he nodded and waved a hand to indicate that she should continue. She finished off her coffee.

"We first heard about Ritva last Wednesday morning," she said. "I went to see her that same day, between five and six, so only a handful of us were aware that Ritva had seen something that could incriminate the men who planted the bomb. In spite of that, she was attacked on Wednesday evening. She was a dangerous witness, and they silenced her. She survived, but she's too scared to talk. Either that or she's telling the truth, and she can't remember anything."

Tommy stared intently at her, drumming his fingertips on the table. Any trace of sleepiness was gone.

"Could Göran Nilsson be the leak? He was supposed to work on a composite image with Ekholm, so he knew about her," he suggested.

"No. He wasn't told which case it concerned, and he wasn't given any contact details for the witness. The message gave Ritva's name and the time she was due to come in, nothing else."

Tommy thought things over for a few moments. "I think you could be right about the leak, but I have no idea who it might be. Any thoughts?"

"No. But we have to assume it could be anyone at the station. We say nothing, but we keep our eyes open. Sooner or later he or she will make a mistake."

"How did you come up with the idea of moving in with me?" Tommy asked.

Irene gave a faint smile.

"I don't think anyone on the team is aware of how well we really know each other—that we've been friends ever since we started training. We haven't hung out much since your divorce, which makes me sad, to be honest, but . . . life changes."

She was a little embarrassed; she wasn't sure how sensitive the issue of their lack of social contact might be. It had been several years since he and his wife had split up, after all; surely she and Tommy should have been able to regain their close friendship, but it just hadn't happened. Krister had also suggested that he and Tommy should meet up, but Tommy had made excuses; neither Irene nor Krister knew why. Maybe she was asking too much of him now? It was a worrying thought.

"I get it. But where are Krister and the girls?" he asked.

"I haven't a clue, and that's the way we agreed it had to be. If Gothia MC get ahold of me, I won't be able to tell them anything."

She told Tommy how they had settled on their plan the previous evening. When they were all in agreement, they had set to work. The girls and Felipe went home and packed enough clothes for at least a week, while Krister also gathered up a few other things that he thought might come in handy. They were all very clear that they were fleeing for their lives.

At four in the morning Irene and Krister picked up Jenny, Katarina and Felipe in the rented car, an almost new white Megane. Egon was there too, of course. Krister had collected the car from Avis late in the afternoon; it had been in the parking lot outside their apartment on Doktor Bex gata for only a few hours, so Irene didn't think Gothia MC would connect it to her

family. She had fixed the bike rack to the back of the car
and attached her bicycle. They drove to a cash machine
on Södra vägen, where each of them took out as much
money as they were allowed on their various cards. They
had to stick to cash over the next week. Then they filled
up the car at the gas station in Ullevi before heading
straight over to Jonsered, where they dropped off Irene
with her bicycle and her bags. She hugged them all
tightly and shed a tear, but she knew they were doing the
right thing. She pushed her bike the last few hundred
yards to Tommy's house. She wanted to arrive without
being spotted by any nosy neighbors. She hid her bike in
the bushes by the visitor's parking space so that no one
would wonder what a lady's bike was doing outside
Tommy's front door.

"It's a good six miles from here to work," Tommy
pointed out.

"Good thing I'm fit, then." Irene managed a half-
smile. "There's no point in going to a hotel. They'd find
me right away. Nobody must know I'm staying with you.
We'll arrive at the station at different times, leave at different times. We don't travel in the car together, we
don't talk about anything connected with home—what
we're having for dinner and so on. Sometimes I'll cycle
in, sometimes I'll take the bus if I'm sure no one is following me."

"I understand why you've come up with the plan, but
are you really going to carry on working?"

"Of course! That's the only way I can be safe: surrounded by cops! I don't think the leak is prepared to
facilitate an attack in the station, or when we're out on
a call," she said, her smile a little bolder this time.

"And how are you going to keep in touch with Krister and the girls?"

"Through you," she replied cheerfully.

Tommy raised an eyebrow.

"Krister is going to buy a pay-as-you-go card for his cell phone; he'll send a number to your cell, but without a name attached. You pass that number on to me, and I'll call him from a new cell, which I'm intending to buy today. Again that will be pay-as-you-go."

"Good idea. But what if anyone starts wondering why the whole family has disappeared? Apart from you, of course."

"We're in luck there. Katarina and Felipe are free for the next two weeks before the next semester starts. Jenny is going to speak to her temporary employer today and tell him that her dad isn't feeling too good after the incident with the car bomb, and that she needs to be around to support both him and me . . . Well, you get the idea. And I'll contact the maître d' and the head chef at Glady's and explain that it's all been too much for Krister. He's going to be out sick for at least a week, probably longer. I'll also inform them that the police have concluded that the restaurant is a possible target for further attacks, given the car bomb and the murder of Jan-Erik Månsson and that it must remain closed for another week."

Tommy nodded. "That could well be true, of course. Is Krister likely to head for the cottage in Sunne?"

"No, we agreed that wasn't a good idea. Far too many people know we own a place up there, after what happened . . ."

Just thinking of the cottage and the bog made Irene's

stomach tie itself in knots. Tommy knew how traumatic it had been for her, and changed the subject.

"Okay, so you and I are housemates. I've got a course this evening, but what shall we have for dinner tomorrow?"

"As we're both equally crap at cooking, I suggest you pick up a couple of pizzas on the way home," she replied with a laugh.

Bearing in mind that she hadn't slept for more than two hours, Irene felt surprisingly bright. She arrived at work fifteen minutes after Tommy. They greeted each other as normal, and no one could possibly have guessed that they'd had breakfast together.

Once again the team was supplemented by colleagues from the Organized Crimes Unit; Superintendent Stefan Bratt, Fredrik Stridh and Ann Wennberg arrived together just before the briefing began. All three were carrying take-away coffees. No morning prayer without a cup of coffee, that was Irene's golden rule. Today Ann was wearing a pale blue short-sleeved blouse with a dark blue linen pencil skirt and blue ballerina pumps. *As fresh as a cornflower*, Irene thought with a stab of envy. She hadn't even managed to have a proper wash after cycling all the way in from Jonsered. There was a decent shower in the changing room, but she had only had time to splash some water under her arms and apply a slick of deodorant.

"Good morning. It looks like it's going to be a lovely day, but we're unlikely to have the opportunity to enjoy the weather. We've got more than enough to do," Tommy Persson began. He turned to Jonny. "Anything new on the murder of Jan-Erik Månsson?"

"Yes . . . I'm waiting for the preliminary report from the pathologist this morning. But Sara has been taking a look at CCTV," he said, nodding in the direction of his colleague.

Typical. Jonny was sitting around waiting, while someone else was saddled with the boring stuff. To be fair, he had definitely perfected the art of looking busy, Irene thought sourly.

Sara clicked on her computer keyboard and a slightly blurred image from the CCTV camera was projected onto the white wall. It was a Renault Megane, and Irene was pretty sure Jan-Erik was driving. There was no one beside him, but she could see a dark figure in the back-seat.

"We went through the footage from various roads leading to the spot where the body was found, and we picked up Jan-Erik Månsson's car. It passed a camera at the Råda intersection at 4:17 on Monday morning and turned onto Säterivägen. Bearing in mind where the car was found, it must have taken minor roads from then on, where there are unfortunately no cameras. However . . ."

Sara paused as Jonny raised his hand and made a V-for-victory sign. Trying to take the credit for her hard work. *Typical*, Irene thought again.

". . . we also noticed a dark-colored Audi A4 with a sunroof following the Megane," Sara continued, ignoring Jonny.

"Could you see the driver of either car?" Fredrik asked.

"Yes. Månsson was driving his own car, but there was someone in the backseat. The Audi was carrying false plates, of course, but not the same plates as in the incident involving Ritva Ekholm. This number belongs to a Volvo V50 which is registered in Kungsbacka; however, the driver matches the description of the guy who was behind the wheel when the bomb was planted under the Huss family's car, and when Ritva Ekholm was assaulted. We're sure it's the same Audi in all three cases, even though they've switched the plates, but it's not possible to identify the driver because as usual he's wearing a baseball cap pulled well down over his forehead."

"Can we check out the tattoos on his hands? They're pretty clear in these images too," Jonny suggested.

"The Audi reappears at the Råda intersection at 5:06, heading back into the city."

Sara ended her report with the relevant images; the driver looked the same, and sitting beside him was Andreas Brännström.

"So we know that Månsson was alive at 4:17 on Monday morning," Tommy summarized. "Andreas Brännström was in the backseat, and forced him to drive to the location in Landvetter where we found the car. It seems likely that he was killed almost as soon as they arrived; the time of death is somewhere between 4:35 and 4:55. There are no reports of smoke or flames by the lake, which is hardly surprising; no one lives around there, and people aren't likely to be out and about at that hour in any case."

He informed them that a call had gone out for Andreas Brännström, but with no luck so far. There were images from the previous day of a lone motorcyclist traveling across Öresund Bridge. He had no logos on his helmet or jacket, but his physique matched Brännström's description. He might have left the country, which would explain why Interpol was now looking for him. He could have been supplied with a false passport by associates in Copenhagen and boarded a plane with an unknown destination. At this point he could be anywhere in the world.

It didn't take him long to find out he'd been identified, Irene thought.

"Have you spoken to Kazan Ekici?" Stefan Bratt asked, looking at Ann and Fredrik.

Fredrik nodded. "I interviewed him yesterday, but he denies being anywhere near Kolgruvegatan. He claims that he and his friend Fendi Göks were on their way to a party out in Lillhagen. They'd borrowed Daddy's car, but they took a wrong turn after the Tingstad tunnel and ended up on Ringögatan. They tried to pick up their route via the Branting intersection, but they went wrong again and decided to skip the party. They drove back the same way and went to a bar instead. Fendi Göks tells exactly the same story. We spoke to the bartender who was on duty on Saturday night, and he confirms that Kazan and his pal arrived some time before eleven. We have no evidence to suggest that Kazan and Fendi have anything to do with the murder, so they were released."

"Who's Fendi Göks?" Irene asked; she had never heard of him.

"He just turned eighteen and has a brand new driver's license. He has a record for minor violations, but nothing serious. According to Kazan, he and Fendi are cousins, but I don't know if that's true. They live at home with their respective parents in Gunnared," Fredrik clarified.

"Thanks for the information, Fredrik, and for conducting

the interview. We still have people on vacation, but we'll be back to full strength on Monday," Tommy said.

Stefan Bratt leaned forward. "Speaking of full strength: we're also a little short-staffed at the moment. This evening we're supposed to check out an interesting party: Danny Mara, the leader of the Gangster Lions, is having a fortieth birthday celebration at a conference center in Sävedalen. Or just outside Sävedalen, in fact. The place is owned by a property company that Danny runs with his brother. It's important to have a legitimate business for money-laundering purposes."

He sat back with a meaningful smile.

"So the mafia king is holding court. Fascinating," Jonny commented.

"That's right. I'm sure most of the gang will be there. Those who aren't on our wanted list or behind bars, anyway," Bratt said, his smile even broader now. He quickly grew serious and nodded toward the picture of Brännström and his associate in the Audi.

"We've also heard from various sources that a new war is brewing between Gothia MC and the Gangster Lions. It seems likely that Gothia will want to avenge the murder of Patrik Karlsson; what better time to strike than when the Gangster Lions are partying?"

"Partying . . . you mean totally wasted on booze and narcotics. Keeping an eye on those bastards is always a fucking nightmare; it costs a fortune and it means extra work for us. Can't we just forget the whole thing? Let them sort it out among themselves? Cheap and . . . self-cleansing," Jonny said with a grin.

Stefan Bratt raised his eyebrows. Tommy glared at his inspector, but Jonny didn't let it bother him one iota. To her surprise, Irene noticed that Ann Wennberg was smiling at Jonny. Did she really find him funny, or was it more of a supercilious smirk?

Bratt considered for a moment before responding.

"There are definitely those who take that view, but right now Göteborg is a city under extreme pressure from gangs. Politicians and public servants are being bribed; those who can't be bribed are threatened. It's endemic, and even innocent citizens are dragged down. It's all about power and money. The mafia gangs control drug dealing, prostitution, human trafficking, illegal gambling, protection rackets plus several other grey areas, not least in the building and catering industries. The mafia is a financial power factor. This affects all of us, one way or another. And now we have a new gang war, which once again is about who is in charge of these lucrative interests. Which means it's our job to get in there and put a stop to it."

Jonny shrugged, but didn't say anything. However, his expression made it clear that he hadn't changed his mind about the way in which the gang problem should be solved.

"So is there any chance that you guys could help us out tonight?" Bratt asked, glancing around the room.

Irene thought fast. It was better to spend the evening with her colleagues than trying to stay out of Gothia MC's way on her own.

"I'm in," she said.

"Me too," Sara said.

Tommy Persson looked troubled.

"I'm at a conference in Stenungsbaden. I'm leaving after lunch and I won't be back until tomorrow afternoon."

Which Irene already knew, of course.

"Unfortunately I can't help—family reasons," Jonny said firmly.

"At least that's two extra bodies, and I'll be there too. It'll be good to get out in the field again," Bratt said enthusiastically.

STRAIGHT AFTER THE meeting Irene borrowed an unmarked car and drove home to Guldheden to pick up her uniform. When she tried on the pants, which she hadn't worn for a couple of years, her suspicions were confirmed: they were pretty tight around her waist and over her backside. There was no denying that she had put on a few pounds, which was annoying.

Krister wasn't due to hand over the money to Gothia MC until the evening, so it was too early for them to realize that something had gone wrong. Just to be on the safe side, Irene gave the plants an extra drink of water. She checked the refrigerator just to make sure there was nothing in there that was going to start stinking over the next seven days.

She also called Glady's on the landline; as she had expected, the maître d' was devastated to hear that the restaurant would have to remain closed for at least another week. However, when Irene explained that the staff and customers could be in danger because of the car bomb and the murder of Jan-Erik Månsson, he didn't protest. He promised to call everyone who had already made a reservation.

Before Irene left the apartment, she took a good look around. The place really was lovely now they had finished all the renovations. Every room had been redecorated, and they had bought several new pieces, but it still retained that cozy, familiar feeling. She was happy there; she didn't want to live anywhere else. No fucking lowlife gangster was going to force her out! Resolutely she locked the front door behind her, but she couldn't ignore the heaviness in her heart. She had no idea when she would be able to come back home.

IT HAD JUST stopped raining, and the flashing blue lights of two parked squad cars were reflected in the wet tarmac. Superintendent Stefan Bratt was in one car, with Irene, Sara, Fredrik and Ann in the other. Two officers from the security detail who had arrived with Stefan had positioned themselves on either side of the imposing gates of the conference center; their job was to check the ID of all arrivals before they drove onto the complex. Stefan himself stayed in the background, keeping an eye on proceedings. As he worked for the Organized Crimes Unit, he recognized most of those who turned up; he also made a point of memorizing some of the younger party-goers. He knew it was only a matter of time before he came across them again.

Irene could see smartly dressed people moving around in the lobby; she too recognized a number of faces. Before they parted company after the meeting, Stefan had shown her and Sara some photographs taken by a surveillance team at an earlier party; the Gangster Lions had been celebrating the release of some of their older members from various jails at roughly the same time. That particular party had also been attended by scantily clad girls who, according to Bratt, were neither the wives nor the girlfriends of the "gentlemen" who were there.

The parkland surrounding the venue itself was an odd shape—long and narrow. Apparently it was because the palatial manor house had been constructed on a plot in between two pieces of land, one owned by the church and the other by a family of noble birth. A wealthy trader had built the "shopkeeper's palace," as it was known locally, in the 1880s. The head of the noble family had refused to cede a single square yard to the "upstart grocer." They became bitter enemies, and the trader had an exceptionally high wall erected all the way around the parkland, making a point of separating himself from his neighbors.

The sturdy wall made of Bohuslän granite was still just as solid as the day it went up. The only way to see what was now the conference center from outside was to stand in front of the impressive gates. Irene had learned that there were two smaller gates set into the wall, one halfway down each long side. They provided access to the park, but it was impossible to see the front of the center from either gate. The police had had no choice but to stick to the main gates if they were to have any chance of monitoring what was going on. At the same time, their obvious presence acted as a warning signal to the Gangster Lions: we're watching you.

Irene could see Danny Mara standing in the middle of the crowded lobby beneath an ostentatious crystal chandelier. Two enormous heavies behind him were checking out anyone who came near their employer; they might as well have had "bodyguard" stamped across their foreheads. Irene recognized them right away: the Iranian brothers Ali and Omid Reza. They had been part of a gang that had split because of internal squabbles over drug money, which had ended with two dead and one seriously injured. The rest of the gang got stuck serving long sentences in jail, including the Reza brothers. They had a reputation for being real tough guys. As soon as they were released, Danny Mara contacted them and said he could use them as his personal bodyguards. And when the leader of the Gangster Lions makes an offer, everyone knows you have no choice. It was non-negotiable; it was an order. They had accepted immediately.

One by one, Danny's guests walked up to him, shook hands and gave him a present. Mostly envelopes, as far as Irene could see. She noticed their stiff posture, and how uncomfortable many of the tattooed men looked in their dark suits and new shirts. Their attitude to their leader was one of respect; some even bent over his hand as if to offer a kiss. Behind Danny, Irene could just see a younger guy: his brother and right-hand man, Andy Mara. The two of them were very much alike, although Andy was perhaps a little slimmer than Danny.

A young woman was standing beside Danny with two children, the smallest in a stroller. He was sucking enthusiastically on a pale blue pacifier that bobbed up and down as he watched everything that was going on, wide-eyed. His older sister was clutching her mommy's hand and gazing down at her shiny red shoes. Occasionally she would glance up and smile shyly when someone spoke to her. The girl couldn't be more than four years old, but it was already clear that she looked just like her mom; she was a pretty child. Her mother was elegant and slender, with long dark brown hair tumbling in loose curls down her back. Her dress was an off-the-shoulder dream in ivory silk.

"Is the woman in the stunning dress Danny's wife?" Irene asked.

"Yes, Elif," Ann replied. "Six years ago she was the prettiest eighteen-year-old in Göteborg. She caught Danny's eye, and he made up his mind; he usually gets what he wants. They married after a very short time, and everyone was happy. But not anymore—at least as far as Elif's family are concerned."

"How come?"

"You see the heavily pregnant girl behind them, on the stairs?"

Irene could hardly miss her; she looked as if she was ready to pop at any moment. Unlike most of the other guests she had a Nordic appearance, with pale blonde hair and blue eyes.

"She's nineteen, her name is Jannike, and she's been Danny's mistress for the last year. Officially she's Andy's girlfriend, but everyone knows the score; that's Danny's baby she's carrying."

"And what does Andy have to say about that?" Irene asked.

"Andy's always been single, and rumor has it that he prefers guys. But that would be completely unacceptable within both the gang and the family, so I guess this arrangement suits him too. They say his last girlfriend was also Danny's mistress."

"So Danny is notoriously unfaithful to his wife?"

"So it seems."

Their attention was diverted by a white limousine pulling up by the gates. The tinted rear window slid down and a face appeared. The man's bleached locks were slicked back in a style that looked ridiculous on someone who was well over forty, with thinning hair. With some difficulty he fished a wallet out of the inside pocket of his smoking jacket and waved his ID at the uniformed officers. One of them took it and examined it at some length, his face expressionless, before handing it back with an exaggerated bow. The man in the backseat grabbed his ID card and the window silently closed. The car slowly rolled forward to the wide steps leading up to the main entrance; the passenger got out and chivalrously held open the door for his female companion. She appeared to be distinctly unsteady on her feet as she tottered out of the car; the man in the smoking jacket tightened his grip on her arm and steered her up the steps.

"Wow! The mafia's lawyer, Christoffer von Hanke, in person. We are honored!" Fredrik exclaimed.

Irene watched as the couple was absorbed by the crowd.

The radio crackled to life, and Stefan Bratt's voice informed them that there were now one hundred and thirty-seven guests inside the building. The party had begun.

THE GUESTS HAD settled down in the dining room. The laughter and the hum of conversation pouring out of the windows increased in volume with every toast. Irene, Sara, Fredrik and Ann stayed in the car, drinking coffee that tasted like dishwater and making small talk to pass the time. As it was a private party in a private venue, the police had no authority to go through the gates, but nobody could prevent them from monitoring the event from outside.

"Did you fix your motorbike?" Fredrik suddenly asked.

"I did. It was just some moisture in the engine," Ann replied with a wry smile.

Ann had a motorbike? Irene raised her eyebrows and gave Fredrik a quizzical look. He nodded eagerly in response.

"She's got a massive machine; it refused to start yesterday," he explained.

At first Irene was completely taken aback at the news that a colleague who was investigating criminal biker gangs was actually in the habit of riding around on a powerful motorbike, but then her curiosity got the better of her.

"So did your job inspire you to start riding?" she asked.

"No, I grew up around cars and motorbikes. I've been riding for sixteen years. My father was a car dealer, but he specialized in bikes as a kind of sideline, mainly the heavier models. My two older brothers run the business today, and of course they ride too. And so do their wives. My eldest nephew is about to get his license, so . . . you could say it runs in the family," Ann said.

"Ann's knowledge of the biker world was one of the reasons why she became part of the team; she knows the culture inside out. And she can fix her own bike," Fredrik said with an unmistakable note of admiration in his voice.

Several young men in suits emerged onto the steps for a smoke, laughing and pointing at the police cars. They were joined by another man holding a large glass; as he staggered out of the door he realized the glass was empty, and angrily hurled it onto the ground. It shattered on the concrete and the shards flew in all directions. The others laughed, and one of them offered a cigar to his drunken companion, who somehow managed to insert it between his lips. He waved his hands around, and someone offered him a light. In the glow of the flame, Irene recognized Kazan Ekici. The heavy gold chain around his neck glinted, and as he cupped his hands around the lighter, Irene and her colleagues saw the glimmer of his gold watch.

"That guy likes his bling," Fredrik commented.

"That's not bling, that's the real deal," Sara said firmly.

They sat in silence for a while; it was beginning to feel unpleasantly warm and damp inside the car.

"Maybe we should stretch our legs," Ann suggested; she was unable to suppress a yawn.

All four of them got out and tried to ease their stiff muscles. Irene was feeling restless; she needed to move. It was a huge effort to keep her thoughts about Krister and the girls at bay. They were safe right now, but what did the future hold? What would the situation be in a week's time? A month? A year? She pushed aside her worries and tried to focus on the here and now.

"How about a walk around the perimeter wall?" Ann suggested.

"Good idea," Irene agreed.

"It's probably best if we go in opposite directions and meet in the middle," Ann said. She tucked her arm playfully under Fredrik's and set off, while Irene and Sara went the other way.

The trader had certainly built a thick, high wall. It was just possible to see the odd tree top above the parapet. The area close to the house was well-lit, but as they moved further away from the building, it got darker and darker. There was no lighting at all at the far end of the parkland, and any illumination from the back of the house was effectively blocked.

Irene and Sara had to switch on their flashlights in order to see where they were going. There was a narrow path running alongside the wall, but their progress was impeded by bushes and undergrowth. Eventually they reached one of the side gates. It was about four times smaller than the showy main gates, but it was still pretty impressive. Irene gave it a tentative shake, but it was securely locked with a heavy chain and padlock. As she peered in through the bars, she could just see the outline of a summer house on the far side of the lawn, with the other side gate behind it, a black rectangle in the wall. Several men were moving around nearby; even from this distance Irene could see that they were taking a leak.

As she and Sara rounded the corner, an extensive field opened out before them. It was surrounded by an electrified fence, and Irene could hear the sound of animals in the darkness. The acrid smell of dung hovered in the air, and just as Irene was wondering what the occupants of the field might be, a loud chorus of bleating answered her question.

The weather was still mild, but thick clouds drifted across the sky, hiding the full moon. It could start raining again at any moment.

They carried on along the back of the wall and met Fredrik and Ann halfway.

"Have you seen anything?" Sara asked.

"Nothing," Ann replied.

"Same here."

"See you at the front," Fredrik said.

Both pairs turned and set off the way they had come.

They had gone no more than a couple of yards when they heard two shots in rapid succession, echoing through the night.

"What the fuck?" Fredrik shouted.

All four of them drew their guns, crouching down and peering in all directions.

"I think it came from the other side of the wall," Sara said.

They started running back toward the main entrance, Sara right behind Irene. Irene stopped at the smaller gate she had just tried; she thought she might be able to climb over it, but it was impossible. The spikes on top were designed specifically to keep out intruders, plus she couldn't get a grip with her heavy uniform shoes.

"Keep going!" she yelled to Sara as she jumped down.

They had to follow the beam of their flashlights to avoid stumbling. As they approached the conference center they could hear screams and agitated voices; all four of them raced through the main gates together and headed for the brightly lit building. The lobby was empty, and so was the dining room, but the tall glass doors leading onto the terrace were wide open; that was where the noise was coming from. Several women were sobbing, clinging to one another, but most people were on the lawn down below. Irene spotted her uniformed colleagues in the crowd. When she reached the edge of the terrace, she heard Stefan Bratt's voice.

"Move! The ambulance is on its way . . . Move, I said!"

Irene, Sara and Ann pushed their way through to Stefan in the middle of the sea of people. The two uniformed officers were doing their best to push back the increasingly hysterical partygoers.

Danny Mara was lying on the ground; he had obviously been shot. The front of his body was covered in blood from a bullet wound near his heart, but the bleeding had more or less stopped, presumably because most of his blood was no longer in his body; he was dead. There was another bullet hole right between his eyebrows, like a horrific third eye.

The two bodyguards were standing beside Danny looking as if they had no idea what to do. Presumably they had plenty to worry about, as they had clearly failed in their task.

In her peripheral vision Irene became aware of a movement as the crowd parted to let Andy Mara through. His tie was loose and the top two buttons of his shirt were undone. His face was bright red, and he looked terribly upset. His eyes were unnaturally bright and his pupils dilated, Irene noted.

"Fucking cops! If you're going to ruin the fucking party and hassle the guests, surely you can at least do your fucking job? Or have you been bribed to look the other way? Is that it? For fuck's sake!"

His voice gave way; he was shaking with rage. Stefan Bratt's eyes narrowed to thin slits as he contemplated Andy's agitation.

"And where have you been until now?" he asked calmly. "It's been several minutes since the shots were fired."

Andy gasped, but didn't respond. For a fraction of a second, pure terror was reflected in his eyes.

In the distance Irene could hear the sound of sirens. Several emergency vehicles were on the way, but for Danny Mara it was much too late.

IRENE MANAGED TO sneak off to one of the rest rooms at the police station to get a few hours' sleep. When she woke up she felt as if a small furry animal had crawled into her mouth and died overnight; judging by the taste, it was already in an advanced state of decay.

She had slept in her uniform, using her jacket as a blanket. Fortunately her civilian clothes were in her locker. In the pale light of dawn she crept along to the changing room and the blissful prospect of a shower. She stood there for a long time, the needles of hot water bringing her weary body back to life. It had been an intense and difficult night.

After using the products in her emergency toilet bag, she looked positively presentable. She always kept a supply of free samples and miniature packs of assorted cosmetics in her desk drawer. She even managed to dig out a mini-mascara from the bottom of the bag.

She went to the canteen and picked up a cheese sandwich; Stefan Bratt had called a meeting for 8:00. A quick glance at her watch revealed that it had probably already started, but there was no need to worry. After all, she had been out with the team for the whole evening and well into the night. She took her

time fetching two cups of coffee from the machine—
and no, she wasn't going to share. They were both for
her, and she had every intention of defending them
with her life, if necessary. At least that was how she
felt right now.

As she slipped in through the door of the large conference room, she could see that the meeting hadn't quite
begun. Stefan Bratt was standing at the whiteboard, his
expression grave. He had dark shadows under his eyes,
and his thin features looked angular in the harsh morning
light flooding in through the tall windows. *Welcome to life
in the field*, Irene thought, smiling to herself behind her
first cup of coffee.

She found a seat next to Fredrik Stridh; Ann Wennberg
was on his other side, and a little further along Sara
Persson was chatting to the two officers from the security
detachment who had been with them in Sävedalen the
previous evening. Irene waved to her; she really liked Sara.

"Okay, let's start," Stefan said, glancing around the
room. He opened a bottle of mineral water and poured
the sparkling liquid into a glass, then continued. "We'd
decided to keep an eye on Danny Mara's party in Sävedalen; we believed there was a significant risk that
Gothia MC would turn up looking for revenge for the
murder of Patrik Karlsson. We wanted to be there partly
to deter any such measures, and partly to monitor what
was going on. With hindsight, the evening was perhaps a
little more dramatic than we might have expected."

He gave a wan smile, provoking the odd burst of
laughter among his audience. He clicked the computer
mouse in front of him, and pictures of Danny Mara's
blood-soaked body appeared on the whiteboard.

"The operation began exactly as planned. We checked the identity of each guest as they arrived, then patrolled the area outside the grounds of the conference center. There were no reports of any unusual activity until 11:34, when two shots were fired in rapid succession. No silencer was used; we know this because we've found the gun. I'll come back to that later. By the time we entered the building, the guests had already moved out onto the terrace and the lawn at the back. We realized someone had been shot, and discovered a man lying on the ground. He had been shot in the heart and the head, and had suffered major blood loss from the wound in his chest. In my opinion he was already dead when we reached him; death was confirmed in the ambulance."

Stefan fell silent and gazed at his colleagues.

"According to one of his bodyguards, Ali Reza—who isn't entirely unknown to most of us—Danny Mara had said he was going over to the lilac bushes by the wall to take a leak. The bathrooms indoors were occupied, and apparently it's normal for the guys to piss in the garden at Gangster Lions' parties. Let's revisit the pictures from the party in May, the ones we looked at yesterday."

This time the picture was taken at twilight and showed the back view of two men facing the lilac bushes, one with his arm around the other's shoulders. Perhaps one of them needed some support. *The male tradition of pissing in the open air always comes out after a few drinks,* Irene thought.

"As you can see, these poor unfortunate lilacs have been used as an outdoor facility on previous occasions. Ali Reza says Danny wanted to be alone while he did what he had to do. The other bodyguard, Ali's brother Omid, took a walk around the perimeter wall. When the shots went off, he was at the far end of the parkland; he says he'd heard voices on the other side of the wall, which would have been our colleagues on patrol. Ali Reza was still on the terrace steps. He saw Danny head off toward the bushes, then he turned around because Danny's wife Elif started talking to him. That means Ali was facing away from the garden, and didn't see the flash when the shots were fired. Danny's wife noticed something in her peripheral vision; she claims they came from the summer house, which is less than fifteen feet from the gate on the long side of the wall."

An image of the summer house appeared; it must have been taken on a different occasion, because it was daylight and there was a thin covering of snow on the ground. The place was in dire need of renovation. A fresh picture, taken much more recently, showed the door hanging off its hinges. Without making a comment, Bratt moved on to one of the side gates. Irene could see that it was the one that lay just a few yards from the gentlemen's outdoor toilet and the summer house—not the one she had tried to climb, but the one on the opposite side. Next came a close-up of the chain and the padlock, taken with a flash. The details were crystal clear. There was only one problem. Both the chain and the padlock were lying on the ground, and the gate was open.

"Hang on. Did no one check this gate last night? I checked the one on the other side, and it was securely locked," Irene said.

"Yes, I checked both the chain and the padlock, and everything was as it should be," Fredrik assured her.

"Was that on the way down toward the field, or on the way back?" Irene wanted to know.

"On the way down. We ran back because we wanted to get inside as quickly as possible," Fredrik replied, unable to hide his irritation.

"Someone must have cut the chain after we'd passed by," Ann said.

"It's strange that neither of us saw or heard anything suspicious around there either before or after the shooting," Fredrik said, echoing Irene's thoughts.

"But weren't there more than a hundred people at the party?" someone muttered behind Irene.

Fredrik nodded. "Absolutely, and that's kind of what I mean. We didn't see anyone outside the wall, so maybe the chain was cut in order to make us think that the killer got in and out that way, whereas in fact he—or she was already there . . ."

Stefan Bratt interrupted him, bringing up a fresh picture: a patch of trampled-down grass illuminated by a portable floodlight. "The CSIs have secured fresh footprints in the damp earth outside the gate. They're deep, so whoever made them weighs around 220 pounds. The impressions don't match our shoes. These are Red Wing biker boots, size forty-five, and they cost a fortune! The tracks continue into the vegetation beyond the path, so this is where the marksman was hiding. It's only a few steps from the gate. Then the tracks run alongside the wall and down toward the field, where presumably our perp disappears among the sheep. The CSIs are checking that out right now. There's a road beyond the field, where a car or a motorbike could have been parked."

The weariness was clearly audible in his voice; he looked as if he hadn't slept at all in the last twenty-four hours.

"You said the gun had been found." The speaker was an older officer from the Organized Crimes Unit; Irene didn't know his name.

"That's right. It was lying on the ground by the gate," Stefan said, sounding a little more enthusiastic. He clicked on a close-up of a gun lying in the grass.

"A Baretta 92S. Fifteen bullets in the magazine. A precision firearm."

"A professional job," Fredrik commented.

"Definitely. Forensics is examining the weapon."

It could have been thrown out through the bars of the gate, Irene thought. And the chain could have been cut earlier, from the inside, as Fredrik had said.

Sara waved her hand, and Stefan Bratt nodded to her. "Just an idea: Could it be someone from Elif's family? Revenge for the fact that Danny was being unfaithful to her, dishonoring their name, something like that? Or maybe they were afraid that Danny would divorce her now that his mistress is pregnant."

"We certainly can't rule out that possibility," Stefan agreed.

He turned and stared at the picture of the Baretta.

"Of course there could be any number of people who wanted Danny dead. We could be looking at an internal dispute here; maybe Andy is sick of dancing to his brother's tune, and wants to be the leader of the Gangster Lions. However, we have no evidence to suggest this is the case. We do know that Gothia MC has unfinished business with the Lions, though. I think it's high time we paid them a visit out in Gråbo," he said grimly.

"Today?" Fredrik asked.

"No, tomorrow afternoon. Today I want us to focus on

the Lions, interview those who were at the party last night. We need to get as clear a picture as possible of what happened. And keep your ears open for any indication that something else might be going on."

LAST NIGHT'S HEAVY rain clouds had dispersed during the early hours of the morning, and it looked as if it was going to be a beautiful day. It was the final weekend before the schools went back for the autumn semester. Irene and Sara headed out to Gunnared, where Kazan Ekici lived. Tommy Persson had decided he wanted to take a closer look at Kazan in connection with the murder of Patrik Karlsson. They might not be able to prove that he'd been on Kolgruvegatan, but thanks to the CCTV footage they knew he'd been in the area, which was suspicious in itself, in Tommy's opinion. Irene agreed.

Kazan was still registered at his parents' address. They lived in a residential area made up of yellow-brick houses that looked as if they had been built in the early '80s. Several of the owners had attached short flagpoles to the wall by the front door; Irene could see Swedish, Finnish and above all Turkish flags, plus others she didn't recognize. There was a flagpole at Kazan's parents' home, but no flag was on display. The flower beds were packed with roses and lavender, filling the air with a faint perfume. Before they had time to ring the bell, the door was opened by a small, neat woman in a blouse with a tiny yellow floral print and a mid-length denim skirt. Sirwe Ekici stood in silence. Her thick curly hair was peppered with grey, and she wore it loose. Her lovely eyes were discreetly made up; it was obvious that "Handsome" Ekici had gotten his looks from his mother.

"Yes?"

Her tone wasn't overtly hostile, but it wasn't particularly welcoming either. *As usual we've got "police" stamped on our foreheads,* Irene thought. *Everyone knows we're here before we even ring the doorbell.*

She and Sara produced their IDs.

"Good morning. We'd like to speak to Kazan; I'm sure you're aware of what happened at Danny Mara's party last night," Irene said, getting straight to the point.

"Yes, I saw it on the news this morning."

"May we come in?" Irene made a gesture encompassing the surrounding houses; she had noticed movement behind most curtains. Presumably Sirwe had made the same observation; without a word she stepped aside and let them in.

The narrow hallway was cramped. The coat stand was laden with outdoor garments of all types and sizes, and beneath it several pairs of shoes were neatly arranged on a rack. Irene had read the notes on Kazan, and knew that he was the eldest of four siblings. He was the only one born in Turkey; the others were born in Sweden. The application forms for Swedish citizenship stated that the family was Turkish-Kurdish. Under the reasons why their application should be given special consideration, they had written: "Man Turk, woman Kurd." The form also said that Zeynep Ekici had reverted to her Kurdish forename of Sirwe, and her son Günes had taken the Kurdish name Kazan. Her husband, Melek Ekici, ran a bakery and café together with a cousin. According to the latest tax data, the business was doing well. Sirwe was a trained nurse and worked at a home for the elderly in Gunnared. Kazan had been six years old when his parents applied for citizenship. His two sisters were fourteen and ten, and his brother was seven. Irene had gathered all this information, plus Kazan's criminal record, in less than fifteen minutes on the Internet.

Sirwe showed them into an over-furnished living room with an enormous TV on one wall. The floor was covered in a large rug, and Irene admired the lovely pattern and bright colors. She and Sara took an armchair each, while Sirwe perched right on the edge of the red leather sofa, which made her look small and fragile. She wrapped her arms around her body as if she were freezing; no doubt she realized that a visit from the police didn't bode well.

"Kazan is sleeping," she said quietly.

"It's almost eleven o'clock. Could you please go and wake him?" Irene said.

Sirwe shrugged and avoided meeting her gaze. She kept her eyes fixed on the rug and mumbled, "Difficult. He is tired. He does not feel good."

"I'm sorry to hear that, but I'm afraid we need to speak to him right now."

"He has been . . . drinking." Sirwe risked a quick glance at Irene, but Sara jumped in before Irene could speak.

"Where's the rest of the family?"

"Melek is at the café. So are the girls. Washing dishes. To earn some money during the holidays. Emre is at my sister's house. Playing with his cousin."

"So Emre is your youngest son?" Sara asked.

Irene wondered if she should take back control, but maybe Sara was going down the family route for a particular reason. Sirwe certainly seemed to have relaxed a little.

"He is seven," she said.

"Such a lovely age, and it's great that he has a cousin the same age. So your sister lives here too. Did you come over at the same time?" Sara sounded genuinely interested.

"Yes. She came with us. Melek and me and Kazan. My sister met her husband here."

"I see . . . There's a big age difference between Kazan and his siblings." It was a statement, not a question. Sirwe gave a start and seemed to hesitate before she spoke. Sara was watching her closely.

"Kazan's father . . . my first husband. He was killed. My sister and I took Kazan and fled. We stayed on a farm with Melek's parents. We worked there. Melek and I fell in love. That meant we could not stay there. Forbidden. His family . . . no. No good." She shook her head.

"So Melek isn't Kazan's father."

Sirwe gave Sara a mournful look and shook her head. Irene glanced around the cozy living room. It was spotless, and the whole house was filled with the aroma of freshly baked bread. Kazan's parents were decent people who worked hard to give their children a good upbringing and a future, and still the handsome young man had been drawn to the criminal gangs in the city. He had hardly even started his high school career when he had ended up in a juvenile detention facility for drug dealing. According to his latest tax declaration, his income for the last year was in the region of 72,000 kronor, allegedly earned from a series of modeling jobs. Kate Moss wouldn't even get out of bed for that kind of money. But last night

Kazan had been sporting a heavy gold chain around his neck and a striking gold watch. These two items alone had to be worth at least double his stated income. Irene decided she would take a little walk around the neighborhood when they were done here just to check on a couple of things.

"No. Melek and I have three children," Sirwe murmured, her eyes drawn to several framed photographs on the wall around the television, some more recent than others: happy children with gappy smiles.

"Could you please go and wake Kazan? Otherwise we'll have to do it," Irene said sweetly.

She knew it wouldn't be possible to question Kazan with his mom around; they would have to take him down to the station. Sirwe shifted uncomfortably on the sofa.

"Kazan is . . . not well. He . . . took a pill. To sleep."

Irene thought fast. Kazan was obviously out of it, and last night he had been extremely drunk. There wasn't much point in trying to talk to him if he was semi-conscious, so perhaps it would be best to defer the formal interview. However, she didn't want to have come all the way out to Gunnared for nothing. She stood up and said firmly, "Okay, but I'd like to take a look at him before we leave. See if it's possible to have a quick word."

Sirwe nodded resignedly. She led the two officers through the hallway to a closed door. She knocked and said something in a language that was presumably Turkish, or perhaps Kurdish. She knocked again, but there was no reaction whatsoever from inside the room. After a moment Irene pushed down the handle and went in. She stopped dead and almost backed out again; the stench of vomit was overwhelming.

"Oh no! I didn't know he was so sick!" Sirwe rushed over to her son's bed. She dropped to her knees, calling out to him in her own language. Kazan lay motionless; there wasn't even a flicker of movement in the long eyelashes. Irene and Sara edged closer. He was lying there in his own vomit, still wearing the same dark suit from the previous evening. His pants were undone, but a large stain at the front revealed that he hadn't made it to the bathroom. What worried Irene was the fact that he seemed completely unreachable. She took his wrist and searched for a pulse; when she eventually found it, it was weak and irregular.

The blinds weren't fully closed, and a small amount of daylight was seeping into the room. Irene noticed the king-size bed, the black leather Jetson armchair, and the wall-mounted Bang & Olufsen music system. Together with the gigantic speakers, it must have cost at least 50,000 kronor. This boy had plenty of money. Even allowing for the fact that he lived at home and probably didn't pay any rent, there was no way he could have bought all this with his declared income, Irene thought.

Kazan's face was a horrible shade of grey, and covered in a thin sheen of perspiration. When Irene lifted his eyelid, he didn't react to the light. His pupils were dilated and his skin felt cold, even though he was sweating.

"We need to get him to hospital," she said. "Too much booze, too many pills." She placed a gentle hand on Sirwe's shoulder as Sara called an ambulance. Kazan's mother seemed oblivious to what was going on as she sat on the floor in the middle of a pool of vomit, clutching her son's hand and weeping.

• • •

THE AMBULANCE WAS there in no time, and the still unconscious Kazan was whisked off to Eastern Hospital. Irene offered Sirwe a lift since they were going back into town that way, and she accepted gratefully.

When they reached the lot where Irene and Sara had parked the unmarked police car, she looked around and saw it straight away, just as she had expected: a gleaming black BMW 6-series Coupé. A very expensive car, especially for a young man. She didn't believe for a second that it belonged to Melek; if it did, he would have driven off to work in it that morning.

"How long has Kazan had his BMW?" she asked casually.

"A month . . . or two . . ." Sirwe sobbed.

When she realized what she had said, she stiffened.

"Not Kazan's. Melek's."

It wouldn't make any difference if the car was registered in his stepfather's name, Irene thought. It was illegal to handle goods that could come from the proceeds of a criminal act. According to the law passed on 1 July 2008, all of Kazan's luxury possessions could be confiscated if the crime of which he was convicted carried a jail term of at least six years, and if they could prove he was involved in the murder of Patrik Karlsson, he would go down for a lot longer.

BY LATE AFTERNOON Irene and Sara had questioned almost all the guests from the party in Sävedalen who were on their list. They hadn't managed to get in touch with two of them, and would catch up with them later. Danny's young widow, Elif, was also one of theirs, but after speaking to her mother on the phone, they had decided to wait a while. Apparently she was still in shock and heavily medicated.

The team gathered in the conference room. Irene had stocked up with two large cups of coffee and a sticky Mazarin cake from the machine. Once again she had no intention of sharing the coffee, though she might give them a taste of the cake. Tiredness had begun to catch up with her, and she needed her caffeine.

Irene reported on the visit to Kazan Ekici's house; Stefan Bratt was very interested in her comments on Ekici's finances. For a moment his weary eyes lit up.

"We've used the law prohibiting anyone from profiting as a result of criminal activity on several occasions. In the past we weren't able to confiscate assets, however obvious it was that they'd been acquired with stolen or dirty money, but now we can. And the cash from the sale of these goods goes to the state, so all Swedish citizens benefit," he said with a smile.

When the laughter died down, Fredrik asked, "Do we know what caused the overdose?"

"No. I called the hospital a while ago; he's still unconscious, but he is stable and they expect him to make a full recovery," Sara said.

They discussed the results of the day's interviews, which were sparse to say the least. To be fair, no one had expected anything else, since the witnesses at the party were all old acquaintances with a record as long as your arm. It seemed that Danny's guests were neither willing nor able to help solve his murder. Many of them spoke poor Swedish, or pretended to—particularly the women.

Some refused to talk to the police at all, mainly on principle. However, some of the men had hinted that they were planning on taking care of both the investigation and the punishment of those responsible, which definitely wasn't what Stefan Bratt wanted to hear. With a sigh he commented that a major gang war was getting closer and closer, if it wasn't already in full swing.

"Danny Mara was shot at 11:34, which probably means that the killer was in hiding for a couple of hours beforehand. Has he left any traces of DNA in the summer house, or in the bushes outside the gate where he was standing?" Ann Wennberg asked.

Stefan shook his head. "Not as far as we know at the moment; in fact the CSIs were surprised that he'd left nothing but footprints."

Irene pictured a big man creeping around among the sheep in size 45 hand-stitched biker boots without being seen by either the police or Danny's own security guards. "In my opinion it took more than cold-bloodedness to carry out this murder. And I don't believe the perp was standing there for hours; if that were the case he would have left his DNA," she said.

"So what's your take on this?" Stefan Bratt said, looking energized.

"Okay, so maybe cutting the chain doesn't require inside knowledge, but the rest of the operation definitely does. And the longer he hung around, the greater the risk that someone would see him."

Irene fell silent, giving herself a few seconds to think things through.

"He knew that Danny and the other guys were in the habit of going outside to piss in the bushes by the wall, which means he was familiar with what went on at their parties."

She was convinced that the killer knew the bushes were always used as an outdoor toilet; the execution of the crime depended upon it.

"Okay, I'm with you so far, but how did he manage to slip away without anyone seeing him?" Stefan wondered.

"He walked across the path and returned to his hiding place. Fredrik and Ann passed within a few feet of him as they raced back to the main entrance. When they had gone, our perp simply returned to the path and ran in the opposite direction, across the field to the other side, where he had some form of transport waiting—probably a car, but it could just as easily have been a motorbike."

When Irene had finished speaking, everyone spent a little while considering what she had said, while she took the opportunity to polish off her second cup of coffee.

"I think you've given us a very credible scenario," Stefan Bratt said pensively.

However, Irene wasn't quite done.

"I've been thinking about the pictures you showed us this morning—the ones from the Gangster Lions' party back in May. Several featured guys pissing in the bushes, and there were also photographs of the summer house. Who else has seen those pictures?" she asked.

Everyone looked at her in surprise. Where was she going with this? After a few seconds they realized why she was asking the question, and one or two looked more than a little annoyed.

"I've seen them," Stefan said, raising his hand.

Fredrik Stridh, Ann Wennberg and two more members of the Organized Crimes Unit followed suit.

"Plus our colleagues in Narcotics; it was one of them who took the pictures." Stefan added.

"I know. Sara and I were shown these photographs in the briefing before Danny Mara's party. My point is that no one else, apart from the people you've just mentioned, knew about the Gangster Lions' little outdoor facility, and the strategic position of the summer house in relation to the lilac bushes," Irene said.

"Maybe we weren't the only ones spying on their parties," Sara objected.

"You mean another gang?" Stefan asked.

Sara shrugged, but didn't say anything. She was right, of course, Irene thought; Gothia MC could well have done the same thing.

"But would Gothia MC really dare to hang around when the Lions were having a party?" she said. "They would be in real danger of being caught. Then again, Narcotics managed to take the pictures, so it's not impossible."

"No, and that's why we're going to pay a little unannounced visit to the boys out in Gråbo. We'll meet here at ten o'clock tomorrow morning to go through the details; we leave at noon. We'll take the SWAT team and a dog with us." Stefan Bratt got to his feet; the meeting was over.

JUST BEFORE FIVE the police in Lerum called to say that a man out training his hunting dog in the forest had seen a burned-out car at the bottom of an abandoned quarry, not far from Björbo. It turned out to be an Audi A4 with a sunroof; the registration plates had been removed. As there was an alert out for a car of that type, the discovery was immediately reported, and the CSIs were already on their way.

Those who had been at the party in Sävedalen the previous night were gathered in the conference room. It had been an intense day, and the atmosphere was subdued.

"I checked on our hospital patients," Sara began.

"So that's our responsibility as well, is it?" Fredrik complained.

Ignoring his comment, Sara continued. "Ritva Ekholm is making a good recovery and will be discharged on Monday."

"Anything on the painting?" Stefan Bratt asked.

"No; we're monitoring various auction sites, but there's no sign of it yet," Fredrik said.

"It's probably not that easy to sell; no doubt it will go on the black market." Stefan attempted to hide a yawn behind his hand and blinked a couple of times.

"As far as Kazan is concerned, his condition is unchanged and he remains stable," Sara continued. "We might be able to talk to him tomorrow, but there are no guarantees."

"In that case I suggest that as we've been working for a day and half, we all go home and get some sleep. A meal and a good night's rest will make us much more effective tomorrow," Stefan concluded.

IRENE STAYED IN her office for a while; it was still too light outside for her to be able to sneak into Tommy's house unnoticed. They had both agreed that it would be best if the neighbors didn't see her; it would only lead to gossip. However, they did have a cover story ready if it became necessary: Irene was his cousin. She had lived in Karlstad for many years, and was staying with Tommy while she was taking a course in Göteborg. They had decided that Tommy's "cousin" worked as an emergency nurse at the central hospital in Karlstad; the idea was that a practical course in the emergency department at one of the city's largest hospitals would explain Irene's comings and goings at odd times. It ought to work, Irene thought, but it would be best if they didn't have to use it at all. She was determined not to be seen.

She could feel the exhaustion like a weight behind her eyeballs. It was almost seven o'clock; definitely time for something to eat.

AS SO OFTEN in the past, she headed for the pizzeria on Färgaregatan. It wasn't far from the police station, and the pizzas were excellent. Many of her colleagues went there, and at the moment that was something Irene regarded as a major point in its favor.

The coleslaw was delicious; Irene hoped it would compensate at least in part for her poor intake of fiber and vitamin C over the past few day. Neither bread rolls nor Mazarins contain much in the way of those particular nutrients.

Irene had almost finished her Hawaiian pizza when she suddenly became aware that she was being watched. She looked up and saw Ann Wennberg standing just inside the door. Ann smiled and came over.

"Hi. Mind if I join you?"

It would have been extremely rude to say yes, so Irene forced herself to smile.

"Of course not."

Ann sat down; a waiter appeared immediately and took her order for a calzone and a large glass of iced water. "If I drink anything alcoholic I'll fall asleep on the table," she said.

"Same here." Irene pointed to her glass, which by now contained nothing more than a half-melted ice cube.

"Very sensible."

"Sara and I haven't had a proper meal all day."

"Nor me. I guess Sara's gone home? I think she mentioned a boyfriend?"

"Yes, she lives with her partner."

The waiter arrived with Ann's water, and set out silverware and a napkin. He gave her shiny red hair an appreciative glance, but she didn't seem to notice.

"I hear your husband's a chef. Is he working this evening? As you're eating here, I mean," Ann said.

"No."

Irene was immediately on her guard. Admittedly Ann's questions could be interpreted as friendly interest, but Irene didn't like them. She had no wish to discuss what her family was doing right now. The truth was that she didn't actually know, but she had no intention of telling Ann that. In order to avoid further interrogation, she decided to turn the tables.

"How about you? Do you have a partner?"

"No, I'm divorced. It was a short marriage, and we parted as friends."

"Was that why you moved to Göteborg?"

"No. I applied for a job with the task force and got it. The first female in that role in Sweden, in fact. I've been with the Organized Crimes Unit for six months now. And Göteborg is a much better city for a single woman," Ann said with a smile.

"I can understand that." Irene forced herself to return the smile.

Ann's steaming pizza was placed on the table, but the smell made Irene feel sick. She broke out into a cold sweat, and knew she had to get out of there. She was so tired that she felt ill.

"I'm sorry, but I don't feel well. I haven't had much sleep this week, and I haven't really eaten properly; my pizza feels like a lead weight in my stomach," she said quickly.

"It's okay, you don't have to wait for me. Are you heading home now?"

Irene was a little taken aback by Ann's question, then pulled herself together.

"Absolutely. Straight home to bed."

"Would you like a lift?"

"No thanks. I've got my bicycle."

"Okay. See you tomorrow," Ann said, spearing a large piece of pizza on her fork. A string of melted cheese dangled between fork and plate, and Irene's stomach contracted. She turned and hurried out of the restaurant.

SHE HAD NO strength left; the thought of cycling all the way out to Jonsered seemed like an insurmountable obstacle. She decided to leave her bike at the station; she walked to the Central Station, then on to the Nils Ericson bus depot. There was a bus to Jonsered in seventeen minutes. She noticed there was no line at the Café Expresso counter, so she went over and ordered a coffee to go. That was exactly what she needed to keep her awake on the journey. Clutching the warm cardboard cup in her hand, she went into a drugstore that stayed open pretty late. It was about to close, but she explained to the very pleasant assistant that she needed tampons and panty liners. After making her purchases she put down her coffee on an empty table outside McDonald's, feeling pretty pleased with herself. She sent a text and received her bus ticket via her cell phone. *Fantastic. How on earth did we manage before cell phones came along? Smoke signals? God, I must be really tired*, Irene thought, sniggering out loud at her childish musings. She looked around in some embarrassment, which was why she saw him before he spotted her.

Jorma Kinnunen, second in command with Gothia MC.

He was walking through the doors between the station and the depot. He was wearing mirrored shades, but Irene recognized him right away. He stopped and turned toward the main entrance, where there was the biggest crowd. Irene was half-hidden in one of the side passages. She hadn't taken a single sip of her coffee, but suddenly she was wide awake. What the hell was Kinnunen doing here at this moment? Was he looking for her? Had he followed her from the pizzeria? Probably, because by now Gothia MC must have realized that Krister had disappeared. Would they really go after her to try and make her tell them where he was hiding? Answer: yes. Were there more members of the gang in the station complex? More than likely; she had to work on that assumption.

Cautiously she reached for her cup and took a few steps back into the side passage, then walked calmly toward the café as she feverishly wondered how to get out of there without Kinnunen or any of his associates seeing

her. Clearly the risk was greatest around the entrances
and exits, but she had to take a chance. Which door was
she least likely to choose? She headed for the one leading
to the Östra Nordstan mall; the police station lay in the
opposite direction. It was sheer luck that she had noticed
Jorma; he was one of the few members of Gothia MC
who had actually met her. The others were presumably
working from a description.

She had to try and change her appearance. She
marched purposefully into a souvenir store and picked up
a pair of sunglasses with slim, dark brown plastic frames.
She didn't bother trying them on, but took them straight
to the checkout.

"I'll take these, please; I don't need a bag," she said to
the young assistant.

"Nine hundred ninety-nine kronor," the girl said, continuing to chew gum and looking bored to death.

In Irene's world, sunglasses were something that disappeared during or after every vacation, so she never paid
more than a hundred kronor for a pair. Without hesitation
she produced her credit card and handed it over. The girl
snipped off the tag, and Irene put the glasses on and left
the store without so much as a glance in the mirror.

Forcing herself not to hurry, she moved toward the
exit she had chosen, her eyes constantly surveying her
surroundings behind the dark lenses. Any man who
looked even vaguely suspicious was carefully scrutinized.
Just inside the exit leading to Drottningtorget she
glimpsed the back of something that looked like a biker
vest, but she kept on walking. There was a florist's store
just inside the Östra Nordstan exit; Irene slipped in and
pretended to be interested in the showy flower

arrangements on display. This enabled her to look out through the glass doors. Apart from a group of boozers who seemed to be in fine form, she didn't see anything suspicious. Before the smiling assistant reached her, she was out of the store and hurrying through the tunnel to the shopping mall.

Irene felt it was safe to increase her pace now. She kept glancing at her watch, as if she were late for an appointment. The mall wasn't crowded; most of the shops were closed, apart from the large department stores. A handful of homeless people were wandering around or sitting on a bench, passing the time until they had to face another night outdoors.

Irene went straight through and out onto Gustav Adolfs torg. She looked around to see if anyone from Gothia MC was waiting for her, but the coast appeared to be clear. A cab with its FOR HIRE sign illuminated was coming straight toward her, and without a second's hesitation she waved it down.

THE CAB DROPPED Irene off just over half a mile from Tommy's house. She thought it would be nice to take a walk, plus a cab pulling up outside his door would attract too much attention.

The evening was chilly, and the smell of charred meat lingered in the air. She could hear loud laughter from the backyard of one of the neighboring houses; she supposed someone had left the sausages on the barbecue for rather too long. Or maybe there was a crayfish party in full swing, with sausages for the kids. She felt a stab of longing for company, good food and wine. She missed her family; she wanted her life back.

PROTECTED BY THE SHADOWS   151

Tommy was sitting on the terrace overlooking the garden in the darkness, a candle flickering in a lantern on the table in front of him. When Irene suddenly appeared he gave a start, and almost knocked over his glass.

He offered to heat up some soup for her, but she declined. She also refused a whisky. All she wanted to do was to fall into bed and sleep, but she knew she had to fill him in on everything that had happened over the past twenty-four hours while he had been away. She updated him on the murder of Danny Mara and what the investigation had come up with so far: very little, unfortunately. Finally she told him about seeing Jorma Kinnunen at the Central Station, and how she had shaken him off.

When she was finished, Tommy sat in silence for a long time. Eventually he said, "Sending Krister and the girls away was definitely the right thing. We couldn't possibly have protected them."

He took his cell phone out of his pocket and scrolled through until he found the message he was searching for. Smiling broadly, he handed the phone to Irene; the display showed a number. Irene leapt to her feet and ran inside to grab the cheap pay-as-you-go phone she had bought the previous day. With trembling fingers she keyed in the number; when she heard Krister's voice the lump in her throat prevented her from speaking for a few seconds.

"Hi, sweetheart!" He sounded bright and cheerful. She swallowed hard several times.

"Hi, yourself. How's it going?"

"Great! It doesn't feel as if we're on the run at all. But listen, it might be a little tricky to reach us over the next few days; we're going to—"

"No, don't say anything. It's better if I don't know," Irene said firmly.

"Of course, I forgot. And how are things with you?"

Irene had no intention of telling him what had been going on. "Fine; things are happening, we're doing our best . . . I'll try to contact you if there's anything major, otherwise I'll speak to you in . . . shall we say two days?"

They had agreed in advance to keep their conversations very short, but suddenly she didn't want to hang up. Just hearing his voice made her feel better; the knowledge that her family was okay was a huge solace. At the same time, she knew it was only a temporary solution; this game of hide and seek couldn't go on forever.

"Two days it is. Felipe and the girls send their love. And Egon, of course. We all miss you. Love you, honey."

"I miss you too. Love you. Bye now."

As she ended the call she was filled with conflicting emotions. On the one hand she missed them so much it was like a physical pain in her chest; on the other hand she was so glad they had managed to escape from Gothia MC and their threats. She was determined to nail those guys, one way or another, but at the moment she had no idea how to go about doing it. Perhaps tomorrow's raid on their place at Gråbo would provide enough evidence to put the whole gang behind bars for years. If nothing else, it would weaken the organization significantly if several of their members went down for narcotics or firearms offenses. Best-case scenario: they would be able to arrest one of them for the murder of Danny Mara, but she knew that was a pipe dream. So far there was nothing at all to prove that anyone from Gothia MC was involved in his death; all the police had were the footprints left by expensive biker boots.

"Irene, did you tell anyone you were going to the Central Station? Before you left work, I mean," Tommy said when she reappeared on the terrace.

"No. I thought I'd feel better after I'd had something to eat, and I'd be able to cycle back here, but instead all the air just went out of me. When I left the pizzeria I decided to take the bus; I didn't even know my plans myself until then."

He nodded slowly several times, as if a suspicion had just been confirmed.

"I'll come in with you tomorrow. Go to bed; I'm going to sit here for a little while," he said with a reassuring smile.

Irene was almost dizzy with tiredness. She managed to drag herself to the bathroom and brush her teeth before she fell into bed. She was asleep almost before her head hit the pillow.

IRENE WOKE UP to the sound of her cell phone ringing. She fumbled around on the bedside table and eventually managed to grab it.

"Irene," she mumbled, still half-asleep.

"Good morning! Breakfast is served," Tommy's cheerful voice informed her.

"Okay. Thanks."

Irene checked her incoming calls list and saw that Tommy had rung her on his landline. Good. If anyone tried to check, there would be nothing odd about her boss calling her before a raid on a biker gang's HQ.

She summoned up all her strength and willpower—not that there was much of either, she thought gloomily—and managed to swing her legs over the edge of the bed. After taking a long shower and putting on clean clothes and discreet makeup, she felt better. Her hair was still damp, but she couldn't be bothered to use the drier; it would dry while she was having breakfast.

Tommy had laid out toast, coffee, eggs and herring.

"We've got plenty of time," he said firmly.

"I need to check when there's a bus," Irene said.

"I've been thinking about that. I don't want you any-where near Central Station. Gothia MC have worked out that you're in hiding somewhere, and that you were planning to catch a bus from the Nils Ericson depot," he said, his expression deadly serious.

"But I left my bike at work," Irene objected.

"I know. I'll drive you into town and drop you off at Sankt Sigfrid's Square; you can take the tram from there, which means you'll be coming from a different direction. That ought to tax their tiny minds if they're looking out for you," he said with an encouraging smile.

Irene felt anything but encouraged. The thought that Gothia MC were following her and keeping an eye on her whereabouts made her feel sick. Before yesterday evening she had seen nothing to suggest that she was being watched. All of a sudden the last piece of herring in mustard sauce smelled positively rancid, and she couldn't bring herself to eat it. She lost her appetite completely and pushed away her half-eaten egg.

She was being followed. What was it Krister had said about being "protected by the shadows"? A shadow is always with you; you can't get rid of it. Would these shadows be with them for the rest of their lives? She knew that was an impossibility; they would never cope, either financially or mentally. On paper Gothia MC would become part-owners of Glady's, but in reality they would make all the decisions. The gang needed the restaurant for money laundering purposes, and to give the illusion that they were running a legal business. Irene already knew of several restaurants in the same position; they had tried to resist, and had suffered violent harassment as a result. Or their owners had ended up like Soran Siljac and Jan-Erik Månsson.

• • •

THE BRIEFING BEGAN at ten o'clock. They were divided into teams and given their instructions. First of all the SWAT team would go in and secure the area, then Irene's group would move in along with three colleagues from Narcotics, plus Frode and his handler. Frode was a springer spaniel on loan from Customs and Excise. The previous year he had won the accolade of Sniffer Dog of the Year; nothing escaped his nose, according to his proud handler. Given that drugs were the main diet of Gothia MC, there was a risk that he might mess things up completely, Irene thought with a certain degree of satisfaction.

Ann Wennberg wasn't present, and Stefan Bratt explained that this was because he wanted as few individuals as possible within biker circles to know that Ann was investigating the criminal biker gangs. Some of them probably knew she was a cop, but they didn't need to know her exact role. As things stood at present she was able to move pretty freely within the biker world, which of course was a huge advantage when the Organized Crimes Unit was trying to monitor their activities.

IRENE, SARA PERSSON and Fredrik Stridh were in an unmarked car being driven by Stefan Bratt, with Tommy Persson beside him. They were following the two SWAT team SUVs, and they were all wearing bulletproof vests made of Kevlar, which were unpleasantly warm. Their colleagues on the SWAT team were also outfitted with helmets and semiautomatic weapons. Bringing up the rear was the Narcotics team with Frode in a Volvo station wagon. This was a major operation, and Irene sent up a silent prayer that it would produce a positive result.

They almost had a pile-up as the convoy was about to turn onto the narrow road leading to Gothia MC's base. The first SUV nearly collided with a large trailer that came speeding along and swung out onto Östadsvägen without stopping. The SUV skidded as the driver slammed on the brakes, and the vehicle behind had to take evasive action. With screeching tires the SUV slid over onto the opposite side of the road; fortunately there was nothing coming, but the second SUV almost hit the trailer as it swayed alarmingly. Irene could see the driver of the trailer yelling, her mouth wide open. Her fellow passenger looked terrified, and the faces of two children were peeping between the front seats.

"Fucking idiot!" Sara yelled.

It was unlike her to express herself in such terms, but no doubt she was as shocked as everyone else in the car.

"I'm pretty sure that was Per Lindström's wife, and I'm guessing the two kids were theirs too," Fredrik said when he had pulled himself together.

"How did you manage to see that?" Irene asked. She had noticed only that the driver was a woman with streaked blonde hair, and that her passenger had short jet-black hair.

"It's my job to know who's who on the organized crime scene, and that means knowing their families and friends too," Fredrik explained.

When they arrived at the target location in Gråbo, they were met by open gates and a banner proclaiming WELCOME TO GOTHIA MC! As they drove in, the officers could see children and adults wandering around among gleaming motorbikes.

"What the hell . . ."

Fredrik broke off, but Irene was thinking exactly the same thing. Whatever they had been expecting, it certainly wasn't this.

As they got out of the cars, they could smell barbecue. *Not again*, Irene thought as she suppressed a sigh. Something told her this wasn't going to turn out as planned. The raid hadn't even started, and already a feeling of resignation had come over her.

Inside the high fence, which was topped with barbed wire, the place was a hive of activity. At least thirty kids and twice as many adults were moving between the highly polished bikes and a variety of food, coffee and soda vendors; there was even a little fish pond. Speakers had been placed by the open windows, facing onto the yard, and the soundtrack from *Mamma Mia!* came pouring out. In the middle of the yard an oil drum had been cut in half lengthways to serve as a gigantic barbecue. Frode was clearly very interested in the sizzling sausages and burgers.

Per Lindström himself was chief cook, with Jorma Kinnunen by his side, popping burgers and sausages into bread rolls. A third guy, who was no more than fifteen years old but was already sporting a Gothia MC vest, was adding plenty of ketchup and mustard before handing the finished product over to a stream of satisfied customers. The vest was probably borrowed; it was far too big for him.

Lindström gave the police convoy a dirty look, then saluted them with a long pair of barbecue tongs.

"Well, would you look at that! The boys in blue have come along to our family day!" he chortled with feigned joviality.

The temperature had risen to almost twenty degrees, and the heat from the coals had inspired him to strip above the waist. Virtually every inch of visible skin was covered in tattoos. It could have been his arm that Ritva Ekholm had seen reaching up through the Audi's sunroof outside the entrance to the backyard at Glady's, but though he was muscular, he was much too squat and flabby. The CCTV footage showed a man who was tall and athletic. Irene quickly glanced around at the other guys in Gothia MC vests, but as she had expected, there was no sign of Andreas Brännström. Unless he was completely stupid, he would have gone into hiding after the murder of Jan-Erik Månsson and the attack on Ritva Ekholm; he was probably in southern Europe, or even some far-flung corner of the world.

"Sausage?" Lindström called out, a big grin plastered across his face.

"No thanks. We've come to search this place," Stefan Bratt replied.

"What the hell for?"

Any pretense at geniality disappeared. Lindström froze with two sausages firmly gripped in the tongs, then waved them around in an angry gesture; the sausages fell apart and flew in all directions. Frode was as well trained as a dog can be, but when a piece of sausage, smelling utterly delicious, landed less than an inch from his nose, not even he could resist. The tasty titbit was gone before his handler could blink.

"And I don't want your fucking dog eating our sausages!" Lindström snapped.

Frode lowered his head, thoroughly ashamed like the good dog he was. He knew perfectly well that he had done something he shouldn't have. Lindström glared at the intruders, then turned away and put a fresh batch of burgers and sausages on the grill. When three little boys came racing over demanding food, his sweaty face broke into a smile. The boys jumped up and down with delight when they were each given a can of Coke to go with their burger.

Several members of Gothia MC, along with their girl-friends, wives and children, were sitting on garden seats. Irene noticed that both the men and the women were wearing strikingly ostentatious gold chains and rings.

A pit bull tied to the leg of a chair went absolutely crazy when Frode passed within a few feet of him. The hair on the back of his neck stood on end, and he started barking and spraying saliva everywhere. Frode didn't even glance at him; he was now totally focused on his job, which was to search for narcotics. He stopped and signaled several times, but when the police checked, they found nothing. Or almost nothing. There were traces of white powder and tiny flakes of what could have been cannabis in the pockets of some of the vests, and they also managed to scrape together a few white grains in the bottom of a closet. There was nothing in the untidy shed or the filthy barn either. Taken altogether, they didn't even have enough to charge someone with the possession of narcotics for personal use. They also found an old Mora knife that was so blunt it wouldn't even have been any use for slicing bread, let alone as a murder weapon. Nothing else.

The gang members watched their activities with

scornful grins. They knew the cops weren't going to come up with anything. The whole place had been literally cleansed of any trace of drugs; the acrid smell of Ajax was everywhere.

On the way back, everyone sat in silence until the car entered the parking lot under the police station.

"They knew we were coming," Fredrik said grimly.

AFTER AN HOUR'S lunch break, everyone involved in the raid gathered in the conference room. The atmosphere was subdued; the only sound was the buzzing of a sleepy bluebottle trying to escape through a solid pane of glass. The older officer from the Organized Crimes Unit put an end to the irritating noise with the culture section of *Göteborgs Posten*. Irene was too tired and disappointed to even try to remember his name.

They had failed. Gothia MC had gotten away with it and still posed a major threat to her family. She wanted to lie down on the floor and scream. It wouldn't solve the problem, but it might relieve the pressure building up inside her. She felt as if she was about to explode. A few years ago, one of the first wars between the biker gangs had ended when one of them fired a well-aimed shot from a bazooka straight into the headquarters of the other. Right now that seemed like the only possible solution, but where could she get her hands on a bazooka?

"I know how disappointed you all are," Stefan Bratt began. "But to be honest, I'm not really surprised. In fact this is more or less what I expected."

A murmur of astonishment quickly spread around the room; Stefan raised a hand to silence it.

"Per Lindström and his associates knew we were coming.

They know we have images of Andreas Brännström, linking him to the murder of Jan-Erik Månsson and the attack on Ritva Ekholm. They also know that we have images showing that he was in the area around Glady's restaurant when the Huss family's car was blown up. Everything indicates that Gothia MC was behind these crimes. After Danny Mara's murder, Lindström realized we were bound to turn up. They must have cleaned that place like crazy!"

He raised an eyebrow and gave a wry smile. The colleague who had flattened the fly spoke up. "How could they possibly know about the CCTV footage, or the fact that we've identified Brännström?"

Stefan Bratt took a deep breath and gave him a long, evaluating look before he answered. "Exactly. There has been nothing in the press. How could they possibly know about the CCTV footage? Or that we knew about the Audi with the sunroof? And how did they manage to tip off Brännström so quickly that he managed to slip through the net before we could pick him up?"

The questions were left hanging in the air. It seemed to Irene that there were other things Gothia MC shouldn't have known, but clearly they had.

As if he had read her mind, Stefan continued. "We have a leak. An informant. Right here in the station."

Most people can be bribed; almost everyone has a price. But the idea that one of their colleagues was working with a biker gang was unthinkable. Irene found Stefan's theory every bit as difficult to take in as her fellow officers, even though she had had her suspicions for a while. It had happened before, of course. A few years ago, an officer in Malmö had been an unofficial member of the Hells Angels, and had supplied the gang with information. She had heard of similar cases in England and the US.

Stefan cleared his throat. "As we have no evidence whatsoever against anyone, I must stress that no one is to breathe a word of this outside the walls of this room."

"That way, if anything does get out, it will have had to have come from someone who is here right now," Tommy said gravely.

As the meeting broke up, Tommy beckoned to Irene. "Do you have a moment before you go home?"

"Sure."

"It's about your annual leave; I just want to check to make sure I've got my facts correct."

Irene followed Tommy into his office, where he unlocked the top drawer of his desk. *Since when does he lock his drawers?* Irene thought.

"Here," he said, handing her a slim folder.

Inside was a sheet of paper torn from a notepad, on which Tommy had scrawled: *Take an unmarked car. Drive around until you're sure no one is following you. Park outside the ICA grocery store and walk the last part.*

Irene knew the small store a few hundred yards from Tommy's house. She nodded.

"Looks right to me," she said, forcing a wan smile.

"Good!" Tommy said, closing the folder.

Irene knew he would destroy the sheet of paper as soon as she had left the room.

After dinner — prawn noodles from a Thai restaurant in Partille—Irene tried to get Tommy to discuss the informant, but with little success. When she returned to the subject for the fourth time, he cut her off impatiently.

"It's for your own sake."

"What do you mean?" Irene was taken aback to say the least.

"There's a leak. We don't know who it is. Your family is in danger. Gothia MC might have threatened you personally. They could be forcing you to pass on information," he said, with a crooked smile to show that he didn't for one second believe the scenario he had just outlined.

At first Irene didn't know what to say, then she got angry. "Have you lost your mind? Do you really think I'd—"

He interrupted her before she went completely crazy. "No, I don't, but Stefan Bratt isn't quite as sure, so it's best if we leave it there."

So Tommy and Stefan had been discussing this behind closed doors. And Stefan suspected that she . . . Irene took a deep breath and tried to calm down. With a huge effort she switched to professional mode, and after a little while she realized they were doing the right thing. They had no idea who the guilty party was, which meant they had to regard everyone as a suspect. The biker gangs' ability to corrupt democracy and the judicial system had reached inside the walls of police HQ. The force itself had been infiltrated.

THE BOMB PLANTED on the steps of the house in Örgryte went off at exactly 7:00 on Monday morning. It was an enormous explosion; the door was blown in, and a fire started in the hallway. Every window at the front of the attractive house was shattered. An elderly man next door received a number of cuts when the window in his living room fell in on him. He and his wife, who was suffering from severe shock, were taken to hospital even though neither of them was seriously hurt.

Fortunately the house where the bomb had been left was empty. Gunilla Åkesson, the prosecutor who lived there, had needed to step in for a sick colleague in Vänersborg on a case with which she was already familiar, and in order to get there on time, she had left home at six. Her husband had flown to a medical conference in London the previous evening, and their two grown-up sons had moved out some time ago.

Gunilla Åkesson had made a name for herself as someone who wasn't afraid to speak her mind; she had been involved in several high-profile trials against the members of various gangs. She was regarded as something of an authority on the subject of organized crime in Västra Götaland.

The case in Vänersborg concerned two men with links to biker gangs in the town. They were accused of extortion and making threats. The plaintiff was the former owner of a small restaurant. He was Iranian, and had worked hard to buy the business. Everything was going well, and at last he could see a brighter future for himself and his family. Until the two men from the biker gang turned up. They explained that terrible things would happen to both his family and his restaurant unless he paid them 200,000 kronor. The owner didn't have that kind of money and went straight to the police.

He and his family had been left with no choice but to go into hiding, and he had been forced to sell the business. He was devastated, but had decided to stick to his accusation.

The parallels with the case in Vänersborg and what had happened to her own family were crystal clear to Irene. There was exactly a week between the detonation of the bomb under Krister's car and the one outside the prosecutor's house in Örgryte.

She shuddered and pulled her jacket more tightly around her; it was a damp, chilly morning. Chunks of the door, still smoking, were strewn across the driveway at the bottom of the steps. For the third time in seven days she was standing at a crime scene that reeked of smoke. Inside she could see the charred remains of something that had presumably been a rug, a chest of drawers and a large mirror. Parts of the gold frame lay among the pieces of the door; maybe the mirror had been a treasured heirloom, or a much-loved item picked up at an auction. Now the glass was in a thousand pieces, sparkling like tiny stars amid the blackened mess.

• • •

IRENE HAD SPOKEN to a deeply shocked Gunilla
Åkesson on the phone, and they had agreed that the
prosecutor would come to the police station at around
four o'clock for a longer conversation. The answers she
had given Irene so far had been encouraging.

There could be links between Gothia MC and the
gang members accused of threatening behavior and
extortion in Vänersborg. Patrik Karlsson's name had
come up during the investigation into the allegations
made by the Iranian restaurant owner, and a few months
earlier, an anonymous witness had said Karlsson regularly
delivered drugs to the biker gang in Vänersborg. There
was no proof, so the tip off was put to one side, but the
information was still there in the case notes, and Gunilla
Åkesson remembered the name when Karlsson's murder
hit the headlines. However, she didn't think it was relevant, so hadn't contacted the police.

Irene spoke to several colleagues in Vänersborg, and
gradually the picture became clearer. Patrik was born in
Trollhättan. His parents divorced when he was ten years
old, and he and his mother moved to Vänersborg. After
a while his mother met someone new, and they moved
again, this time to Göteborg. Patrik kept in touch spo-
radically with his friends in Vänersborg and relatives in
Trollhättan. The Göteborg police were very familiar with
the next chapter in his story because Patrik featured
heavily in both police and social services records less
than a year after his arrival in his new hometown. He
quickly made his mark in the teenage gang known as the
Desperados, and since they were a subchapter of Gothia

MC, his career was already mapped out. It began with break-ins and petty larceny, then moved on to two suspected cases of assault and a conviction for serious assault. He also went down twice for drug dealing. He had achieved all this before he was eighteen, and he finished up in a juvenile detention center. At seventeen he went into rehab for four months, and at nineteen he was sentenced to nine months for dealing. But this time he was in a real jail. He was released thirteen months before his death and had nothing new on his record during that period. By this stage he was a full member of Gothia MC.

Irene was sitting at her computer with all the facts on the screen in front of her, gathered as part of the investigation into his horrific murder. Her thoughts turned to the suspect, Kazan Ekici, the handsome young man who was rumored to go completely crazy when he took too much cocaine, or whatever his narcotic of choice might be. According to the CCTV footage, he had been in the area at the relevant time. It was unfortunate that there were no cameras closer to Kolgruvegatan because then it would have been much more difficult for him to explain why he was there. At the moment he was getting away with it because he and Fendi, who had been driving the car, had stuck to the same story.

Sometimes she wished there was the same density of CCTV cameras in Sweden as in the UK. Some people claimed that it was an infringement of their liberty, and Irene agreed to a certain extent, but the cameras made it so much easier for the police to catch the real criminals. She and her colleagues always had problems investigating gang crime, because there was rarely anyone brave enough to testify. If they did step up, like the Iranian in

Vänersborg, things usually didn't go well for them. Irene often felt frustrated when the courts had to release a suspect, or when she and her colleagues had to drop a case for lack of evidence. The key was to find watertight proof that would stand up in court, but without involving any witnesses. CCTV cameras were a big help.

She was convinced there was a connection between Kazan Ekici and the murder of Patrik Karlsson. All she had to do was prove it.

TOMMY AND IRENE had managed to slip away to a small Chinese restaurant on Odinsgatan. The food was terrible, which was why none of their colleagues ever went there. There was a high staff turnover, and most of the employees spoke very little Swedish, if any. The place could well be involved in illegal immigration and people trafficking, but that was another department's responsibility. Right now Irene needed to speak to her boss and friend without anyone disturbing them. This place was ideal; the customers sat in individual booths, and modern Chinese pop music made it impossible for their conversation to be overheard.

Irene briefly ran through the ideas she had come up with during the morning. When she had finished, Tommy sat and looked at her for a long time before he broke the silence.

"You want to search Kazan's home for drugs, and you want us to go over the car that's registered in his father's name with a fine-tooth comb. And you want to question him again."

She nodded.

He ran his fingers through his thinning hair and went

on. "You also want us to put more effort into seeking links between Gothia MC and the Gangster Lions. I'm with you on that; there have to be several points of contact."

Irene leaned forward over her plate, which was virtually untouched. According to the menu it was supposed to be "three tasting dishes," but in fact it reminded her of something unidentifiable that a child at nursery might have made out of modeling clay. She held up her index finger.

"One. The murder of Patrik Karlsson, which took place in Gothia MC's former HQ. We know that Kazan and Fendi were in the area, so I want their car examined for any possible traces."

She added her middle finger.

"Two. We know that Kazan and Patrik had a common interest: narcotics. Both have a long history of dealing and using. They need money, because it's an expensive habit. There's money in dealing. And somewhere in the middle of all that is the motive for Danny Mara's murder: a turf war over the drug market."

Third finger.

"Three. The bombs. We know that the bomb under our car and the one outside Gunilla Åkesson's front door were exactly the same kind as the car bomb that killed Soran Siljac. Once again, this points to Gothia MC."

She paused for breath, then waved her little finger.

"Four. The attack on Ritva Ekholm. She was the witness who had to be silenced."

Tommy nodded. "As I've often said, you have an unusually well-developed instinct as a cop, and . . . yes, you could be on the right track. But . . ."

Now it was his turn to raise a warning finger.

". . . don't forget our informant. No one must hear about this. Can you take a closer look without anyone else getting a sniff of what you're up to?"

"Yes."

The answer sounded much more confident than Irene felt, but at the same time she realized she had to get going before her colleagues started to wonder what she was doing. She had to stay one step ahead of whoever was leaking information.

"I'll get a search warrant for Kazan's home; it should be ready for this afternoon," Tommy said.

"I can go over there after I've spoken to Gunilla Åkesson."

Tommy shook his head firmly. "No, that will be too late. I'll talk to Åkesson. It's more important that you act fast."

Irene felt a wave of relief, mainly because she wouldn't have to waste time interviewing the prosecutor, but also because she knew that Tommy didn't believe she was the leak. She also had a couple of things to do before she set off.

IRENE HAD FINALLY decided whom she was going to work with. The first was the person who couldn't possibly be the informant. The second was absolutely essential to the investigation and couldn't possibly tell anyone what they found. She would contact the third person with no warning, immediately before they were due to start work.

Perfect, she thought. *Time to get moving.*

DETECTIVE INSPECTOR HANNU Rauhala had returned to work that morning after a three-week vacation, so there was no way the leak could have come from him. Despite the fact that the whole place had been turned upside down after the violent events of the past week, Hannu was calm and collected as always. Irene had learned to appreciate him more and more over the years. Nothing escaped him when he was after a perpetrator or something in their past that they were desperate to hide. His nose led him unerringly to the place where the stench was at its worst, as Superintendent Sven Andersson used to say.

He was sitting at his computer surrounded by piles of paper. When Irene walked in he looked up at her and smiled. His teeth and ice-blue eyes seemed almost luminous against his tan skin, and his sun-bleached hair was verging on chalk-white. Irene could see why her friend and colleague Birgitta had fallen for this taciturn man from the far north. Their son, Timo, was about to start second grade; Birgitta had completed her law degree and had been assigned to the court in Uddevalla as a clerk. She would start commuting on a daily basis in September. Her long-term plan was to become a judge.

Irene quickly filled Hannu in on the situation, and what she wanted him to find out. She didn't even bother to stress that he mustn't tell anyone what he was doing; he never did.

IRENE HAD TO contact the second member of her team, the one who couldn't possibly tell anyone what they found, through an intermediary: Rickard Mellkvist, Frode's handler. Customs and Excise was doing nothing special that afternoon and evening and was happy to help. Rickard was a little taken aback when Irene explained that their destination was confidential and that at this stage she couldn't tell him where they were going, but he readily accepted it when she said it was a matter of routine security. As he wasn't a police officer, Irene was counting on the fact that he wasn't familiar with normal procedures. They agreed that Irene would contact him as soon as the search warrant was approved.

JUST BEFORE SETTING off for Gunnared, Irene called Matti Berggren in forensics; it took a little persuasion, but eventually he agreed to come along. He found it difficult to accept that he couldn't tell anyone he was going with her to an unknown destination; Irene and Tommy were the only two people in the station who knew where they were heading. Irene was determined to stay one step ahead, and to block any possible leaks.

SIRWE EKICI RECOILED when she opened the door and saw Irene, Matti, Rickard and Frode. She stood there in silence as Irene introduced her colleagues and produced the search warrant. There was such deep sorrow in her eyes as she stood aside to let them in that Irene had a lump in her throat. *How could Kazan cause his mother such pain?* The answer was he didn't really care about her or the rest of his family. All he cared about was getting what he thought he deserved: luxury possessions, a high-status car, designer clothes and access to the best clubs and parties. And last but not least: an unlimited supply of drugs.

They went straight to Kazan's room. Irene wasn't surprised to see that it had been thoroughly cleaned; there was no sign of the previous day's chaos. In spite of the overpowering smell of detergent, it didn't take Frode long to find what he was looking for. He stopped and signaled by one of the closets.

The drugs were in a tin box hidden on the top shelf. The lid wasn't on properly, probably because Kazan had helped himself to the contents. It was concealed behind a loose plywood panel, easily removed by pulling on a short nylon cord. A simple but not particularly clever idea.

A thin layer of white powder was clearly visible on the bottom of the tin, which contained eight packages the size of a house brick, tightly wrapped in plastic and sealed with duct tape. There was a small slit in one of the packages, possibly made by a knife; the hole had been covered with ordinary transparent Scotch tape.

"Cocaine. That's what it looks like when it arrives direct from South America; I've seen it before," Rickard Mellkvist said. "It's usually cut in Tenerife or one of the countries on the west coast of Africa before distribution in Europe, and the packaging is different then."

Matti picked up the package with the slit and peeled away the tape. He shook a tiny amount of white powder onto his palm and tasted it with the tip of his tongue. After careful consideration he said:

"Cocaine. Wow, that's strong! Each pack weighs around half a pound. As Rickard says, it hasn't been cut yet; it's very rare to see it in its pure form here in Sweden."

"How much will this be diluted before it's sold?" Irene asked.

"Between five and ten times; the street value of each of these packs will be at least two million kronor," Matti said.

If he was right, they had just found cocaine worth sixteen million kronor in a tin box in Kazan's room. How come Danny Mara had allowed him to store such an enormous amount? Kazan could hardly be regarded as his right-hand man. Or was it a smart move? Under normal circumstances, the police would never have suspected that Kazan was hiding pure cocaine in the closet in his bedroom at his parents' house.

Rickard Mellkvist looked very pleased, and gave Frode a treat. The dog wagged his tail happily, and after a job well done, he and his master headed back to their car.

Irene called Tommy and told him what they had found. He was more than happy with the outcome and said he would call for back up from Narcotics. He would also make sure the BMW was picked up right away. His next job was to inform Superintendent Stefan Bratt; it would look odd if he didn't, as they had confiscated such a large quantity of drugs.

"I'll go to the hospital to see if I can question Kazan," Irene said.

"Good idea."

• • •

WHILE THEY WERE waiting for their colleagues from Narcotics, they carried on searching the room, and found a small-caliber pistol taped to the underside of the bed. Matti photographed the gun in situ before carefully loosening the tape. His face lit up as he contemplated the slender weapon.

"A Morini CM .22 RF—wow! What a little beauty!"

"Another area of expertise?" Irene asked in surprise.

"I've been a member of a shooting club for years. This is a fantastic pistol, but it's quite unusual. The small caliber means it's not exactly a murder weapon; it's more likely to be used in competition."

"Stolen?"

"Probably. Top quality, and it would suit someone with small hands. Six bullets in the magazine."

Was it possible that Sirwe hadn't discovered the gun when she was cleaning her son's room? Hardly. She kept her house spotless; she would never have missed something like that.

How involved were Kazan's parents? It seemed likely that they were well aware that Kazan's money came from criminal activities, but preferred to pretend they had no idea. Maybe they had resigned themselves to the situation. That was what usually happened, in Irene's experience.

NARCOTICS ARRIVED IN less than thirty minutes. They couldn't understand why Irene had requisitioned a dog from Customs rather than one of their own, but accepted her explanation that it had been the quickest solution.

She mentioned the BMW in the parking lot, but informed them that it wasn't to be touched. She suspected that it contained trace evidence relating to the murder of Patrik Karlsson, so it was to be transported to the station where Matti Berggren could go over every inch of it.

Sirwe was sitting on the stairs, her tears dripping onto the head of the boy she was clutching to her chest. He stared at the police officers, but there were no tears; his eyes burned with hatred. This must be Emre, Kazan's half brother.

"Kazan hasn't done anything! You're trying to frame him!" the child hissed.

He was trying to sound tough, but his lower lip was trembling.

Irene stopped in front of them and said calmly: "Your brother is in hospital because he took so much cocaine that he almost died. He's very sick. We found an enormous amount of coke in his room; it would be impossible for the police to get ahold of that much in order to frame someone. He hid it all himself so that he could sell it to other dealers. He risks people's lives just to make money. They die because of the drugs he supplies. But he doesn't care about any of that."

Sirwe looked as if someone had slapped her across the face. The boy probably didn't really understand what Irene had said; the look in his eyes hadn't changed. *Why bother telling a kid all this?* Irene thought. But deep down she knew why: she was sick of taking crap from all sides and constantly being challenged. In a few years this little boy would be throwing stones at the firefighters and police officers who were called out to some suburb because a gang of teenagers was setting cars on fire. Perhaps he would take on his brother's mantle and begin his progress toward the higher echelons of gang culture. The fact that his parents were decent people made no difference; money and the sense of belonging that came with the gang had a more seductive appeal. Respect, easy money and identity were the key words. Those young men wanted to go their own way. Unfortunately they were on an inexorable downward spiral, sinking deeper and deeper into the morass of drugs and crime.

MATTI BERGGREN STAYED to wait for his colleagues from CSI. Working in tandem with Narcotics, they would search the Ekici house. Sirwe had gone over to her sister's house with Emre; she lived just a short distance away.

Irene tried to think straight as she drove to the hospital. There were several new pieces of the puzzle, and a picture was beginning to take shape, despite the fact that some pieces were still missing.

Kazan had had an enormous amount of cocaine in his possession, but he was well below leadership level in the Gangster Lions. They were hardly likely to trust him with such a valuable asset, particularly given the fact that they must have known about his own problems as a user. Which meant he probably wasn't hiding the coke on their behalf. So whom did it belong to? Another gang? Surely Danny Mara wouldn't have stood for that. And Danny had been killed—by Kazan? Again, unlikely. Besides, Kazan had a watertight alibi; he had been out on the terrace with plenty of other people when the shots were fired, and he was already as high as a kite by then.

But Kazan was a user; had some of the coke been intended for personal use? After all, he had overdosed on pure coke; he probably didn't realize it was several times stronger than usual.

Matti had said that it was very rare for such a pure form of the drug to reach Sweden. Irene remembered a narcotics course where she had learned that cocaine is cut several times on its journey from South America to Europe. A common additive is a worming powder that contains tetramisol. It gives the same corrosive feeling on the gums when the major dealers are testing the purity of the drug. The side effects of tetramisol are fatal to both people and animals. Other common adulterants are crushed painkillers that can no longer be sold, and are therefore easily and cheaply available on the black market. The in-crowd are basically inhaling baking powder, crushed painkillers or worming powder, spiced up with a tiny amount of coke. *Fools*, Irene thought, pursing her lips.

The question that overshadowed everything was where the hell Kazan had gotten all that cocaine from. Had he bought it? Stolen it, more likely. The logical follow-up question had to be: From whom? That was where things got tricky. He could have stolen it from the Gangster Lions, but would he even get near that quantity? Irene knew from past experience that only the top tier within a gang had access to drugs, even if they weren't directly involved in dealing. The dealers ran the greatest risk of being caught, so they used errand boys to do that particular job.

So the question remained: Where had Kazan gotten the cocaine? She had every intention of asking him as soon as he was fit to be interviewed.

• • •

A FRIENDLY BUT stressed nurse in the intensive cardiac care unit informed Irene that Kazan had been moved to a general cardiac ward. Irene took the elevator up to the relevant floor. The nurse in reception gave her a sharp glance when she introduced herself and said that she would like to speak to Kazan Ekici.

"Just a moment; I know Dr. Enkvist wants to have a word with the police first," she said, pressing a button on the intercom.

A male voice answered right away: "Enkvist."

"There's a police officer here, asking to see Kazan Ekici."

"Show him to my office."

"Will do, but it's a woman."

The doctor didn't hear her; he had already disconnected the intercom.

Irene followed the nurse as she bustled along the corridor; she stopped, knocked on a door and waited until a voice called them in. Only then did she proceed.

"Police Constable Irene Hysén," she announced.

"Detective Inspector Irene Huss," Irene corrected her.

The middle-aged doctor peered at her over the top of a pair of cheap reading glasses. Exhaustion and many years of smoking had etched deep lines in his thin face. The room stank of smoke, and a packet of Marlboros lay on the desk in front of him. He made a clumsy attempt to smooth down his thin hair, which was sticking out in all directions. He made a move to stand up, then sank back down on his chair.

"Please sit down, and I'll see what I can do," he said.

You say that automatically to everyone who walks in here, Irene thought, feeling vaguely irritated. However, she forced herself to thank him and smile. Dr. Enkvist leaned forward, resting his elbows on the desk. Slowly he took off his glasses and folded them up. After a little fumbling he managed to push them into his breast pocket among a multitude of pens.

"I said I'd like a word with the police before Kazan was interviewed," he began. Before Irene could respond, he waved a dismissive hand and continued. "I know, it's essential for your investigation, etcetera etcetera. But the patient's welfare is my responsibility, and in my view Kazan is definitely not well enough to be questioned. Let me explain why."

He fell silent and looked down at his hands, clasped together on the desk. The fingertips on his right hand were stained yellow with nicotine. Irene decided to bide her time.

"Kazan has taken a huge overdose. He has stopped breathing several times, and is still suffering from severe arrhythmia. His heart is badly damaged; there is also a significant risk that he has suffered brain damage. He is on a high dose of a range of medication, mainly for his heart; he is also sedated, which makes him a little confused. We don't yet know what his long-term prospects are, but . . ."

He spread his hands wide and looked at Irene with his expressionless eyes.

". . . given the current situation, I don't want him placed under any stress."

He leaned back and folded his arms, underlining his decision. *For God's sake!* Irene thought, trying hard not to let her irritation show.

"I understand what you're saying, but during the past week we've had three murders here in Göteborg, with clear links to biker gangs. We believe Kazan is one of the leaders of the Gangster Lions. I'm telling you this in confidence, of course. We've just searched his house and found cocaine with a street value of at least sixteen million kronor. That's one of our biggest finds ever. You'll be able to read all about it in the papers tomorrow," she said.

Sometimes you just have to tell the odd white lie, let the end justify the means and all that jazz, she thought. Dr. Enkvist raised one eyebrow, and something glimmered in his eyes; she had clearly gotten to him. Irene had mentioned that Kazan was probably one of the gang leaders in order to add weight to her request, and she decided to press home her advantage.

"We also have good reason to suspect that Kazan was involved in last week's brutal murder; a man had gasoline poured over him and was set on fire while he was still alive."

The doctor gave a start, and his eyes darted around the room. Most people would find the murder of Patrik Karlsson utterly repugnant. Irene didn't give him a chance to come back at her.

"I'm very happy for you to be there when I talk to Kazan. This interview is extremely important. He has information that could help us solve one or more of these homicides, and prevent additional deaths."

Enkvist swallowed and cleared his throat nervously. His chair suddenly seemed to have become extremely uncomfortable; he started shuffling around. He took a deep breath and said, "Okay. But stop when I say so. Otherwise I'll throw you out."

Good luck with that, Irene thought as she tried to hide the triumph she was feeling.

• • •

THE ROOM STANK of sweat and urine, and "Hand-some" wasn't exactly living up to his name. His face was grey, his hair plastered to his scalp. No one would have the slightest desire to run their fingers through those curls now. Blue-black stubble highlighted the pallor of his skin, which was marked with angry blotches. Only the shadow of his eyelashes falling on the high cheek-bones gave any hint that he was a good-looking guy. His hands lay peacefully folded on top of the yellow blanket— *small, well-formed hands with manicured nails*, Irene thought. Matti had said that a Morini CM .22 RF would suit someone with small hands.

Electrodes were attached to his upper body, the slender wires leading to an ECG machine. The screen showed the rhythm of the heart in the form of a graph. Even Irene could see that in several places there were two spikes very close together. This must have been the arrhythmia Enkvist had mentioned. She knew that the plastic clamp on one finger was there to register his blood pressure, which was also shown on the screen: 92/50. Wasn't that pretty low? A pouch of clear liquid attached to a stand by the bed was dripping slowly down a tube and into Kazan's left hand via a catheter. The back of his right hand was black and blue from previous needles.

Dr. Enkvist leaned over the motionless figure and gently touched his shoulder.

"Kazan? Can you hear me?" he asked softly.

The long eyelashes twitched, and after a little while Kazan opened his eyes a fraction. He blinked two or three times, and mumbled something unintelligible.

Suddenly his eyes were wide open and full of sheer panic, his hands waving frantically in the air. The drip stand rattled alarmingly and began to sway.

"It's okay, Kazan. Calm down. It's only me, Dr. Enkvist. How are you feeling?"

His tone was still warm and soothing, and it seemed to have an effect on Kazan. After a moment the fear subsided, and he looked straight at Irene.

"Hi, Kazan. My name is Irene Huss, and I'm a police officer. I have a few questions I hope you'll be able to answer."

"Go to . . . hell," he managed to force out.

Demonstratively he turned his head away; there was no point in addressing the back of his neck. Irene had to get him to look at her.

"We found the cocaine you hid in the closet," she said calmly.

She saw his body stiffen under the blanket. He didn't move for a long time, then slowly he turned his head back.

"You . . . no, no. Fuck! Fuck! I'm a dead man . . . fuck!"

It was clear that the last few words came from a place of sheer terror. Dr. Enkvist began to move his lips, and Irene was afraid he was going to put a stop to the interview before it had even started.

At that point an alarm went off out in the corridor. This time it was the doctor who stiffened. With a dubious glance at his patient, he said, "I have to go."

"Of course. I'll stay here," Irene said quickly.

Enkvist was already half-running. The door closed behind him with a soft hiss. *Saved by the bell*, Irene thought. *Or rather the alarm.*

"As I was saying, Kazan: we've found the lot. Eight big fat packages of cocaine. You could say we hit the jackpot."

He was certainly paying attention now.

"I'm . . . toast. They're . . . they're going to kill me. Fuck!"

Irene leaned closer, trying to keep her tone measured. "Who's going to kill you?"

Kazan clamped his lips together and looked as if he wasn't going to say another word. Irene could almost see the thoughts flying around like terrified birds in his befuddled brain. Before she could rephrase her question, he seized her wrist. His grip wasn't tight, but she could feel that his palm was sticky with sweat.

"I need . . . I need . . . protection! A new . . . identity!" he gasped.

"Why?"

"Because . . . they're going to kill me!" His last words were no more than a whisper as he loosened his grip.

"You can't have a new identity just because you claim you're in danger. You have to tell me why. Otherwise, no chance."

There was a shimmer of tears in Kazan's brown eyes; the color reminded Irene of dark amber.

"I know . . . something. Fucking . . . huge!" he said with sudden eagerness.

"Big enough to merit a new identity?"

He nodded and grabbed her hand, as if he were trying to draw her closer to make sure she heard every word.

"Meeting . . . Thursday."

"This Thursday? The twenty-fifth?"

He nodded, and the fear in his eyes began to give way

to a glint of wickedness. It almost looked as if he was smiling.

"The twenty-fifth . . . that's when it all goes bang!"

Irene hadn't misinterpreted his expression; he really was smiling. And wasn't what he had just said a line from the chorus of a Magnus Uggla hit from years ago, "King for a Day"? Surely Kazan couldn't be referring to the song, or could he?

"What do you mean, it all goes bang?"

He was still smiling even though he found it difficult to speak. "Meeting . . . Pravda . . . restaurant."

"Who's having a meeting?"

Kazan swallowed a couple of times, then pointed to the glass of water on his bedside table. Irene helped him to insert the straw between his dry lips. He sucked greedily at the tepid water, then sank back on his pillow.

"Our bosses . . . and theirs."

"You mean the Gangster Lions and Gothia MC?"

"Yes."

"What are they going to discuss?"

"The war. Disrupting their . . . business."

Irene heard the sound of agitated voices and running footsteps in the corridor. Clearly something serious had happened. She knew she didn't have much longer; the over-protective Dr. Enkvist would be back at any moment. She had to get Kazan to talk about the cocaine they had found, and the murder of Patrik Karlsson. Time to stop pussy-footing around.

"This war began when you and Fendi set fire to Patrik Karlsson. Am I right?"

The light in Kazan's eyes died, and he clamped his lips firmly together once more.

"Remember you have to tell me the truth, or I can't help you," Irene went on.

She had absolutely no authority to promise him a new identity, but in his befuddled state, Kazan didn't seem to realize this.

"Patrik . . . thought . . . he was selling to . . . another gang."

"He didn't think he was selling to the Gangster Lions?" Irene was taken aback.

"No . . . no . . . Latin Kings."

The name was vaguely familiar, but it took Irene a few seconds to place it. The Latin Kings were a relatively new gang that had emerged in the western part of the city over the last couple of years, consisting mainly of South Americans and the odd individual with a different ethnic origin, usually the Balkans.

"So you and Fendi claimed that you were members of the Latin Kings. You arranged to meet Patrik to buy drugs in the old Gothia MC HQ on Kolgruvegatan. Right?"

Kazan nodded and closed his eyes, as if to indicate that the conversation was over as far as he was concerned. Irene continued implacably:

"So where had Patrik gotten the drugs from?"

"Enrico . . . Gonzales."

She certainly hadn't expected that name to come up in this context; Gonzales was a major dealer who had been found shot dead, along with his companion David Angelo, on board a luxury yacht in the marina on the island of Getterön outside Varberg. They had been murdered on the morning of Sunday, 1 May, almost four months earlier. As the season was just getting started, there were no other boats in the marina, and no one in the nearby houses had heard or seen anything. Both men were riddled with bullet wounds from an automatic weapon. Two hidden storage compartments were found on the yacht: one was empty, but the other contained several pounds of cocaine. All the indications were that a deal had gone wrong. Gonzales and Angelo had been robbed of the narcotics that had been concealed in the empty compartment, but the killers had missed the other one. There were no traces of the perpetrators, but a witness claimed to have been woken up by the sound of powerful motorbikes heading toward Getterön at around three o'clock that morning.

Narcotics and the Halland police were in charge of the investigation, which was going nowhere fast. No one was talking; anyone who might know something was too scared to speak up. Was that where the gang war had started to escalate?

"So Patrik acquired over four pounds of cocaine after the murder of Gonzales and Angelo, and he wanted to sell. Why didn't he want Gothia MC to have it?" Irene pressed on.

"Needed . . . money. He owed . . . the gang."

It wasn't unusual for gang members to get into debt, then find they couldn't pay. Instead they were forced to carry out tasks that no one else wanted to touch—high risk projects like murder, for example. It seemed that Patrik Karlsson had made a big mistake.

"But how did you come into contact with each other? Did you already know him?"

"No . . . Fendi. Bought from . . . Patrik before. Friends."

"Did Patrik know that Fendi belonged to the Pumas, one of the Gangster Lions' subchapters?"

Kazan shook his head slowly.

"So Fendi got in touch with Patrik, who told him he had a lot of cocaine to sell. Fendi passed the information on to you, and you decided to call Patrik and pretend that you wanted to do business with him. Is that correct?"

In her peripheral vision Irene saw the ECG graph spike twice in close succession, but Kazan didn't appear to feel any ill effects.

"Kind of," he mumbled.

"But you never intended to give him any money. You and Fendi beat him up and set fire to him. Didn't you?"

Eyes still closed, Kazan nodded.

"We never meant to . . . kill him. He had . . . huge fucking knife."

Patrik's long knife, adorned with a skull, had been found on the floor, with only his fingerprints on it. Maybe there was some truth in what Kazan said.

It was possible that Irene's summary of the course of events was correct, but at the same time she knew something didn't fit.

"Why would the Gangster Lions buy drugs from a member of Gothia MC? You have your own suppliers."

Kazan started laughing silently and opened his eyes. They were sparkling, but not with merriment. The look he gave Irene was pure evil. How could she have ever thought that his eyes were beautiful?

"Who says . . . the Lions were buying?"

Had he totally lost it, or had she misunderstood?

"But you belong to the Lions. Or have you gone over to the Latin Kings?" she asked.

"I don't belong . . . to anyone," he boasted.

"You don't belong to anyone?"

It took a second or two before she realized what he meant.

"You're telling me that you and Fendi were buying for yourselves," she said dubiously.

"Yesss!"

Kazan smiled, looking very pleased with himself. Maybe the idiot really didn't understand what he'd started. His coke-addled brain had simply come up with a crazy idea: he was going to become a major player in his own right, start his own gang. That was why he needed capital, which was where the theft of the drugs came in. When he had sold the stash they had found in his closet, he would have plenty of money to buy more drugs. After a while he would be top dog—or so he thought. In reality he had no chance. He wasn't smart enough, plus he was too much of an addict himself. He hadn't even been able to resist the temptation to try the product; the overdose must have come as a nasty surprise.

Now Irene could see why he was demanding a change of identity. The Gangster Lions would find out that he had been doing his own thing, aiming to set up in competition with them. He would also be in danger from Gothia MC once they knew for sure that Kazan had killed Patrik Karlsson. Thanks to the police informant they already had a good idea that Kazan and Fendi were responsible. It didn't matter which of the gangs got a hold of Kazan first; the outcome would be the same. Maybe they had already dealt with Fendi; that would explain why the police hadn't been able to track him down since his initial interview with Fredrik.

Irene decided to push a little harder on the subject of the meeting. "This restaurant, Pravda, where is it?"

"Gårda."

Irene had never heard of a restaurant by that name, but if it was in Gårda, it was no more than half a mile from the police station. Was he lying? Or delirious?

"What makes you think this information is worth a new identity?"

Once again she saw that glimmer of suppressed amusement in his eyes. He whispered, "The twenty-fifth, that's when it all goes bang . . ."

He broke off and looked past Irene at the door. She heard it fly open and heavy footsteps approaching from behind. Before she could turn around, she felt something cold and hard on the back of her neck. The barrel of a gun.

"Stand still! Keep quiet!" a voice hissed roughly.

The man was standing so close that she could smell his disgusting breath. She looked down into Kazan's amber eyes, which were wide with fear. His lips were moving, but he was incapable of making a sound. A movement behind her and to the side indicated that there was another person in the room. The pressure on her neck remained unchanged. She heard the rustle of clothing as the other man moved toward the foot of the bed. She realized that he wanted to stand on the other side to get a better firing angle. Right-handed. She caught a glimpse of a pistol with a long barrel. Silencer.

That was her last lucid thought before the darkness closed around her.

Irene was vaguely aware of being lifted and placed on a gurney. People were talking to her. They opened her eyelids, shone a light into her pupils. If it hadn't been for the constant pain at the back of her neck, she would have told them to go to hell and leave her alone so that she could get some sleep.

Slowly she grasped what had happened. Something had gone wrong, terribly wrong. She tried to sit up, but the pain in her head made her sink down again.

"Steady. You have a concussion," a professional female voice informed her.

Irene tried to ask about Kazan, but her attempt at communication was cut off immediately.

"Take it easy. Your colleagues will be here at any moment. They'll talk to you, tell you everything you need to know. Here's the doctor," the nurse said.

Dr. Enkvist's concerned face appeared in Irene's limited field of vision. She might not have been fully conscious, but she thought he had aged ten years.

"You were struck with the butt of a pistol. You have a concussion," he said.

Once again Irene tried to speak, but he had already turned to the nurse.

"We'll keep her in for observation overnight," he said firmly.

"But we don't have any beds," the nurse objected.

"Then she can stay in here."

"But I have to . . ." Irene protested feebly.

"Right now you don't have to do anything, and in fact you're not capable of doing anything. There is a possibility that a blood vessel has been damaged, which means you could suffer internal bleeding between the cerebral membranes or deeper inside the brain. It happens fast, and it can be fatal. You need to be in the hospital," he said, his grave expression leaving her in no doubt of the seriousness of the situation.

Irene started to feel nauseous. She couldn't stop herself from throwing up; fortunately the nurse saw what was about to happen and managed to get a kidney dish under her chin. It had been a long time since Irene had eaten, so she didn't have much to bring up. Food was the last thing she wanted, but she was thirsty. She had a desperate, burning thirst. She started retching again.

IRENE WAS AWARE of the nursing staff checking on her at regular intervals; they didn't allow her to sleep until the early hours of the morning. The bed was pretty uncomfortable, but she slept deeply. Waking up wasn't much fun. Her head felt as if she had been to one hell of a party the night before, apart from the fact that she didn't usually have lumps on the back of her neck to accompany her hangover. At least then the pain was self-inflicted, unlike now.

It was seven-thirty by the time she came round properly. Tommy was standing beside her bed, looking serious.

"Are you awake? And how are you feeling?" he asked.

Irene tried to moisten her dry lips with the tip of her tongue, but the result was depressing. Her tongue felt as if it were covered in coarse sandpaper, just like the rest of her mouth. Eventually she managed to croak:

"Awake, yes. Feeling—not so good."

"I understand. The doctor says you have to rest for at least a day or two. And that's non-negotiable," Tommy said when he could see that she was about to protest.

Irene realized she wasn't going to be able to work that day. *Better to rest and come back with fresh energy,* she told herself. She had a drink of water and suddenly felt ravenously hungry. She could hear voices and the clink of crockery out in the corridor; was she hallucinating, or was the seductive aroma of coffee drifting into the room? Breakfast would definitely be very welcome.

"What happened to Kazan?" she asked, even though she already knew the answer.

"They shot him. He died instantly."

Irene closed her eyes and let out a groan. The only witness who had been prepared to talk had died, literally before her eyes. Although that wasn't entirely true; she had no memory of the shooting. It must have happened when they knocked her out, or just after.

"So what did he say to you?" Tommy asked.

Irene quickly went through what she recalled of the attack itself, and what Kazan had told her. When she told Tommy that he had confessed to the murder of Patrik Karlsson, his troubled face lit up. The information that the drugs Patrik was intending to sell came from the Gonzales/Angelo homicide cheered him up even more.

"Wow, the first real lead in a double homicide! Our colleagues in Halland will be delighted. And the killers came from Gothia MC . . . But why did Kazan and Fendi have to kill Karlsson?"

"According to Kazan, that wasn't their intention, but Karlsson pulled a knife on them."

They wouldn't find out the definitive truth about the course of events unless they found Fendi Göks, and he seemed to have vanished in a puff of smoke.

"Is that why Kazan wanted a new identity? Because he was afraid Gothia MC would want to avenge Karlsson's murder?" Tommy said.

"Yes, plus there's the stolen cocaine of course. Even if Gothia MC don't know about that yet, they soon will, thanks to our informant. And they'll think it's their property."

"So Kazan and Fendi were acting on behalf of the Gangster Lions?"

"Not really . . . I think the little guys were planning on going solo. When I asked Kazan why the Gangster Lions needed to buy from Gothia MC, he told me he wasn't buying for the Lions, but was posing as a Latin King to Karlsson. He insisted he hadn't gone over to the Kings, and boasted that he didn't belong to anyone."

"So he claimed there was an indirect threat from the Gangster Lions too? In that case he needed all the protection he could get!"

A nurse came in with a tray. She chirruped a bright "Good morning!" and wanted to know whether Irene would prefer tea or coffee. And of course Irene's visitor was also welcome to a cup, she added when she saw Tommy's tired face.

"Have your breakfast in peace," he said when Irene had been provided with coffee and two cheese rolls. "I'll just sit back."

She ate greedily, and gulped down the coffee as fast as she could without scalding her mouth. After a top-up she was starting to feel more like herself, apart from the dull ache at the back of her head.

"Kazan said something else: the leaders of Gothia MC and the Gangster Lions are having some kind of meeting on Thursday to discuss the escalation of the gang war. Apparently it's disrupting their business—that's the way he put it."

"Are they indeed? Any idea where they're meeting?" Tommy said, looking very interested.

"He talked about a restaurant called Pravda; it's supposed to be in Gårda."

Tommy thought for a moment, then said hesitantly, "I think there used to be a place with that name . . . but if it's the one I'm thinking of, it closed down long ago. That area is due for demolition. I'll check it out."

"He said it all goes bang on the twenty-fifth."

"The twenty-fifth as in this Thursday?"

"Exactly. It reminded me of the Magnus Uggla song." She began to hum the melody of "King for a Day."

"Yes, I remember it; one of those terrible summer hits. But is that what he meant?"

"I have no idea; it just reminded me of the lyrics."

"Hmm. Maybe he just wanted to stress the importance of the meeting. Make himself sound a bit more interesting," Tommy mused.

"Maybe."

Somewhere deep inside Irene's pounding head, a little voice protested, but she couldn't quite make out what it was trying to say. Perhaps it was just her shaken brain, sloshing around as it tried to find its way back to normality. Or perhaps it wasn't. Her colleagues would have to sort things out for themselves; today she was going to rest, and forget all about biker gangs and their violent way of life.

IRENE WAS DISCHARGED, and Tommy drove her back to his house in an unmarked car. When he got back to the station he would tell everyone that she was recuperating with a close friend. If anyone tried to find out more details, he would be keeping a close eye on them. They still didn't know who was leaking information to Gothia MC.

• • •

THE HOUSE WAS cool and quiet. The sky was beginning to cloud over, and the weather forecast had warned
of rain in the afternoon. Irene tried to read the newspaper, but found it hard to concentrate. Kazan's death
dominated the front page of *Göteborgs Posten*: BRUTAL
HOSPITAL MURDER! screamed the headline, with the sub-
heading VICTIM KNOWN TO THE POLICE.

Irene forced herself to go through the article. The
killers had walked in during evening visiting hours,
when most of the staff were taking a well-earned coffee
break. The two men arrived separately, a few minutes
apart. The murder was described as well-planned and
cold-blooded. The first man had slipped into a cardiac
patient's room and pulled out all the tubes connecting
him to a monitor and his oxygen supply, which automatically set off the alarm. The patient was an elderly
man who was asleep at the time; all he remembered
was the back view of someone dressed in black as they
went out the door. The staff came running, but none
of them had seen anyone in the hall. Presumably the
killers had hidden in the examination room where
Irene later ended up. When there was no one around,
the two men entered Kazan's room. Irene's presence
was presumably an unforeseen complication, but it
didn't stop them from carrying out their plan. She had
been facing away from the door, so hadn't seen either
man. Kazan was shot in the head, twice. It was assumed
that a silencer had been used. A nurse in the cardiac
patient's room thought she heard two muted bangs,
and looked out into the hallway. She caught a glimpse
of the men as they emerged and saw they were wearing
jeans and black hoodies, but she was unable to provide

any further detail. The police were currently going through the hospital's CCTV footage.

A white Volvo C30 was of interest; it was seen leaving the hospital parking lot at high speed, almost colliding with an ambulance as it turned onto the main road. The paramedics saw two men in dark clothing in the front seats and described them as quite tall, aged twenty to thirty, with baseball caps pulled down low over their foreheads. One was shorter and stockier than the other. The car had been stolen during the afternoon from the parking lot at the Allum mall in Partille. The police wanted to hear about any sightings of the car or the two men; a number for the public to call if they had any information was given at the end of the article.

Let's hope something useful comes in, Irene thought before she fell asleep on the sofa with the newspaper on her lap.

IRENE WAS WOKEN up by the sound of her cell phone. She grabbed it from the coffee table, still half-asleep, and pressed the green button. As she was about to put it to her ear she realized that it wasn't actually ringing at all; the screen was black. So why could she still hear a ringtone? It took another couple of seconds for her to grasp that it was the pay-as-you-go cell; fortunately it was also on the table.

"Hi, sweetheart," Krister's voice said before she could speak.

"Hi, yourself," she croaked in a weak voice. A glance at her watch told her it was quarter past twelve.

"Have you caught a cold?"

Irene cleared her throat before answering. "No, I just woke up. I was . . . working last night."

She didn't want to worry Krister and the girls; there was no need to tell them what had happened over the past twenty-four hours.

"Glad to hear you're resting up, in that case. I just wanted to check that you're okay, and to tell you that we're all missing you. And I love you."

"I miss you too, so much. And I love you!"

That goddamn lump in her throat was back. She really wanted to sob down the phone and tell him what a hard time she was having. Although she was actually feeling a little better, come to think of it. The ache at the back of her head was beginning to ease.

"We're off on our travels again, so you won't be able to reach us before Friday evening at the earliest," Krister went on.

"No problem."

Given the situation it really was for the best, but emotionally the thought of not having any contact with her family for almost four days was devastating. She gritted her teeth, determined not to give away how she was feeling. However, that lump refused to disappear.

"The girls and Felipe send hugs and kisses. And Egon, of course. And me."

"Hugs and kisses to everyone," Irene said, trying to sound bright and cheerful.

The tears came as soon as she ended the call.

THE NEXT TIME Irene's cell phone woke her, she was lying in bed; it took a little while to register that she was in Tommy's guest room. A fine drizzle was falling outside the window, and it felt a little damp indoors too. This time the sound of "Mercy" echoed through the room, so it was definitely her usual cell. The display showed a name she recognized.

"Hi, Hannu."

"Hi. How are you feeling?"

"Better, thanks."

Hannu Rauhala wouldn't call to make small talk; she knew he would get straight to the point.

"You asked me to take a closer look at a couple of things."

"I did."

"I think I've found something, but I just need to check one or two points."

Irene could feel the tension rising; she was wide awake now. "What's it about?"

"Unexpected connections," Hannu replied after a brief silence. He wasn't the kind of man to waste words, and sometimes he drove Irene crazy. Like now, for example. As if he sensed her frustration, he continued.

"I'm almost certain, but I need to be a hundred percent sure before we move on this. Are you coming in tomorrow?"

"Absolutely," Irene said, sounding more convinced than she felt.

"Morning prayer is at eight; can you meet me at seven-thirty?"

"Sure. You can't tell me anything now?"

"No, it's better this way. In case I'm on the wrong track," he said firmly.

You're not, because if you were you wouldn't have called me. But you want to make sure it's a belt and braces job, Irene thought. It was probably a sensible idea, given the incendiary nature of what he had probably found out.

"See you in my office at seven-thirty," Hannu confirmed. "Take care."

"Okay, thanks," Irene said with a sigh.

Could the guy be any more annoying? Nobody could keep their mouth shut like Hannu, but that was exactly why she had chosen him to confide in. She looked at her watch; almost five-thirty. Exactly twenty-four hours ago she had walked into the hospital. It felt like a lifetime.

WHEN TOMMY GOT home Irene was lying on the sofa watching an episode of *Midsomer Murders* that she had seen at least twice before. It wasn't the razor-sharp plots that appealed to her, but the glorious setting. The residents of the small villages lived in picturesque old houses, surrounded by leafy, beautifully kept gardens. Some member of the nobility was often embroiled in the mystery, and terrible crimes were committed behind the idyllic façades. There really were a hell of a lot of murders. Apart from that slight inconvenience, Irene liked the idea of cruising around in a shiny Jag and chatting to people without running the risk of being hit on the head with a pistol. Instead the friendly villagers offered DCI Barnaby tea and scones with homemade jam. Right now that seemed like a dream scenario.

One glance at Tommy's face told her that Midsomer was definitely a better bet. Okay, so nobody had actually hit him over the head, but he looked as if he were about to collapse.

"Hi. There's pizza in the kitchen, and these are the tablets you asked me to get," he said without any spark of enthusiasm.

A tube of Alvedon rolled across the table. Tommy threw himself into his favorite armchair. He closed his eyes, tipped back his head and gave the distinct impression that he was about to go to sleep.

"I'm feeling much better, thanks for asking. The lump on my head has gone down a little, but it hurts like hell if I bump it on anything. The headache has gone though, so things are definitely improving. Thank you for getting the tablets anyway," Irene said.

Tommy didn't open his eyes. "Good, that means you can come into work tomorrow. God knows we need you. This is the worst situation I've known in all my years of service!" He sighed and rubbed his eyes.

"And you want to bring a poor sick person with a severe concussion into the middle of this chaos?" Irene said reproachfully, tilting her head to one side and smiling. She always used to be able to cheer him up by teasing him, but it didn't seem to be having the desired effect now.

He merely gave her a weary glance and said, "After a day like today, you're probably in better shape than the rest of us."

"So it's been one of those days."

"It sure has."

"Tell me."

"Okay, but can we eat at the same time? I'm starving."

He hauled himself out of the chair and headed for the kitchen. Irene was hungry too; she hadn't eaten anything since breakfast at the hospital. She got up cautiously and padded after him. The pizza boxes were on the counter, and Tommy was peering into the refrigerator.

"There's only one beer," he informed her.

"No problem. I'm happy with water."

Irene found a jug, added ice cubes, then filled it up

with cold water. Both of them were perfectly comfortable eating pizza straight from the box, but Tommy set out glasses and cutlery. As they were about to sit down, his next door neighbor went by just outside the kitchen window. The woman turned her head and glanced in. The blinds were pulled down, but both Irene and Tommy had forgotten to angle them so that no one could see in. The neighbor obviously noticed that Tommy had female company, because she quickly looked away, as if nothing had happened.

"Let's eat in front of the TV," Tommy suggested.

They went back to the living room; the windows faced onto the garden, and the overgrown lilac hedge meant that no one could see in. They tucked in with a healthy appetite, and by the time Tommy had demolished three quarters of his pizza, he had recovered sufficiently to tell Irene about his day.

"We held a press conference at ten; there wasn't much to say, except that two unknown men had shot Kazan Ekici and assaulted a police officer who was in the room with him. We also released the information about the drug bust at Kazan's house, and implied that we thought his death was linked to the cocaine we found. Needless to say we didn't mention that Kazan and Fendi had bought it from Patrik Karlsson, nor did we give any details of the quantity involved. It would be dumb to tell Gothia MC that we know they killed Gonzales and Angelo on board their yacht."

He paused and finished off his can of beer, then sighed demonstratively and poured himself a glass of iced water.

"After that the day was just crazy. Patrik Karlsson, Jan-Erik Månsson, Danny Mara and Kazan Ekici have all been killed within the past ten days. We just don't have the resources to deal with this kind of thing, and then there's the new link to the double murder outside Varberg. At least Interpol, Narcotics and the Halland force are taking care of that one."

Irene raised her glass to him. "Right now I'm dreaming of a transfer to Midsomer. People are dying right, left and center there too, but they do it an orderly manner. And the cops drive around in luxury cars, spending lots of time in cozy pubs," she said.

A tired smile flitted across Tommy's face. "We've tried to impose some kind of order on this mess. We've interviewed everyone who was at the hospital, particularly in the cardiac unit when Kazan was shot. The perps were seen by several people, but no one was able to provide a good description."

"CCTV?"

Tommy nodded. "We found footage of both men. They entered the building at 6:02 and left at 6:17, so the whole thing took no more than fifteen minutes; they were well prepared. Unfortunately there's no chance of identifying them. They were wearing jeans and hoodies with no logos. The one who went in first was powerfully built; he was responsible for disconnecting the cardiac patient's oxygen supply and the cables leading to the monitor."

Irene put down her glass with a bang. "Hang on. How did they know exactly where Kazan was? I only found out when I went to the intensive cardiac care unit, and they sent me to the right place. And yet these two guys seem to have gone straight to the right unit and the right room."

Tommy stared down at the remaining slice of pizza for a long time. Suddenly he took a deep breath and turned to face Irene. For a second something glinted in his eyes; it could have been fear, but she wasn't sure. He looked away and addressed the pizza.

"I got a call from the hospital informing me that he'd been moved. I was given all the details, including the room number. Unfortunately I didn't get around to calling you until almost half an hour later. Stefan Bratt contacted me in the meantime; he'd heard about the drugs raid at Kazan's house, and he was pretty pissed because he hadn't been kept in the loop. It's a sensitive issue, given that we're supposed to be running this investigation together. A point he underlined several times."

"But it was because of the leak—" Irene began.

Tommy waved an impatient hand. "I know. I was the one who told you to follow your judgment, and that's exactly what I explained to Stefan. Then I immediately gave him everything I knew about the raid; I also told him that Kazan had been moved out of intensive care. He took the details of the new unit and the room number; we talked about putting a guard outside his door, not for Kazan's safety but because of the risk that he might take off. As he was in such poor shape we decided to wait; we thought the chances of him disappearing were negligible. By the time I called you, you were already at the hospital and you'd . . ."

". . . switched off my cell phone," Irene finished the sentence.

"Precisely."

"What time was that?"

"Just after five-thirty."

Which was exactly when she had read the notice by the main doors and switched off her cell. She had gone up to intensive care, been redirected, then spent a few minutes with Dr. Enkvist. She had probably been in the hospital for half an hour or so before she actually saw Kazan.

"Tommy, did you tell anyone else that Kazan had been moved?"

"Nope. And I asked Stefan if he was alone before I passed on the information, and he assured me he was."

"So only you and Bratt knew Kazan's room number?"

"Correct."

Their eyes met.

"Oh my God. Stefan Bratt," Irene whispered.

Tommy tipped back his head and closed his eyes. With an audible sigh he said, "You can understand why it's been such a difficult day."

"I can't believe it."

"Me neither. But there's no other explanation."

Irene nodded. The very idea sent her brain into over-drive: the head of the Organized Crimes Unit was Gothia MC's informant. Superintendent Stefan Bratt was no ordinary cop; he was responsible for monitoring organized crime within the whole Västra Götaland region.

"He must have contacted Gothia MC straight after he'd spoken to you. And they must have had the killers waiting outside the hospital. Or nearby, at least," Irene said.

"Nearby is more likely; we have two witnesses who saw a white Volvo C30 in Torpa, which is only a few minutes from the hospital. And the CCTV cameras in the hospital parking lot picked up the car, but unfortu-nately they didn't capture the men as they got out; the intervals between the pictures are too long. But we did get them when they returned to the car—only their back view, but the license plate is clear. It's the car that was stolen in Partille a few hours earlier."

"It hasn't been found?"

Tommy shook his head. They'd probably driven it to an isolated spot and torched it, Irene thought. That was still the most common way to dispose of a stolen car, although some perps sprayed the interior with a fire extinguisher instead, which was guaranteed to destroy DNA. The drawback was that they needed access to a foam extinguisher; fire was easier, and Irene suspected they would soon receive a report about a burned-out Volvo C30.

"Have you checked outgoing calls from the station? Bratt must have called as soon as you put down the phone," she said.

"I asked Hannu to check it out this morning. A text was sent at 5:37 from a cell phone inside the building, but it can't be traced."

"That's exactly what I'd expect of our informant. No evidence."

There was a brief silence, then Irene continued. "So the killers set off right away and parked close to the main doors. Then they joined the stream of visitors entering the hospital. They knew we didn't have a guard outside Kazan's room."

"Because Stefan had told them," Tommy added gloomily.

Something occurred to Irene. "By the way, did Hannu mention anything else in relation to the case?"

"No, he just came in and told me about the text message at around six o'clock. I didn't see him again before I left."

"Hmm. I asked him to look into a couple of things before I went over to Kazan's house yesterday. He called me a little while ago; we're meeting at seven-thirty tomorrow morning. He wouldn't tell me what he'd found out; I got the impression he was still waiting for confirmation."

Tommy's face brightened a little. "That guy is like a bulldog; he never lets go. If he thinks he has a lead, he won't give up. He didn't give you any indication at all?"

"Nope."

"Typical Hannu," Tommy said with a wan smile.

THE BARREL OF the gun was being pressed into the back of her neck, harder and harder. Sinews and cartilage began to break down; soon the pain would be too much. She looked down at Kazan's ashen face, his terrified eyes wide open. He was pushing back into the pillow in a desperate attempt to escape. His lips were moving, but she couldn't hear what he was saying. The agony in her neck was unbearable now. She knew that the gun would be fired at any second; she could see it in Kazan's eyes. He knew that death was approaching. The shot came as an explosion of deep red and dazzling white, but it wasn't the head on the pillow that had been blown to pieces, it was her own.

Irene woke up with her heart pounding, and stared into the darkness. The aftermath of the nightmare lingered on, not least because of the pain; she was lying on her back, and the pillow was pressing on the lump. Tommy had given her a tube of painkiller gel that one of his kids had left in the bathroom cabinet. She sat up with a groan, found it amid the mess on the bedside table and applied a generous amount. It was almost three-thirty, and she knew she wouldn't be able to get back to sleep. She settled down on her side and waited for dawn. But she might have fallen into a doze after all; she had a vague memory of seeing Stefan Bratt's face just before the alarm on her cell phone went off.

ONE LOOK AT Tommy told Irene that she wasn't the only one who had slept badly. *This is a bit much for all of us*, she thought. *Including me.* Her family slipped into her mind, but she immediately pushed them away. There was a risk that she would lose her ability to act decisively if she allowed herself to dwell on the danger they were in, but it was there at the back of her mind, chafing at her consciousness. How could they get back to their normal lives? It seemed hopeless right now; the gangs were fighting to increase their strength and control. *So many of us are in their power*, Irene mused. The number of victims of extortion, drugs, human trafficking, abuse and murder was growing all the time, not to mention the families of those victims. As long as people were prepared to pay for what the gangs could supply, their sphere of influence would continue to spread. Wherever there was easy money, that's where the gangs could be found. Given the inexhaustible desire for cheap labor, sex and drugs, it seemed like a hopeless situation.

"You look terrible," Tommy said.

"You don't exactly look like a dew-kissed rose yourself."

"Ouch. I've made the coffee extra strong . . ."

"You know how to please a woman," Irene joked in an attempt to make up for snapping at him.

"I've never had any complaints," he replied with a smile.

It hadn't occurred to her before, but she suddenly

realized how charming he could be when it suited him. She had never even considered it during all the years they had known each other, but now she could see that he was an attractive man. Okay, so his hair was thinning and his midriff was thickening, but on the whole he was in pretty good shape. Those sparkling brown eyes and that smile could melt a iceberg in no time. In spite of that, he hadn't seemed interested in actively looking for a new partner after Efva Thylqvist. Irene assumed his self-esteem had suffered a severe blow and would take a while to be built up again. The betrayal had been too great.

"What are you thinking about?" he asked.

Irene gave a start, feeling caught out. "I'm just wondering what Hannu's come up with," she improvised quickly. Tommy seemed to swallow the lie.

"Yes, it will be interesting to hear what he has to say." He picked up the daily paper and laid out the different sections on the table. "What do you want first? Culture?"

"Sports," Irene said as she pulled it toward her. *My God, we sound like an old married couple*, she thought. Then again, she never read the culture pages. They ate their breakfast in silence as they skimmed the latest stories.

IRENE WALKED INTO Hannu Rauhala's office at precisely seven-thirty. He was already there, as expected, with two mugs of coffee waiting on the table. He tried asking how she was feeling, but she made light of her aches and pains and started questioning him instead. He held up his hands to stop her.

"Let me start from the beginning. With several homicide inquiries going on at the same time, things are a little chaotic around here, which is why it took a while to get the confirmation I was waiting for."

He cleared his throat and sipped his coffee. Irene knew it was horribly sweet, but that was the way he liked it. As far as she was aware, that was his only character defect.

"Patrik Karlsson was born in Trollhättan. He was very much the baby of the family; his brothers were twenty and eighteen when he was born, and his sister was thirteen. The parents had problems with alcohol, and his sister was like a mother to him. His parents divorced; Patrik moved with his mom to Vänersborg, where she met a new man, and the three of them then came to live in Göteborg. This new guy was also a drinker. Nobody was keeping an eye on Patrik, and he soon became a member of the Desperados. His biological father died of a stroke when Patrik was fourteen, and Patrik's brothers took over his car repair workshop."

Hannu paused to catch his breath and to have another sip of coffee. Irene was amazed. She had never heard so many consecutive sentences come out of his mouth, and they had been working together for almost twelve years.

"The new guy took off, leaving Patrik alone with his mother. She was a physical and mental wreck, constantly in and out of the psychiatric unit. His sister tried to help, but Patrik was a delinquent teenager who was determined to go his own way. However, they kept in touch and seemed pretty close."

Hannu fell silent again, then took a deep breath before delivering the killer blow.

"Patrik's sister, Ann, became a police officer. After a few years she married a colleague called Wennberg. They divorced twelve months later, but she kept the surname."

Irene stared at him, completely lost for words. Was this really true? "Ann Wennberg was Patrik Karlsson's sister?"

Hannu nodded. "There's no doubt. They're siblings. The brothers took over their father's business, and Ann became a cop. They all share an interest in motorbikes."

"Right," was the best Irene could come up with.

She was utterly flattened by the news, and it turned yesterday's theory about who the informant might be on its head. It had to be Ann Wennberg, but Stefan Bratt had told Tommy that he was alone when he was given the details about Kazan's location in the hospital. So what did that mean?

"What do you know about Stefan Bratt?"

Hannu didn't seem in the least surprised at the change of subject. "Forty-four years old, divorced, no kids. Stellar career path. He's a lone wolf, but allegedly one of the good guys," he said calmly.

Irene merely nodded in response. Her head was spinning. She had to speak to Tommy before morning prayer.

IRENE FOUND HER boss in his office, twisting his new chair from side to side and staring at the computer screen. His gaze was unfocused, however, and she knew he was thinking about something else entirely.

She didn't waste any time. "Have you spoken to Bratt?"

"He'll be here in a minute," he replied without even looking up.

"Good. He's not the informant."

"What?" She definitely had Tommy's full attention now.

"Hannu's on his way to tell us what he's found out."

"But who—"

Tommy broke off as Stefan Bratt walked in carrying his cell phone. He glanced at the screen, then turned it off. He too bore the signs of the heavy workload they were all carrying. There were dark circles under his eyes, and lines of fatigue around his mouth. The fine blond hair wasn't quite as carefully arranged over his bald patch as it had been at the beginning of their association, but he was impeccably dressed as always in chinos, a pale blue shirt and a beige linen blazer.

"Morning, morning," he said, nodding to Irene and Tommy.

"Morning," Tommy said, still looking totally confused. Much to his relief, Hannu appeared in the doorway.

"Sorry to interrupt. Tommy, I thought you said you wanted to speak to me privately before the briefing?" Stefan was trying to sound polite, even though he had no idea what Irene and Hannu were doing there.

"I did, but things have taken an unexpected turn."

Tommy asked his colleague to sit down: Stefan Bratt perched on a chair, his expression wary. He was still holding his cell phone. Tommy nodded to Hannu, who began to speak with his usual calm demeanor. As he talked Stefan grew paler and paler, although he didn't move; he hardly even blinked.

By the time Hannu had finished, Stefan looked like a ghost. It was just as well he was sitting down, or he would have keeled over. The blue eyes had narrowed to slits, and his mouth was a thin line.

"Did you know about any of this?" Tommy asked him tentatively.

At first Stefan didn't appear to have heard the question, but after a few seconds his lips moved.

"No. I didn't know she and Patrik were siblings. I didn't even realize they knew each other."

"Did it ever cross you mind that Ann could be the leak?"

"Never . . ." His voice broke and he fell silent.

"You told me you were alone when I gave you the details about Kazan's hospital room. Was that true?" Tommy went on.

Stefan shook his head slowly and let out a deep sigh. He swallowed several times before he straightened his back and spoke. "Yes and no. When I called to ask you about the drugs that had been found at Kazan's house, I was alone in my office. But while we were talking Ann came in with some files. She heard part of the conversation, and could well have seen what I'd jotted down on my notepad on the desk: Kazan's name, the ward he was on, and his room number."

His face was expressionless. The only sign of agitation was the movement of his slender fingers, constantly playing with his cell phone. After a moment he went on resolutely.

"She put the files on my desk and signaled that she would come back later, then she left. I saw her through the glass wall, heading for the bathroom. That must have been when . . . when she contacted them."

His voice let him down again.

"So you think she could have seen the notepad when she came over to your desk?" Irene asked.

"Yes."

"Does Ann know we're going to discuss our strategy for the gang leaders' meeting at Pravda tomorrow?" Tommy asked.

Stefan shook his head once more. "No, I haven't had

time to tell anyone what Kazan said to Irene. She's in her office at the moment," he added.

"In that case we can limit the damage by removing her from the investigation right away," Tommy said, getting to his feet.

It was obvious how relieved he was now that the leak had been exposed. Stefan Bratt's face told a very different story. He seemed to be taking the fact that someone on his team had been supplying information to Gothia MC as a personal insult.

WHEN MORNING PRAYER finally got under way, the two senior officers looked serious but composed. Ann Wennberg was not with them.

Tommy Persson smiled warmly as he addressed the team. "Sorry to keep you waiting; things just got a little complicated. Anyway, we're here now; the plan is to outline our strategy for tomorrow."

They clearly had no intention of revealing that the person responsible for the leaks had been tracked down; Irene wondered if that was a wise decision, given the speed with which rumors spread throughout the station.

Tommy began by talking about Kazan's last words to Irene; a meeting between the leaders of two major rival gangs was of particular interest, and had to be monitored.

"Kazan mentioned a restaurant called Pravda, but it was closed by Environmental Health fifteen years ago. The place is falling down, and the whole block is due to be demolished in a few weeks. Meanwhile, there's no one around," Tommy went on.

"So how have the gangs gained access?" Jonny Blom wanted to know.

Stefan Bratt answered. "One of our guys checked it out yesterday. The building is owned by the same people who own the conference center out in Sävedalen: the Mara brothers and Christoffer von Hanke, the mafia lawyer. The Gangster Lions, in other words."

Tommy took over again. "Exactly, and it's the perfect place to meet because the area is deserted. The street is closed off, and traffic has been redirected via Åvägen. Which presents us with a problem: How do we keep the restaurant under surveillance? How do we get close without being seen? Plus we don't know exactly what time the meeting is due to begin, so we need to be there from early in the morning until something happens."

"What if there's nothing going on? What if Kazan was just making it all up?" Jonny chipped in.

Irene took over.

"That's possible, of course, but he was terrified when I told him we'd found the cocaine. He knew he was a dead man walking as far as both Gothia MC and the Gangster Lions were concerned. I believed him when he talked about this meeting."

Tommy leaned forward and clicked on the laptop in front of him. A map of Gårda was projected onto the wall. He pointed out a number of locations where he wanted surveillance units stationed; some of the team would go over there straight after the meeting to work out the best approach. Someone suggested setting up a camera overnight, but there was a risk that the Gangster Lions had already installed their own camera, which meant they would be able to see any police activity. The warning lights would start flashing, and no one would turn up for the meeting. The idea was quickly discounted.

Instead they agreed to park a surveillance truck in a strategic spot. The most important thing was to be able to listen in to the meeting so they could find out what the gang bosses were plotting. The truck was still a risk, but it was the best they could come up with.

"We need to split up into several groups; it's essential that their lookouts don't keep on seeing the same faces in the area. They might not have anyone posted today, but we have to assume they'll be out in full strength tomorrow," Tommy said.

He and Stefan divided those present into teams; they would work out a schedule shortly. Everyone was allocated a role apart from Irene. Tommy turned to her.

"I have a special task for you; I'll see you in my office straight after the meeting."

Irene was well aware that she couldn't be sent out to Gårda with the others; plenty of the Gangster Lions' members knew who she was after the night when Danny Mara was killed. Plus of course Gothia MC would no doubt recognize her by now; the two who had murdered Kazan had probably been bawled out for not shooting her at the hospital when they had the chance. Maybe they had been totally focused on the job of killing Kazan, and hadn't realized who she was. She was unlikely to be so lucky next time she bumped into one of Gothia's henchmen.

SHE WENT TO Tommy's office via the coffee machine. He was already at his desk; Irene put down a mug of coffee in front of him, and his face brightened as he thanked her. The smile reached all the way to his eyes, and he almost looked back to normal. The knowledge that they had a fifth columnist inside the walls of the police station had weighed heavily on his shoulders, and now that burden had been lifted he seemed to be filled with renewed energy. Which was good, but a little odd. They still had six homicides, if you included the double murder outside Varberg, two bomb attacks and a gang war to deal with. They were also facing a major operation with no idea what it would bring.

"So what's happened to Ann Wennberg?" Irene asked.

"She's being held in an interview room downstairs, with no cell phone or any other way of communicating with the outside world. The guards have been told not to let her out under any circumstances. They were a little surprised, but didn't ask any more questions when I said she was a suspect and would shortly be arrested."

"Will she be charged?"

"Absolutely. And she's facing a long jail term, plus of course she'll be kicked out of the force," he said dryly.

"Why didn't you say anything during the briefing?"

"We decided to wait a few hours. We'll know more when she's been interviewed; at this afternoon's meeting we'll tell everyone the informant has been exposed," he said, looking pleased.

For a second Irene felt sorry for Ann, but then she thought of all the damage she'd caused. The investigation had been sabotaged because the perps were warned in advance. People had died because of the information Ann had passed on to Gothia MC, and it was thanks to her that they had almost managed to grab Irene at the bus depot. No, there was no reason to feel any sympathy with Ann.

"I thought you and I could be the first ones to question her," Tommy said.

• • •

THE SHINY RED hair was as beautifully styled as
ever. The eyes were discreetly highlighted with eyeliner
and mascara. Not a trace of tears. Nothing in her erect
posture suggested any trace of remorse.

Irene and Tommy sat down and began the interview,
but Ann answered either in monosyllables or not at all.
It took almost half an hour before she started to give
slightly more detailed responses. She confirmed what
Hannu had discovered about her family circumstances.

"I did what I could as far as Patrik was concerned, but
it wasn't enough. I was too young."

She sounded as if she were apologizing, and for the
first time Irene could see that she was genuinely moved.
Patrik was her Achilles' heel. Irene decided to change
tack. Gently she asked, "Why didn't your older brothers
look out for Patrik?"

"That's exactly the reason: they were older. They left
home when he was born," Ann snapped.

"But you stayed."

"Yes."

Ann swallowed and looked away. Patrik must have had
a hard time when he was growing up. The adults around
him had had more than enough to deal with, coping with
their own problems; nobody had paid much attention to
him. Apart from his sister, who had done her best.

"I was only thirteen when he was born. He . . . he was
so little, and . . ." Ann suddenly let out a sob. Tears
poured down her cheeks and she asked for a tissue.

Tommy passed her a box of Kleenex while Irene
poured her a glass of water, which she took with shaking

hands. They waited while she pulled herself together, then resumed the interview.

"You trained at the police academy in Stockholm, then you worked in Trollhättan for a number of years. Why did you go back there?" Irene asked.

"I met my husband. He was a DI in Trollhättan and knew about my family. I didn't have to pretend, although in fact there wasn't a great deal to hide. My dad went down a few times for being drunk and disorderly in a public place, but that's all. Neither of my older brothers has done anything illegal, apart from speeding and minor tax evasion. They were both convicted and fined. But Patrik was something else. He seemed to be drawn to crime, and we just couldn't keep him away from it. Particularly once drugs came into the picture."

Her voice hardened and she blew her nose before continuing.

"He was so sweet when he was a child, the kindest little boy in the world. But things didn't go too well at school, so he more or less stopped going. Relocating to Göteborg didn't help; he seemed to thrive when he joined a gang. I suppose it gave him a sense of identity. I moved here to keep any eye on him and my mom, but Patrik was running his own race. All I could do was be around. As you can see, it worked out really well!"

The last sentence was shot through with self-reproach. Ann clearly saw the fact that Patrik had been murdered as a failure on her part. She hadn't been able to protect him, so she blamed herself for his death. Irene recognized the pattern, which was very common in mothers with sons who had turned to crime and come to a sticky end.

"Was it because of Patrik that you started passing

information to Gothia MC?" Tommy asked. His tone was pleasant, but Ann recoiled as if he had slapped her across the face. A red flush spread up her throat and cheeks, and for a moment she seemed completely knocked off balance.

"I . . . yes . . . I . . ."

She fell silent and stared straight ahead, not looking at either of them.

"Ann, when did you start passing information to Patrik's associates in Gothia MC?" Irene asked.

At first it seemed as if she wasn't going to answer, but then she murmured almost inaudibly, "After . . . after those bastards killed him. He . . ."

She fell silent, blinking away the tears.

"Gothia MC had never contacted you before?"

"No."

"Which member of the gang called you?" Tommy wanted to know.

This time she met his gaze, her expression defiant.

"They didn't call me. I called them."

"Why?" Irene managed to get the question out, even though she was taken aback by Ann's response.

"Because I knew that we . . . the police . . . wouldn't catch the killers. As far as you . . . the police . . . were concerned, Patrik was just a criminal, a member of a biker gang who got what he deserved. But he was my little brother!"

The last sentence came out as a scream. *There's something about her eyes. She doesn't look well,* Irene thought. Was there some kind of mental instability, an additional component in all this? That might at least partly explain Ann's actions, but it wasn't something Irene could judge; that was up to the psychiatrists, if they were called in.

"So you're telling us that you contacted Gothia MC and offered to provide them with information on our investigation, in return for a promise that they would deal with the person or persons who murdered your brother," Tommy summarized.

Ann nodded.

"Did you get paid for your services?"

"No, revenge was all I asked for. And I got it."

Ann's words were accompanied by a cold smile, a particularly unpleasant smile. Irene felt the hairs stand up on her arms and the back of her neck.

Tommy decided to push harder. "Who was your contact in the gang?"

Ann merely shook her head and fixed her eyes on a point over his shoulder. He tried to get her to say more, but she just kept on shaking her head.

"I want a lawyer," she said eventually.

WHEN IRENE SWITCHED on her computer she found an email from Matti Berggren. He had found lots of fingerprints from Kazan Ekici and Fendi Göks in the BMW, plus prints from others, but only Kazan and Fendi's contained traces of gasoline.

Matti had also found bloodstains on the front and backseats; they were small, but enough for DNA testing. The blood was Patrik Karlsson's. It must have splashed onto their clothes while they were beating him up, then come off on the seats, Irene thought with a deep sense of satisfaction. This was exactly what they needed in order to tie Kazan and Fendi to Patrik's death.

As she read on, her optimism continued to grow. Matti had discovered traces of cocaine in the trunk that were the same pure quality as in the packages in Kazan's closet. He had also compared the findings from the BMW with the powdery residue they had secured during Sunday's raid on Gothia MC: the result was positive. It was the same batch of unusually pure cocaine; the composition in each sample was identical.

This strengthened the credibility of what Kazan had told her, Irene thought. The cocaine came from the murders of Enrico Gonzales and David Angelo, which in turn led to Gothia MC and Patrik Karlsson. And then to Kazan and Fendi. *We should be able to tie this up before long*, she told herself—and she actually believed it.

She was also beginning to hope that they would be able to nail the leaders of Gothia MC for the double homicide in Varberg, which in turn should weaken their organization to such an extent that they would lose interest in trying to extort money from Krister. The police just had to make sure they had cast-iron evidence to prove that Gothia MC was behind the murders and the theft of the cocaine.

THE AFTERNOON PASSED quickly; every available officer was working at full capacity. The interviews with those who had attended the party where Danny Mara was shot had been completed, but the investigation was making no progress. Over a hundred guests, and no one had seen a thing, including the nine cops who had been there. Stefan Bratt had his suspicions about Omid Reza. The bodyguard insisted he had been at the far end of the park when the shots were fired, which was why it took a while before he reached the spot where Danny lay. No one had contradicted his story, so they had had to let him go.

Fendi Göks was still missing. His mother assured them that her son had never done anything like this before; he was the oldest of six siblings, and had taken on the responsibility for the family when his father walked out. Fendi would never abandon his mother and his younger brothers and sisters. *Maybe*, Irene thought, *but he's still nowhere to be found. And he's a suspect in the murder of Patrik Karlsson.* The crime he and Kazan had committed was horrific. *If he's still alive, I will find him*, Irene promised herself.

TOMMY PERSSON AND Stefan Bratt were in a meeting with the head of Narcotics, Superintendent Lena Hellström. Also present were Irene and Fredrik. Irene ran through her conversation with Kazan at the hospital one more time, and when she revealed that the cocaine had come from Enrico Gonzales and David Angelo, Lena Hellström raised her eyebrows.

"This is an important lead in the murders of two major dealers. As you say, Irene, the trail takes us from Gonzales and Angelo to Gothia MC. So where's the cocaine now—besides what we already confiscated from Kazan? We know it's not hidden at Gothia MC's HQ," Tommy began.

"If we'd been kept in the loop we might have found out by now," Lena said acidly.

She was a tall woman in her sixties, with short, thick steel-grey hair. She wore no makeup apart from bright vermilion lipstick which matched the flamboyant flowers on her blouse. Irene recognized the pattern: Marimekko. Good for interior design, not so good when it came to clothes, in her opinion. Lena clearly didn't agree; around her neck she wore a statement necklace made up of green wooden tiles that rattled every time she moved her head.

"You couldn't have done anything different," Stefan Bratt informed her.

He seemed to have recovered from the morning's shock, and looked more like his normal pale self.

"We've been watching that gang for years," Lena snapped.

"So have we."

"But neither of you noticed them shifting the cocaine, or where they hid it," Tommy stated.

His colleagues looked as if they had swallowed something that tasted extremely bitter, but neither of them spoke.

"Thanks to the powdery residue the CSIs found during the raid," Tommy continued, "we know the cocaine has been at Gothia MC's HQ. Does anyone have a theory as to where it might be right now?"

Lena Hellström nodded with such enthusiasm that her necklace sounded like a rattlesnake.

"I know Per Lindström pretty well. He was involved in drug dealing long before he became the leader of Gothia MC. He's not dumb enough to keep the stuff at home— unlike Kazan Ekici. On the other hand, I don't think he'd want it too far away. I'm sure it's hidden somewhere close to Lindström," she said firmly.

The atmosphere in the room had lightened during the discussion, which Irene found liberating. There was far too much bickering over territory between the different departments, but the Göteborg police probably weren't the worst of the bunch when it came down to it. Over the years, and thanks to the pressure of a growing workload, they had learned to work together reasonably well.

"I think Lindström was intending to lie low after the double homicide, until the worst had blown over," Tommy said. "And then Patrik Karlsson was murdered; that was probably the last thing he wanted."

"Absolutely. Ann Wennberg tipped Lindström off about the raid, and that's why he moved the cocaine," Stefan chipped in, and Tommy nodded in agreement.

"In which case that must have happened the day before we showed up," he said.

They all sat in silence for a few moments, trying to work out what had happened.

Irene suddenly remembered something. "The cleaning," she said.

"Cleaning?" Lena echoed.

"When we were on our way to raid Gothia MC's HQ, the first SWAT team vehicle almost collided with an enormous trailer that was in one hell of a hurry to get away. Fredrik recognized the driver as Lindström's wife. I'm thinking the drugs were in the trailer; that would explain why she seemed so stressed. And they'd cleaned the whole place to within an inch of its life."

"How do you know?"

"We arrived in the middle of a so-called family day; the place was heaving with people. Everything reeked of Ajax, and was spotless."

Tommy ran his fingers through his hair; it was obvious that he was thinking something over.

"How much coke did you find on the yacht?" he asked suddenly, directing the question to Lena.

She pursed her shiny vermilion lips before answering. "Exactly twenty-eight pounds, divided into fifty-six packages, which filled the storage compartment completely."

"So there could have been the same amount in the other compartment, which was the same size. Fifty-six packages . . . that could explain how Patrik managed to squirrel away eight of them without anyone noticing," Tommy said.

"So Patrik stole four pounds, which means Per Lindström has twenty-four pounds of pure cocaine stashed away somewhere, with a street value of around a hundred million kronor," Fredrik pointed out after a quick mental calculation.

They were talking about huge sums of money, which explained the significant loss of life among those who had been involved with this particular shipment.

Everyone jumped when Lena Hellström clapped her hands and said, "I'll call a meeting right away, speak to everyone in my department who's been keeping an eye on Gothia MC recently. Someone might have a suggestion as to where the coke is hidden, and we'll definitely check out the trailer. We'll reconvene on Friday morning."

"Should we bring in Per Lindström and Jorma Kinnunen for questioning?" Fredrik asked.

All three senior officers shook their heads.

"There's no point. We don't have enough to go on," Tommy said.

"All we have is what Kazan told Irene; he's dead, and she was alone with him at the time. We can't prove anything," Lena said, glancing at Irene.

Irene thought about protesting, pointing out that forensics indicated that they were looking at the same consignment all the way along, from the double homicide outside Varberg through to the hiding place in Kazan's closet, but she refrained. To be fair, that was all they had in terms of firm evidence; Christoffer von Hanke would simply claim that the traces of cocaine at Gothia MC's HQ had been planted and proved nothing.

"We need to find the coke first, then we can bring them in," Stefan Bratt said.

Everyone started to gather up their pens and notepads.

"Okay, so we'll meet on Friday morning—nine o'clock in this room," Tommy concluded, getting to his feet. He seemed to have held on to the fresh spurt of energy from earlier in the day; Irene wished some of it would come in her direction.

THE GROUP WHO would be running the surveillance operation on Pravda met again at six. It had never been a decent restaurant, more of a bar. Plain clothes officers had been patrolling the area all day; a couple of smart cookies had borrowed dogs, so that they could stroll around with their four-legged friends looking perfectly natural.

Tommy Persson and Stefan Bratt came up with a plan, which was accepted with one or two minor adjustments. Toward the end of the meeting Stefan informed the team that Ann Wennberg had been passing information to Gothia MC. The revelation received a mixed response. It was obvious that some people had already heard the rumors, but most were devastated and found it hard to believe. Stefan murmured and nodded, without showing what he really felt. As the hum of conversation died down, he said:

"We'll be interviewing Ann again tomorrow, but she has admitted everything. There's a tragic family story behind what's happened; I'll get back to you as and when necessary," he said, making it clear that the discussion on that particular topic was over.

When they went their separate ways shortly before eight, everyone knew what they were doing the next day.

Irene went down to the underground garage and took out an unmarked police car, just as she and Tommy had agreed. She drove out through the electric gates and watched in the rearview mirror as they closed behind her. She spent some time driving around the neighborhood just to make sure she wasn't being followed; then she headed out to Jonsered.

A NUMBER OF cars were parked outside the ICA store in Jonsered. A sign on the door informed her that it was open every day until nine in the evening. During breakfast Irene had noticed that they were almost out of milk and that the cheese looked like a ski slope when the snow has almost melted. They were probably out of eggs too. Time to do a little shopping.

She parked right by the entrance. In order to pay Tommy back at least in part for providing her with a place of refuge, she bought fruit and vegetables as well. She decided two big packs of rolls on sale were definitely a bargain; then her guilty conscience drove her to pick up a pack of heavy, dark brown whole-wheat bread cheered up with a few sunflower seeds, even though she knew neither of them would eat it. Pasta and a ready-made tomato sauce would do for dinner; that was the closest to home cooking she could manage tonight. For the following day she chose pork chops and a bag of frozen potato wedges. Krister would have had a fit— buying expensive frozen potatoes! But what he didn't know couldn't hurt him, Irene reasoned. To be on the safe side she added two frozen pizzas before joining the line at checkout. She found herself standing next to a big refrigerator full of beer and soda, and grabbed a six-pack of beer. That would brighten Tommy's day.

IRENE DROVE TO the visitors' parking lot opposite Tommy's house because she couldn't carry her shopping all the way from the store. She noticed that Tommy's car wasn't in its usual spot but assumed he would be home soon. She lifted the two bags out of the backseat, one in each hand, and pushed the door shut with her hip.

She spotted a large white Mercedes van with blacked-out side windows a short distance away. In the gathering dusk it was impossible to see if there was anyone in the driver's seat. There was nothing written on the side, and she hadn't seen it in the lot before. It was just an anonymous white van, like thousands of others on the streets of Göteborg. Under normal circumstances she probably wouldn't have paid any attention to it, but circumstances were far from normal, and the van stuck out like a sore thumb. Should she take a closer look? Or get back in her car and drive away?

Before she had time to consider her options, both front doors opened. A man dressed in dark clothing got out of the driver's side and came straight toward her. He was tall and powerfully built, and he was moving fast. Irene heard the sound of heavy footsteps running from the other side of the vehicle. Reflexively she stepped to one side, dropped the paper bag of groceries in her left hand, and took a firm grip on the plastic bag containing the six-pack of beer. The tall man hesitated when he

saw her swinging the bag around in the air, but before
he could work out what was going on, Irene took a step
forward and let go of the bag. It flew through the air like
a missile and struck him full in the face. Without a sound
he fell back and sat down, blood spurting from one eyebrow. Clumsily he tried to wipe it away as it poured into
his eyes, but to no avail. *Yesss!* Irene thought. But then
the second guy appeared. He was a little shorter, but
much stockier. His head was shaven, and he too was
dressed in dark clothing. When he saw his buddy sitting
on the ground, he paused for a second before growling
something unintelligible and launching himself at Irene.
He was holding something in one hand; Irene realized it
was a knife. So they were intending to force her into the
back of the van at knifepoint. An ice-cold rage surged
through her body. Suddenly everything crystallized. She
knew exactly how to handle the situation.

When her attacker got close, she leapt in the air and
started roaring at the top of her voice. At the same time
she jabbed her arms, like a drunk who has just decided to
take up boxing. She darted toward the man; as expected,
he stopped and stared at her flailing arms and distorted
face. Like lightning she bent her right leg and drew it up
toward her chest before putting all the strength she could
muster into a powerful kick, aiming her heel at his knee.
It might not have been quite as vicious as a kick from a
stallion, but it wasn't far short. There was a horrible
crack, like dry wood. In fact it was the sound of a kneecap
being forced into cartilage and ligaments in what had
been a fully functioning joint until now. It would never
be the same again. The man went down with a bellow of
pain, stabbing at the air with a short-bladed knife. Irene

quickly moved back as she fumbled for her cell phone in her pocket. In her peripheral vision she glimpsed someone running; when she turned her head, she saw that it was Tommy.

"Irene! What the hell is going on? Are you hurt?" he yelled.

"I'm not, but they are."

She was short of breath, probably due to the mental strain. The attack itself had been over before it started. Tommy also took out his cell phone; holding it in both hands, he pointed it at the two guys writhing in agony on the ground.

"Police! Stay down!"

Neither of the men made any attempt to get up. In the half-light they couldn't tell whether Tommy was actually aiming a gun at them, but Irene had a feeling they both already knew she and Tommy were cops. He could easily be armed, even though in reality it was very unusual for off-duty Swedish police officers to carry a gun. *We're not like our American colleagues who seem to sleep with a firearm under their pillows*, Irene thought.

Tommy shouted at the man with only one working knee to drop the knife, and without protesting he tossed it a short distance away. His companion was still clutching his eyebrow, while blood poured down his face.

The first squad car arrived within minutes.

INSIDE THE WHITE van they found two Gothia MC vests, cable ties, several yards of twine and a roll of duct tape. Everything necessary for an abduction, in fact.

"At least they were planning to take me alive," Irene said, trying to smile to show that she was joking.

"I wouldn't be so sure. This was also in the back," Tommy said, holding up a roll of thick builder's plastic. The smile died on Irene's lips.

THEY OPTED FOR pizzas and beer; neither of them felt like cooking. The only problem was beer sprayed everywhere when they opened the first can; its flight through the air had given it a good shaking. Tommy simply went out onto the terrace and held the hissing cans over the neglected rose bed, one by one. *Maybe it will give the poor roses some kind of nutrition,* Irene thought. *I'm sure they need vitamin B.* She decided to keep her opinion to herself.

"How did they know where I was?" she said instead.

"Ann."

"Ann? But she didn't know I was staying here, did she?"

"I guess she put two and two together . . . You remember the painkillers I brought you the day before yesterday?"

"I do."

Tommy took a slug of beer; he looked a little troubled when he put down the can. "Stefan and Ann came into my office when I was just about to leave. He asked if I had time to go over a couple of things; I told him I had to get to the drugstore to pick up some painkillers. Ann said she had an unopened pack in her purse, and that I was welcome to take it. So I bought it from her."

Irene rolled her eyes and continued the story. "And quick-thinking little Ann immediately realized the connection between a blow to the head, headaches, and the need for painkillers. So she tipped off her friends in

Gothia MC, suggested they should follow you because you would probably lead them to wherever I was hiding."

Tommy nodded, looking very embarrassed.

"I guess so. I never thought to check whether anyone was tailing me. I was just going home, behaving normally," he said apologetically.

"Of course. You're not to blame."

He immediately looked relieved and finished off the pizza. "I have to say I was impressed by the way you handled those two guys earlier. That wasn't a jiujitsu move though, was it?"

"Hardly, but if you've been training in martial arts for over thirty years, you don't just know the correct holds. You learn the dirty tricks too."

Tommy nodded as if she had confirmed something he had already worked out. "And you scored a direct hit with the six-pack!" he said with undisguised admiration in his voice.

"Top scorer in sling ball in fifth and sixth grade," Irene informed him with a smile.

"Thank God for that," Tommy said. He sounded as if he really meant it.

IT WAS A member of the Narcotics surveillance team who came up with a brilliant plan. When he told Lena Hellström about it, she immediately got the preparations under way without consulting Tommy Persson or Stefan Bratt. It was already late afternoon and there was no time for deliberation, she explained when she called to inform them that evening. Neither of them had any objections; they thought it sounded like a great idea.

Narcotics and the tech guys worked flat out all night. At 7:05 the following morning a truck carrying a large construction site trailer arrived in Gårda and parked about fifty yards from the dilapidated building that had once housed the Pravda restaurant. The trailer was unloaded at the top of the street, which had become a dead end thanks to the closure of the route leading to Åvägen. A number of construction workers' huts and storage sheds were already in place, hence the idea of hiding the surveillance equipment in a trailer. Demolition was due to start any day, so with a bit of luck no one would give it a second glance.

The trailer was spacious and modern and included both a small kitchen and a bathroom. Admittedly it was only a chemical toilet, but if it worked on boats, it would work there, Irene thought. She was with Hannu Rauhala, Stefan Bratt and Fredrik Stridh. They had been joined by two detective inspectors from Narcotics, who were every bit as secretive as usual, but at least they introduced themselves as Malin and Lasse.

Tommy Persson and Lena Hellström were back at the station, and would be in constant contact with the team in the trailer.

There was a small dirty window in the short side of the trailer, facing Pravda, with a camera in the bottom corner. It couldn't be seen from outside, and was disguised as a flashing intruder alarm. A sticky label on the glass stated that the trailer was alarmed. The other two windows were outfitted the same way; they also had thick, closed curtains, and screens behind these curtains made it impossible for passersby to see any internal lights. There was another camera concealed in a broken external light by the door, which meant they could see in all directions.

The small room behind the window overlooking Pravda contained only a rickety table and four mismatched chairs. The door to the other room was closed, and the keyhole was plugged to stop any light from seeping through, just in case anyone decided to peer in. The trailer was supposed to look empty, ready and waiting for the demolition crew who were due any day now. Behind the closed internal door, however, the place was a hive of activity. Four screens registered everything that was going on outside, and the listening equipment was on a separate table. Directional microphones could easily pick up conversations inside the old wooden building, because there was nothing in the way. Everyone had been provided with headphones.

The empty building opposite Pravda was now occupied by twelve heavily armed officers from the SWAT team. They had been driven in through the gates at the back in two anonymous black minibuses under cover of the lingering darkness at around four in the morning. The buses reversed into the yard, and the officers quickly jumped out and made their way inside, locking the door behind them as the minibuses drove away. The entire operation had taken less than a minute. The men headed for an apartment on the second floor, overlooking Pravda. Broken Venetian blinds still hung crookedly at two of the windows, and the last tenant had also left behind some thin, incredibly filthy curtains. The police had an excellent view, but no one could see them in the dim light of the apartment.

Stefan, Tommy and Lena had decided to maintain the patrols by plain clothes officers, so yesterday's borrowed dogs were once again on duty. None of them could understand why they were being walked around this boring area yet again, but they were all well trained and obediently trotted along beside their temporary masters and mistresses.

"I think we've got a pretty good handle on the situation," Stefan Bratt announced. He looked a little pale, but there was nothing wrong with the intensity in his eyes. Irene thought he seemed totally focused on the day's task.

All they needed now was for the leaders of the Gangster Lions and Gothia MC to actually show up. As Jonny Blom had said, there was a risk that Kazan had made the whole thing up, but deep down Irene didn't think that was the case. Kazan had believed that the information he

had given her was enough to guarantee him a new identity. Maybe he was also hoping that the cops would bring
in the major players, giving Kazan and Fendi the chance
to escape the gang's revenge for the murder of Patrik
Karlsson and the opportunity to build up their own business dealing drugs. It wouldn't have worked in the long
term, of course. The gangs always get their man. The
bosses would simply have issued their orders from jail,
and the end result for Kazan would have been the same:
death. Had Fendi already paid with his life? If so, it was
just a matter of finding out which gang had gotten to him
first.

The morning crawled by uneventfully. The officers
inside the trailer discussed why Pravda had been fitted
with a new front door; three shiny locks gleamed
against the sturdy oak. The two large windows looking
out onto the street were boarded up; there would be no
possibility of seeing inside once the meeting started.
However, they would have no problem listening to
everything that was said.

Nothing of interest happened until around eleven-
thirty, when a small red van appeared with DELI
SERVICE—LEAVE THE PARTY PLANNING TO US! on the side,
and CATERING AND PARTY SERVICE in smaller letters
underneath. Two men got out; Irene recognized both of
them from Danny Mara's party. One was Ali Reza, the
bodyguard, the other was a young man in a waiter's uniform. He had been among the group laughing on the
stairs when Kazan smashed his glass. Reza had a good
look around; he stared at the trailer for quite some time
as everyone inside held their breath, keeping their eyes
on the screen.

After what seemed like an eternity Reza turned his attention to a young woman coming toward him with a springer spaniel on a leash. She smiled at the well-built young Iranian as she passed by; he watched her hips swaying beneath her thin skirt before once again focusing on the buildings around Pravda. If he had known that the dog in question was Frode, last year's Sniffer Dog of the Year, and that the young woman was part of the Narcotics surveillance team, he would have shown a little more interest. In fact he would probably have shot them both with the revolver that was clearly visible under his jacket, Irene thought with a shudder. The very idea brought her out in a sweat and made her blouse stick to her back—or maybe it was just getting very hot inside the trailer.

Fredrik whispered, "All right. Something's happening."

Ali Reza went over and unlocked the heavy oak door. He disappeared inside, and after a few minutes he said, "We can unload."

Everyone jumped; they hadn't expected to hear him quite so loud and clear in their headphones.

Ali reappeared. The other guy had already opened the rear doors of the van, and they started to carry in several large Styrofoam boxes. It seemed as if lunch was being provided for those attending the meeting. There were also cases of beer and bags containing bottles. Presumably successful negotiations would be followed by a celebration. What would happen if those negotiations broke down didn't bear thinking about.

For almost an hour Irene sat listening to Reza and his pal moving around inside the restaurant: the scrape of furniture being shifted, the clink of crockery and glass as they set the tables. From time to time they spoke to each other in Swedish, but said nothing of interest to the police.

A sudden flash of sunlight reflected on metal alerted Irene to an approaching car. It was a white Lexus, last year's model. It had been parked outside the conference center in Sävedalen, and she knew it had belonged to Danny Mara. It glided smoothly to a halt in front of the oak door, and four men in sharp suits got out. One of them was Andy Mara, the new leader of the Gangster Lions. They looked as if they worked in the financial sector, and maybe they did. All four walked straight into Pravda without knocking. The driver remained in the car; most cops and criminals in Göteborg knew him as "The Cobra." He was a short, overweight middle-aged gangster who had been with the Lions right from the start. After a serious bullet wound to one hip, he now worked as a right-hand man and driver for the bosses.

The conversation inside came through the head-phones:

"Everything under control?" Andy Mara asked.

"Yes, boss," came Ali Reza's deep bass voice.

Then Andy said something in a foreign language. A younger voice replied, and Irene guessed it was the waiter. Then Andy reverted to Swedish.

"When everyone has helped themselves to food, you and Casim can leave."

"Okay, boss."

It was fortunate that Andy Mara, who was Turkish, had to speak Swedish with the Iranian Ali Reza; other-wise the cops wouldn't have understood a word.

A long conversation in Turkish between Andy and the three men who had arrived with him then followed, and it was recorded for translation later.

After a few minutes, a black Mercedes pulled up behind the Lexus and the leaders of Gothia MC climbed out. It might have been Irene's imagination, but she thought the car gave a sigh of relief as the undercarriage lifted a couple of inches off the ground. Three of the four burly occupants were easily identified as Per Lindström, Jorma Kinnunen and Andreas "The Dragon" Brännström. The fourth was tall and athletic with a baseball cap pulled down low over his forehead. Beneath his Gothia MC vest he was wearing a black sleeveless T-shirt, and his muscular arms were completely covered in tattoos, right down to his fingertips.

Their driver also stayed in the car. He was a younger guy, identified by Fredrik Stridh as Alexander Svensson. Irene thought he seemed too young to have a driver's license; in spite of all the external trappings, including tattoos and a shaven head, he looked like an ordinary kid from the suburbs. However, appearances were deceptive. According to Fredrik, Svensson already had an extensive record. He had been taken into custody by social services, had served time in a juvenile detention center for drug dealing and serious assault, and had resolutely fought his way to the top of the Desperados. He had just turned eighteen, and was clearly regarded as being ready to move on to Gothia MC. The fact that he had been trusted to drive the leaders to this important meeting spoke volumes.

"So Andreas Brännström is still in town!" Fredrik hissed as Pravda's door closed behind the new arrivals.

The temperature inside the trailer rose significantly,

and that wasn't just down to the lack of air-conditioning. Everyone felt the change of pace.

"The tall guy with the tattoos could easily be the man in the CCTV footage from Södra vägen, and from the images we have of Jan-Erik Månsson being forced to drive out to Landsvetter," Irene said.

"He also matches the description of one of the men seen arguing with Soran Siljac a few days before he was blown to pieces," Fredrik added.

"Do you know who he is?" Hannu asked.

Fredrik shook his head.

"It could be Soltan Milosevic," Hannu suggested. "Wanted for war crimes during the Balkan conflict."

None of the others had heard of him.

"He's a psychopath. Vanished without a trace after the war. Distinguishing features are his height, his athleticism and his tattoos," Hannu went on.

No one in the Västra Götaland police force had a memory for people like Hannu did. He could well be right; that would explain why no one had recognized the tall guy in the CCTV footage. He wasn't on their system; he was wanted by Interpol.

"Even if he's living under a false identity, it's strange that he's prepared to show himself so openly," Stefan Bratt said.

"Maybe he's been in Sweden for a long time without any problem. Maybe he's getting careless. That always trips them up in the end," Fredrik said.

"What a coup! We mustn't let any of them slip through the net when the meeting is over!" Stefan exclaimed.

A combination of heat and excitement had brought a flush to those pale cheeks.

Irene could hear the gang leaders greeting one another. She couldn't make out individual words, just a general hum as everyone said hello. After a while she heard Andy Mara's slightly shrill voice:

"Thanks for coming in spite of all the shit that's gone on lately."

"No problem. And let me tell you right now that we didn't fucking shoot Danny, okay? And we haven't heard a fucking thing about who was responsible."

Per Lindström's rough bass voice.

"Sorry for your loss," he added.

"Thanks."

There was a brief uncertain silence before Andy continued.

"Please sit down. We're here, you're over there."

Chairs scraping on the floor, another burst of muted conversation, then Andy again:

"Casim and Ali—drinks, please. Whatever our guests would like."

Champagne corks popped, while the odd click and fizz indicated that some people clearly preferred beer.

"We'll eat first," Andy said briskly.

The suggestion seemed to meet with general approval, and was followed by the clank of metal, presumably as the lids were lifted off the large food containers, and various comments such as: ". . . I don't mind potato wedges, but what the fuck are those pine needles doing in there . . . Whadya mean, rosemary? What the fuck?" and "Whadya mean, there's no fucking sauce?" It was clear that Ali Reza and Casim had their hands full keeping the guests satisfied.

Once things had calmed down, Andy said, "I'll call you when you can pick up the dishes."

"Okay. The desserts are in that box and . . ."

Ali was rudely interrupted by Andy: "Just leave."

"Okay."

Shortly afterward Reza and Casim could be seen emerging through the front door. They jumped into the little van and shot away with a screech of tires, disappearing in the direction of Åvägen in a cloud of dust. The drivers in the other two cars were sitting smoking, and didn't even bother glancing at the lackeys. They were ignoring each other equally studiously.

"Let's talk business while we're eating," Per Lindström suggested in his deep voice.

Everyone seemed to agree; the clatter of knives and forks already formed a wall of background noise.

Andy Mara nervously cleared his throat several times before he began. "As you're all aware, it was my brother, Danny, who convened this meeting. He wanted us to call a truce. Per, I know when he contacted you he assured you that the Gangster Lions weren't responsible for Patrik Karlsson's death. It was a horrific, brutal murder, and we absolutely distance ourselves from it. None of us had a personal issue with Patrik; we're as much in the dark as you guys. And now the murder of my brother . . . we think . . . well, I think . . ."

Andy Mara paused for effect. Both the cops in the trailer and Göteborg's gangster elite held their breath. Instinctively Irene and her colleagues cupped their hands around their headphones, pushing them closer to their ears to make sure they didn't miss a word:

". . . there's a third gang fucking around with us."

There was silence as his words sank in.

"What the fuck . . . You mean another gang took out

both Patrik and Danny?" Per Lindström exclaimed. His voice was full of suspicion, but there was something else, as if the idea wasn't totally new to him.

Andy cleared his throat yet again.

"That's . . . that's what we think."

Per Lindström seemed to be considering what the new leader of the Gangster Lions had just said.

"That would explain everything! So we're being fucked over by . . . who exactly?"

The listeners in the trailer were also very interested in the answer to that question, even though they knew that Kazan and Fendi were responsible for the murder of Patrik Karlsson. They only had Kazan's verbal confession, of course; they needed evidence. With a bit of luck, the Gangster Lions might have come up with something.

"I have no idea," Andy said.

The disappointment was equally palpable in both locations.

"Anyone want more food?" he went on. He had taken over hosting duties following his brother's death, so it was important to make sure the guests were satisfied.

"No? Okay then, we'll clear away. The desserts are in that box over there: ice cream and some chocolate thing. Of course there's more booze! Wine? Beer? Just help yourselves!"

The clatter of dishes being stacked up meant that it was impossible to hear what the men around the table were saying. Everyone in the trailer had their eyes fixed on the screen showing the main door of the restaurant and the two drivers, still smoking away.

Irene noticed something in her peripheral vision; there was a movement on the screen beside her, the one transmitting images from the camera pointing west, in the direction of the closed-off side street leading to Åvägen. When she turned her head, she saw a scooter slowly approaching. The rider was wearing a full helmet with a black visor, white sneakers, jeans, a white T-shirt and a dark-colored padded vest. He stopped just before reaching the street on which Pravda lay. Neither of the drivers appeared to have heard him; they were both looking in a different direction. Irene noted that he was thin and wiry, and just below average height. In spite of the helmet, there was something familiar about him. When she spotted the heavy gold watch on his left wrist, she knew exactly who he was: Fendi Göks. Either he had inherited Kazan's watch, or he had an identical one. The sunlight caught it when he reached into his pocket and took out a cell phone. To Irene's surprise he held up the phone and took a picture of Pravda and the cars parked outside. Before she could alert her colleagues, she caught a glimpse of something behind Fendi: a little boy on a bicycle, heading for the trailer at full speed. He zoomed past Fendi, and as he reached the trailer Irene heard Andy Mara's voice in her headphones:

"What do you mean, you can't get the lid off? Just get a good grip, for fuck's sake . . ."

A pair of amber-colored eyes with a malicious glint flickered through Irene's mind, and Kazan whispered: *"The twenty-fifth . . . that's when it all goes bang!"*

An ice-cold hand clutched her heart as she realized what was about to happen. Her colleagues were astonished when she leapt up and ripped off her headphones. She strode to the door and turned the key, ignoring the agitated voices behind her: "Irene! What the hell are you doing? Are you crazy?" She dashed outside and ran after the little figure on the bicycle. He was only a few yards away, and she was moving as fast as she could. When she caught up with him, she yelled:

"Stop!"

He took no notice of her. Irene flung her arms around him and pulled him off his bike. The shock wave reached them as they landed on the ground. Over thirty years of training in how to fall meant that they had a soft landing, but she felt her face hit the tarmac because she couldn't use her hands to protect herself. Quickly she rolled over and pressed herself against the wall with the boy underneath her as debris rained down on them. Neither of them moved; presumably the child was paralyzed with fear. It was almost impossible to breathe; Irene found herself inhaling dust and sand. There wasn't a single clear thought in her head, just an instinctive urge to protect the boy with her own body. She pushed harder against the wall in a vain attempt to give the projectiles hammering down a smaller target area. She lay motionless with her eyes closed for what seemed like an eternity.

Irene didn't lose consciousness, but felt battered and dizzy when she was lifted onto a gurney. The blast had also deafened her, and she couldn't hear what those around her were saying, even though their facial expressions told her they were yelling. Fredrik had taken care of the little boy, and was leading him gently toward a second ambulance. As the child stepped inside he suddenly began to sob helplessly. Fredrik place a protective arm around his narrow shoulders, speaking reassuringly

to him as the paramedics closed the doors and drove
them to Queen Silvia's Children's Hospital.

SUPERINTENDENT TOMMY PERSSON'S face was
pale and strained; he was as shocked as everyone else
over what had happened. Irene forced herself to give him
an encouraging smile, but it was a pathetic attempt. She
couldn't speak. Her hearing had started to return, but
with a loud, irritating buzz deep in the ear canal.

Through the noise she suddenly recognized a familiar
voice.

"Don't you think it's time you considered a change of
profession, fru Huss? Being a police officer doesn't seem
to be particularly good for your health," it said dryly.

Dr. Enkvist was standing in the doorway of the examination room. Irene was about to tell him to go to hell
when he came over to her. His face was even more hag-
gard than before, but he was actually smiling, much to
her surprise. *Good grief, he was making a joke!* The occasion hardly could have been more inappropriate, but
Irene didn't have the strength to tell him. Instead she
closed her eyes, pretending to be worn out. The next
moment she was fast asleep on the gurney.

". . . COVERED IN bruises, but no fractures. Miracu-
lously, it appears that the head wasn't struck by any
heavy objects. The fact that she fell asleep is due to
exhaustion, not a fresh concussion."

So Dr. Enkvist was still there. Irene opened one eye a
fraction; Tommy was by her bed talking to the doctor.
Bed? Yes, she was actually in a bed. When she opened her
eyes properly, she discovered that she had been moved to

an ordinary ward. *Good. Much more comfortable*, she thought as she closed her eyes and went back to sleep.

IRENE STIRRED WHEN the food trolley clattered by in the corridor. She hadn't eaten since breakfast and was starving. A young nurse appeared and asked if she would like something.

"Yes, please, a large portion of anything at all. And lots of water."

"What time is it?" Irene asked when the nurse returned with a tray.

"Almost five. How are you feeling?"

"Okay, if I don't think about it too much."

In fact it was the pain that had woken Irene. Her entire body was throbbing like one huge bruise, and her cheek was itching. When she raised her hand to scratch it, her fingertips touched a large dressing holding a pad in place. Presumably she had grazed her face when she threw herself on the ground. She had no recollection of any pain at the time; the adrenaline rush had no doubt prevented her from feeling anything.

"Do you know if the little boy on the bicycle is all right?"

"He's fine. Shocked, of course, but completely unhurt. It's all over the Internet," the nurse replied with a big smile.

Irene could imagine how the story of the bomb had spread like wildfire. She was probably one of the few people who didn't know what had happened after the explosion.

"Do you know how many were killed or injured?" she asked as she greedily attacked her sausage and macaroni.

It was a long time since she had eaten anything so utterly delicious.

"No, they just said there were people inside the building, but nothing about the number."

With a reassuring smile the nurse left the room, closing the door behind her.

An hour later Tommy turned up.

"How are you feeling?"

"Pretty good, under the circumstances. I want to go home."

Tommy raised his eyebrows. "Wouldn't it be best to stay here overnight?"

"Not this time. I'm bruised, but not seriously injured. I want to go home to my apartment and sleep in my own bed," Irene said firmly.

"Okay. I'll have a word with the nurse, then I'll drive you home."

"I'm sure they're short on beds; they'll be glad to get rid of me."

It took less than thirty minutes for the duty doctor to discharge her.

"The Konsum store is still open," Irene informed Tommy as they parked in the visitors' lot opposite the apartment block on Doktor Bex gata.

"Okay. I'll go and do some shopping while you take a shower and freshen up."

Tommy smiled, and it occurred to Irene that their relationship was getting back to the way it used to be: good friends through thick and thin. Being there for each other. They'd lost that closeness over the past few years.

A pile of mail, newspapers and magazines was waiting behind the door. Irene pushed the whole lot aside with her foot; right now she didn't have the strength to bend down and pick it up. The apartment smelled of dust and wilting pot plants, but the smell of her family was there too. She felt a lump in her throat. She was home at last.

A glance in the bathroom mirror made her flinch. She had a large white dressing on her cheek, and a smaller one on her forehead. Dr. Enkvist had informed her that she hadn't needed stitches, but that the dressings had to stay on for a few days. She also had dressings on her left palm and on the outside of her left ankle. Her arms, legs and back were covered in angry red marks that were already beginning to turn bluish-black. She would certainly be a colorful sight when Krister and the girls got home! The thought of her family brought tears to her eyes once more, but she resolutely wiped them away and said out loud to her reflection:

"Pull yourself together!"

With that she peeled off her dirty clothes, dropped them on the floor and stepped into a long, hot shower.

IRENE AND TOMMY were sitting at the kitchen table drinking tea and eating ham and cheese sandwiches. Irene was wearing the soft velour leisure suit that her daughters had given her for Christmas.

"So tell me what happened," she said, looking at Tommy over the rim of her teacup.

"Okay, so you know everything up until the bomb went off . . . By the way, how did you know there was going to be an explosion?"

Tommy narrowed his eyes a fraction; was there a hint of suspicion in his gaze? Did he think she was the one who had planted the bomb in the food container? She immediately realized she was being ridiculous; he was simply asking a perfectly reasonable question.

"I saw Fendi Göks appear on a scooter; he stayed just around the corner, then took a picture of Pravda on his cell phone. Before I had time to tell the others that he was there, that little boy came whizzing along on his bike. In my headphones I heard Andy Mara telling someone to get a good grip on the lid because they couldn't get it off . . . and suddenly I realized what Kazan had meant when he said, 'the twenty-fifth . . . that's when it all goes bang.' He meant exactly what he said; there was a bomb. And the kid on the bike was heading straight for the place where it was about to go off. Everything happened so fast . . . I didn't have time to tell . . ."

Irene fell silent as she remembered racing out of the trailer and hurling herself at the unsuspecting child.

"I understand. Thank goodness you caught up with him; it was a hell of an explosion. Everyone inside the restaurant died, plus one of the drivers; a lock flew in through the open side window and hit him on the head."

"That must have been the Gangster Lions' driver; their car was parked right by the door."

"Possibly; we haven't started identifying the victims yet. Nine dead. It's going to take a while."

"What about the other driver, the young guy?"

"Serious head injuries; he's in a critical condition."

Irene gazed pensively into her empty cup, then said slowly, "Do you think either of the gangs will be able to carry on as before?"

"Hardly. Both the Gangster Lions and Gothia MC have lost their key players. This kind of gang can't cope without strong leaders."

Irene swallowed a couple of times before asking the most important question of all. "So does that mean Krister and the rest of the family are no longer in danger?"

Tommy looked at her for a long time before responding. "I believe so. The most-likely scenario is those two gangs will break up, and their members will join other gangs."

"Thank God!" Irene felt such a physical surge of relief that she almost fainted.

"Have you spoken to Krister or the girls?" Tommy asked.

"I tried calling and texting, but he did say it wouldn't be possible to contact them until tomorrow evening, so I guess I'll just have to be patient."

"You really don't know where they are?"

"I haven't a clue!" Irene's smile was so wide that it hurt her injured cheek, but she couldn't have cared less.

Two painkillers and nine hours' sleep did the trick. Irene woke up to sunlight spilling into the apartment, the dust shimmering in the sunbeams like fine snowfall. It was pretty, but it meant she needed to do some cleaning. But that could wait; right now she just wanted to enjoy the moment. For the first time in weeks she felt properly rested, but when she tried to get out of bed, reality made its presence felt. She was as stiff as a rusty suit of armor. Every fiber in her body protested at the slightest movement. She staggered to the bathroom and looked in the mirror, which didn't make her feel any better. The dressings were still in place, but the left side of her face was now covered in a huge bruise. *Jeez!* Her first instinct was to hide away from the world for the next two weeks, but one glance at the headlines covering virtually the whole front page of the morning paper changed her mind. SEVERAL DEAD IN BOMB ATTACK— HAS GANG WAR REACHED ITS CLIMAX?

As she quickly skimmed the article she realized the reporter didn't know much more than had been on the Internet the previous day. A number of people, all known to the police, had been inside a former restaurant in the Gårda area of the city when a huge bomb exploded.

The relatives had not yet been informed, and therefore the identities of the dead could not be published. The reporter linked the incident to the bomb placed under the Huss family's car, and the one planted outside the prosecutor's house in Örgryte.

Irene also found a separate story about a courageous police officer who had saved a little boy cycling along the street just before the bomb went off. The officer's gender and rank were not mentioned, but there was a picture of Hampus, who had just turned nine, and the shiny new bicycle he had been given for his birthday. His father had been interviewed and revealed that the family had recently moved into one of the newly built apartment blocks next to the area that was due for redevelopment. They had been a little worried about letting Hampus cycle along that particular side street, but as it was closed to traffic, they thought it was safe. He had set off at high speed and disappeared around the corner. Even though they could no longer see him, they thought it would be fine because the only vehicle they could see was a parked scooter with a teenager sending a text message. Hampus was supposed to cycle to the end of the street, then turn back. Suddenly they heard a deafening explosion. When his father reached the scene, he was surprised to find the place crawling with police officers amid all the dust and debris. A number of them were heavily armed, like "the SWAT team in an episode of *Beck* on TV," as he put it. Two ambulances arrived almost immediately, and before he had the chance to make himself known, he saw his son being led into one of them. Eventually he managed to explain who he was, and one of the officers arranged for a police car to take him and his wife to the hospital.

When they got there they were told that Hampus had sustained virtually no physical injuries. "Although we don't yet know if there will be any long-term emotional trauma," the article ended.

There was nothing about the condition of the police officer who had saved the boy. Though the physical damage was impossible to ignore, she was well enough to go to work. But she decided to treat herself to a cab on the station's dollar.

THE CAB DRIVER was a plump woman around the same age as Irene. She made no attempt to disguise the fact that she was having a good look at Irene's face in the rearview mirror. Irene gave her destination, and the woman nodded as if her passenger had confirmed something she already suspected. When Irene had paid and was about to get out, the driver turned and said:

"You make sure you report him, honey. Don't believe a word that asshole says. He'll do it again, no doubt about it. You stick to your guns!"

She swung the car around in order to head back down Skånegatan, and gave Irene an encouraging smile and a wave. *If it didn't hurt my cheek so much I'd laugh*, Irene thought.

HER COLLEAGUES WERE surprised to see her, but patted her gently on the back and congratulated her on her heroic contribution the previous day. No one was insensitive enough to mention her appearance. Apart from Jonny Blom, of course.

"I'm not sure that particular combination of eye shadow all over your face does anything for you, Irene."

"Watch out or you'll be wearing the same look," she said grimly. He had worked with her long enough to know not to push it.

Tommy Persson and Stefan Bratt positioned themselves on either side of the whiteboard. The hum of conversation died down, and Stefan began.

"The last twenty-four hours have been quite something. Things didn't exactly turn out as planned . . . to say the least. We're going to start with an up-to-date report on the casualties. Over to you, Tommy."

"Nine people were killed instantly in yesterday's explosion. Alexander Svensson was Gothia MC's driver; he was sitting in the car outside the restaurant, and like the other driver he had wound down the side windows. He was hit by debris and sustained serious head injuries. His condition remains critical. So the tally is nine dead, one badly injured."

Tommy clicked on his laptop and a picture of charred remains, which could have been just about anything, appeared on the wall.

"In order to keep the food for lunch hot or cold as required, it was supplied in metal containers which were delivered in Styrofoam boxes. Dessert was some kind of ice cream. The last thing we heard was Andy Mara telling the person who was trying to open the container to get a good grip on the lid because it seemed to be stuck. You could say the dessert was literally an ice cream bombe . . . Fendi Göks was sitting outside on his scooter. We don't yet know whether he detonated the bomb with his cell phone, or whether it went off when the lid was removed; forensics tend toward the latter. This is what's left of the guests."

He brought up a series of images showing burned corpses and body parts; the pictures seemed unreal, as if they had been taken after a suicide bombing in Iraq or Pakistan rather than in Sweden.

"In order to clarify how this all hangs together, Stefan and I have listed the events of the past few weeks."

Tommy brought up a PowerPoint slide with the heading GOTHIA MC, followed by a series of key points:

1) Double murder of Enrico Gonzales and David Angelo in the marina on Getterön outside Varberg, 1 May

2) Theft of cocaine, 56 packages each weighing 8 ounces = 28 pounds of pure cocaine (Patrik Karlsson took 8 of these packages)

3) Extortion and murder (car bomb) of restaurant owner Soran Siljac

4) Extortion and murder of former restaurant owner Jan-Erik Månsson

5) Extortion and attempted murder (car bomb) of restaurant owner Krister Huss

6) Threats, assault and theft of a valuable painting—witness Ritva Ekholm

7) Murder of Kazan Ekici

8) Attempted abduction of Irene Huss

Stefan Bratt took over once more.

"Narcotics have been working with our colleagues in Denmark and Halland, and have come up with a credible scenario on the double homicide. The cocaine that had already been cut was probably intended for sale to Gothia MC, while Gonzales and Angelo were planning

to ship the pure stuff over to Denmark for further pro-
cessing. They've been having problems in Copenhagen
all summer, with two gangs at war, each blaming the
other for having stolen a large amount of cocaine.
Something tells me that missing cocaine is here in
Göteborg."

He switched to a picture of the empty storage compartment on board the yacht before continuing.

"So Gonzales and Angelo were murdered by members of Gothia MC, including Patrik Karlsson. Since
they were dealing with such a large amount of coke,
fifty-six packages, Patrik somehow managed to nab
eight packages for himself. We know from questioning his sister, DI Ann Wennberg, that he was in
financial trouble. He owed money to the gang for
drugs; his only chance was to make money fast so he
could pay them off."

Stefan paused to refill his glass with mineral water
from the bottle on the table. He took a few sips, then
continued.

"Given the commotion following the double homicide, Patrik decided to keep a low profile over the
summer. At the beginning of August he got in touch
with Fendi Göks. Fendi and his pal Kazan Ekici convinced him that they were members of the Latin Kings,
and wanted to buy as much coke as he could lay his
hands on. The temptation was too great. Instead of
selling the coke in small amounts, he tried to sell the
whole lot at once. Maybe he was running out of time as
far as his debts were concerned."

Stefan clicked on a new slide; this time the heading
was THE THIRD GANG.

1) Murder of Patrik Karlsson
2) Theft of pure cocaine, 8 packages each
weighing 8 ounces = 4 pounds (from Patrik K)
3) Murder of Danny Mara
4) Bomb at Pravda, 9 dead (possibly 10)

He looked at Irene with a smile and a nod.

"It was Irene's conversation with Kazan Ekici just before he was killed which made us suspect that some members of the Gangster Lions were planning to branch out on their own. Since the Göteborg police are more than familiar with Danny Mara and the way he works, we know he would never have tolerated such a thing."

Stefan cleared his throat and drank a little more water.

"The problem for this breakaway group was that they had no start-up capital, which is why the tip-off about the large amount of cocaine in Patrik Karlsson's possession seemed like a godsend. When Kazan and Fendi went over to Kolgruvegatan to seal the deal, they had no intention of paying him; they had no money. They had always intended to kill him."

Irene cast an involuntary glance at the image of Patrik Karlsson's charred body on the board. *No living creature should have to die in such an appalling way.*

"Excuse me, but our friends Fendi and Kazan don't exactly come across as the sharpest knives in the drawer. How the hell did they manage to pull all this off?" Jonny Blom asked, waving a hand at the screen.

He's got a point, Irene thought. Everyone looked attentively at Stefan, waiting for the answer. He nodded to Jonny.

"You're absolutely right. Neither Kazan nor Fendi were

the leaders of this new gang. Ali and Omid Reza were tired of working as Danny Mara's bodyguards; they wanted a slice of the action for themselves, particularly as Ali had started playing around with Danny's beautiful wife, Elif. We know this from interviewing Fendi Göks, who was picked up immediately after the explosion. He had plenty to say, but has refused to answer any questions relating to the murders of Patrik Karlsson and Danny Mara. We know what happened to Patrik because Kazan confessed. As far as Danny is concerned, we can only speculate."

Sara Persson spoke up: "Is there really no proof at all? Just circumstantial evidence?"

"There is one thing that suggests we're probably right: a pair of Red Devil biker boots, size 45. They were found when Omid Reza's house was searched a few hours ago. We've sent them to forensics to check if there are any traces of earth from the field or the parking lot of the conference center where Danny was shot. Fingers crossed . . . No one saw Omid at the time of the murder; he claims he was doing a security check inside the wall, and was at the far end of the grounds. However, we believe he was in or around the summerhouse. He knew that Danny would come out sooner or later to take a leak by the bushes, and of course that was exactly what Danny did. Omid shot Danny when he got close enough to the spot where Omid was hiding. We can assume he was wearing gloves; he immediately threw away the gun, pulled off the gloves, then mingled with the other guests who were milling around on the lawn," Stefan replied.

"But we found traces of someone hanging around outside the gate . . . and what about the chain that had been cut?" Fredrik Stridh objected.

"Red herrings. Ali and Omid had set it all up earlier in the day—although they hadn't actually severed the chain. It was important that various people could testify that the chain and padlock were intact during the evening. Omid probably cut it when he got rid of the gun. Smart move," Stefan said with a wry smile.

"So where are the bolt cutters he used?" Sara wanted to know.

"I've no idea, but presumably the brothers had prepared a hiding place where he could stow them along with the gloves. We're going to go over the summerhouse and the surrounding area with a fine-tooth comb again, but of course he could have disposed of everything by now."

"And yesterday's bomb?" asked a colleague from the Organized Crimes Unit.

"Yesterday's bomb . . . well, that gave the third gang the perfect opportunity to dominate the narcotics market in a single stroke. With the Gangster Lions and Gothia MC out of the picture, there would be a vacuum which the new gang could fill right away. They had four pounds of cocaine, after all; they could start selling immediately."

"Plus with the top tier of both gangs gone, they had reduced the risk of revenge attacks," Tommy added.

Irene thought the two superintendents' analysis of the situation was probably as close to the truth as it was possible to get at the moment. She raised her hand, and Stefan nodded to her.

"Who else have you brought in, apart from Fendi Göks?"

"The Reza brothers. We questioned Casim, the young waiter, but we let him go; he has nothing to do with the third gang."

"Have they said anything?"

Tommy took over.

"As Stefan mentioned earlier, Fendi's talked quite a bit; neither of the brothers has said a word. We have previous experience of those two tough guys, and I'm afraid they're unlikely to crack. We're just hoping that Fendi will decide it's in his best interests to tell us the rest."

"How did he explain his presence outside Pravda?" Irene asked.

"He claims he knew about the meeting and was curious. He wanted to take some pictures with the camera on his phone."

There was a loud knock on the door, and it was immediately flung wide open. Lena Hellström sailed in with a triumphant smile on her vermilion lips. She nodded to everyone and no one before she announced, "We've found the cocaine! All of it!"

"Where?" Stefan Bratt asked.

"In a trailer owned by Per Lindström's mother. She lives in a small house out in Utby, with a brand new trailer parked in the large garden. She went crazy when we turned up with a search warrant, and insisted it was her trailer. However, when we found the cocaine she changed her story and admitted that Per had bought the trailer and asked if he could register it in her name and leave it at her place. Then she denied all knowledge of how a painting by Ivan Ivarson came to be hanging in her living room. According to her she came home one day, and there it was."

Lena Hellström couldn't help laughing.

Irene's cell phone vibrated in her pocket. Discreetly she took it out and saw to her delight that Krister was calling. She slipped out of the room; her colleagues looked at her in surprise, but no one said anything. Irene was desperate to answer before voice mail kicked in. Her heart was pounding and her whole body was trembling, but as soon as she heard Krister's voice, she felt a great sense of calm.

"Hi, sweetheart! We've just gotten back to civilization. Your text came through a little while ago. Is the danger really over?" he said cheerfully.

She could only manage a feeble response: "It is. Yes."

"How come? Have you locked up everyone from Gothia MC?"

"It's . . . it's a long story. Check out the *Göteborgs Posten* website. There's also an article about a little boy and a cop. I'm the cop."

There was a longish silence before Krister spoke again.

"Okay. Even if we share the driving and don't take any breaks, we can't get back to Göteborg before Sunday."

"Wow. Where the hell are you?"

"We're in a place called Kebnats. We sailed here from Saltoluokta this morning; we've been walking in the mountains. It's glorious. We've seen the most amazing things, so many different animals, and the scenery is fantastic. But it hasn't been easy; sleeping in a tent on the mountainside when it's pouring with rain isn't much fun. We didn't dare stay in the mountain stations, because you have to give your name. Maybe we were being a little paranoid, but on the other hand we've certainly had plenty of fresh air. I feel really good. We must do this next year, just the two of us!"

Krister paused for breath. "So how are things with you?"

Irene could see her reflection in the window of the conference room where her colleagues were sitting. The white dressing glowed on her multi-colored face; it was a dramatic look to say the least. But right now she didn't have the energy to go through everything that had happened, so keeping her tone as light as possible, she simply said:

"Oh you know, same as usual."

WHEN SUNDAY FINALLY arrived, Irene made an effort to produce a really good dinner, which meant ordering in food from a local restaurant. She couldn't help shuddering as she took the large Styrofoam box from the delivery guy.

"Just put everything back in the box when you're done; it would be great if you could rinse out the individual containers. Do you want me to pick it up, or will you drop it back?" he asked.

"We'll bring it back," Irene assured him.

She could see he was fascinated by her face, which by now was black and blue. He did his best to hide it, but she could tell from his expression that he understood why she didn't want to go out in public. To be honest, that wasn't why she had decided to order in. She didn't want to be stuck in the kitchen cooking, she wanted to spend time with her family. It felt like forever since they had left. They had been in Lapland, according to Krister, which was as far north as it was possible to go in Sweden. Hiding out in the wilds of nature was a smart idea if you were trying to avoid biker gangs. Outdoor life and physical activity weren't at the top of their agenda.

A little while later all four of them turned up. There

was a lot of hugging and kissing, and plenty of tears were shed. Egon hurtled around like a lunatic, beside himself with joy at being back home with his mistress once more. Irene's heart was positively dancing in her breast. Her beloved family was safely back home. They looked incredibly healthy, which was more than could be said about her. They were horrified by the sight of her bruised and battered face, of course, but at least they were prepared to a certain extent. After spending Saturday recuperating, Irene had called Krister in the evening to explain what had really happened in the explosion. He and the girls had already trawled the Internet and various newspapers and knew the basics. Irene described her colorful appearance, but reassured them that it looked worse than it was.

She opened a bottle of sparkling wine and poured it into champagne glasses, with alcohol-free cider for Jenny. A pleasurable calm suffused her body; it was partly due to the wine, but the main reason was the knowledge that the nightmare they had been living was over at last. In a while they would tuck into the food, but first of all Irene wanted to enjoy this time together. They had gotten their lives back.

Krister sipped the ice-cold wine with enjoyment, then helped himself to a handful of salted almonds. He looked at Irene for a long time.

"What?" she said eventually.

"We were wondering about something when we were on our way back, after we heard what had happened. The bomb at Pravda . . ." He finished off his wine and placed his glass carefully on the coffee table. "I don't supposed you managed to sneak in there *before* the bad guys had their meeting?"

"Before . . . ? What are you . . ."

Irene broke off as she realized what he meant. After everything she had gone through, her own family was accusing her of having planted the bomb inside Pravda! Just as she was about to hit the roof, she saw the glint in her husband's eye, and noticed the girls exchanging glances.

Okay, so they were teasing her. Fine. She was perfectly capable of giving as good as she got. She tipped her head on one side and assumed an expression of wide-eyed innocence.

"Has Tommy been telling tales? It must have been him. He's the only one who knew about my little reconnaissance mission."

She hid her smile behind the rim of her glass as she watched them exchanging glances that were a little more anxious this time. They weren't sure whether she was joking or not. As far as Irene was concerned, they could carry on wondering.

Author's Note

I'VE BEEN THINKING about this book for several years. I have watched with growing anxiety as the criminal gangs have increased in number and acquired greater power. This means that more and more people will be affected by their activities, both directly and indirectly. My aim has been to show how their ruthless violence can impact just about anyone.

Over the years I have discussed the spread of gang violence with several well-informed police officers, and I would particularly like to thank Detective Inspector Torbjörn Åhgren with the CSI in Västra Götaland, who has been immensely helpful.

All resemblance to any person living or dead is coincidental and not the intention of the author, and the events in my books are the product of my imagination. As usual I have taken considerable liberties with geographical facts. I do not adapt my narrative to suit the existing geography; reality is adapted to fit the story instead. And to be honest, Kolgruvegatan isn't quite as rough as I have depicted it here.

Helene Tursten

Continue reading for a preview of *Hunting Game*,
the first book in Helene Tursten's new mystery series
featuring Detective Inspector Embla Nyström.

AFTER NINE ROCK-HARD rounds, the sweat was
dripping from both combatants and their movements
were noticeably slower. The boxer in the red-and-
white top tried a few attacks against the opponent's
stomach but couldn't make a solid hit. The boxer in
blue and yellow immediately rallied and answered
with a quick series of short jabs against the red-and-
white's leather helmet to the heated shouts of the
spectators. A few of the hits landed solidly, and one
made the opponent stagger. The match was even and
the outcome uncertain.

When the gong sounded the referee blew the whistle,
and the fighters went to their respective corners of the
ring. They spit out mouth protectors, and the trainers
gave them dry towels to wipe themselves with. Both
drank some water but poured most of it over their faces
to revive themselves.

The boxers were called up and stood on either side of
the referee. He took their hands and held them along his
sides until the three judges reported their scores. When
he raised the victor's arm toward the ceiling, an ear-
splitting cheer broke out.

"Embla Nyström is the new Nordic light welterweight

champion!" a voice announced, barely audible over the audience's ovations.

All the new gold medalist heard as she raised her arms toward the ceiling was the acclaim of the crowd. In the rush of victory, she felt neither fatigue nor pain. Smiling happily, she stood in the middle of the ring and let the cheers wash over her.

After a glance at her face, the trainer started carefully guiding Embla in the direction of the locker room. She was bleeding above one eye and had to wipe blood away several times with the towel. It didn't bother her in the least; she was radiantly happy.

THE SECRETARY SLIPPED quietly through the doorway with a small tray in her hands and set it down discreetly on the antique mahogany desk. Beside it she placed the day's mail in a neat pile before slipping out again. Anders von Beehn nodded curtly in thanks and continued his phone call.

For a long time he listened to the voice from the other side of the Atlantic. Finally he stretched in his chair and said, "Yes, I'm looking forward to seeing you in New York, too. Bye."

When he hung up his smile faded. Doing business with Americans was quite different than it was with Europeans. Yankees may sound easy-going, but he knew not to let himself relax. After many years at the top of the Swedish business world he was no fledgling and felt rather certain that he would succeed in pulling off the deal. In just a few more months, Scandinvest would be at the top of the list of Sweden's most successful family-owned companies.

A few days off during moose-hunting season felt well-deserved; he had been working hard on this cooperation agreement. The low-key trip to the hunting cabin was just what he needed to wind down and get a fresh burst of energy before the final negotiations.

He always opened his personal mail after morning coffee, and a small padded envelope caught his attention. He picked it up and assessed its weight it in his hand. He squeezed it carefully. Hard and lumpy. *How strange.*

He set it down gently on the desk and pressed the intercom. "Was the padded envelope X-rayed?" he asked.

"Yes. It's a key chain."

Anders von Beehn slit open the envelope and peeked inside. He reached in and fished out a key ring with no keys. He recognized the BMW logo inside the plastic ring at once.

He sat there a long time, looking at the key ring. What was the meaning? Advertising? A joke? He had a hard time seeing what was funny. Over the years he'd had several BMWs. And a lot of other makes, too, for that matter. Right now the family owned four cars, one of which was actually a new BMW, which his wife, Linda, drove.

When he turned the envelope upside-down and shook it, a slip of paper came floating out and settled on the shiny desktop. He read it several times without understanding a thing.

I remember. M.

M? He noted that the text on both the note and the envelope was printed, not handwritten.

Who was M? Suddenly he felt the coffee churning in his stomach. M. That wasn't possible, was it? Was someone trying to mess with him? Trying to scare him? Who knew about M? Jan-Eric, naturally. But he would never do anything like this. He had never even wanted to talk about it. No, not Jan-Eric. Who? Ola. But Ola was dead.

• • •

THE AUTOMATIC GATES slowly closed behind the heavy motorcycle. The driver braked with the engine on idle. He unlocked the mailbox on the inside of the wall and emptied it. He stuffed the letters inside his motor-cycle jacket before he stepped on the gas and continued down the lane with its newly planted trees.

Whistling, he unlocked the door that led into the house from the garage. Purposefully he guided his steps toward the kitchen. Or rather the refrigerator. Sitting with a couple of beers in the warm Jacuzzi was part of his usual evening routine. If he had the energy he would also swim a few laps in the big pool. Nowadays his body got stiff after a longer motorcycle ride. *You're starting to feel that you'll be turning fifty in a few months*, he thought, grimacing at his reflection in the glass door to the patio. Money can take care of many things, but the passage of time can't be stopped. He carefully drew his hand across his thinning hair.

No, he wasn't going to get gloomy now. It was Friday evening, tomorrow he would pack for the moose hunt and later in the afternoon drive to Dalsland. He was truly looking forward to Saturday's traditional hunting dinner.

He tossed the mail on one of the gleaming stone coun-ters. He opened the brushed-steel refrigerator, took out a can of Czech beer, and opened it. As always just hearing the fizzing sound filled him with pleasure.

He opened the patio door wide and went out onto the large deck. With a deep breath he drew the fresh autumn air into his lungs. When he went in to get another beer his eyes fell on the letters. Might as well open them before he got into the Jacuzzi along with a few more beers.

From the magnetic holder over the stove he took down a sharp Japanese steel knife and quickly slit open all the envelopes. One of them gave him pause. It was a small, square, padded envelope. His name was printed on a label: *Jan-Eric Cahneborg*. He turned the envelope over, but there was no return address.

Puzzled, he pulled out a thin, black piece of fabric that was inside. It took a few seconds before he realized what it was. A bandanna? He peeked into the envelope to see if it contained anything else. At the bottom he glimpsed a small slip of paper. With some difficulty he managed to coax it out. The text was printed out from a computer.

I remember. M.

Jan-Eric Cahneborg gasped. His facial color changed to a sickly grayish white, and he had to support himself against the granite counter.

SUNSET TURNED THE white facade of Dalsnäs Manor a shade of pink. A clear, sunny autumn day was coming to an end. Anders von Beehn looked at the weather forecast for the next three days. Temperatures below freezing were predicted at night, with some chance of sun during the days but no warmth, three degrees above freezing max. Cold, but promising. It was important that the hunt be successful, especially since Volker Heinz was coming. Heinz was the owner of DEIGI, one of Germany's largest investment companies and Scand-invest's most important European partner. Besides that, he was a key player in the negotiations with the US because he had been landing deals with the Americans for a long time. Von Beehn had also invited Scandin-vest's lead attorney, Lennart Folkesson. He was a smart strategist and together they could probably handle the good Heinz.

Within half an hour three new luxury cars were gleaming on the well-raked gravel roundabout in front of the manor. A short distance away was a Hummer H3 Alpha. The big car was von Beehn's pride. He had imported it directly from the US. The Hummer was extended, classified as a limousine, and could take eight passengers with no problem. The back seats could be laid flat when you needed extra room for your baggage. As he liked to say, the engine drank gas as if someone had fired a hail of large-bore buckshot into the fuel tank, but the heavy car could go anywhere and was built like a small tank, which was a prerequisite for navigating the roads up to their destination: the Hunting Castle, as they had taken to calling it. The Hummer was used only for transport during the hunt; otherwise it was parked in the garage at Dalsnäs. Now his new Jaguar XJR was parked there instead. It would have been nice to have it out on the yard, too, simply to show off its beauty, but it would have been a bit cramped.

Last of all Greger Liljon skidded in front of the steps with his new Maserati. The young man, who was recently appointed as CEO of one of Scandinvest's smallest companies, was hanging on a slender thread. Greger was surely aware of his standing, but Von Beehn intended to speak with him about it after the hunt. The most recent quarterly reports had been catastrophic. Actually it was Greger who was the catastrophe. *Incompetent*, von Beehn thought, but he did not let his face betray his thoughts. With a warm hug, he welcomed his nephew.

The host escorted his guests through the hall and up the broad stairs to the upper floor, where the doors to the terrace were open. They stepped out to admire the view of the lake. The last rays of the sun glistened on the slightly rippled surface. Here and there a bright red maple blazed among the deciduous trees ringing the lake.

As beautiful as an ad, von Beehn thought contentedly. Smiling, he handed a glass of Champagne to each of the guests. Once everyone was holding a glass he said in impeccable English, "Dear friends, welcome to Dalsnäs. Cheers to a good moose hunt!"

He raised the Champagne flute and the sun's last streak of light reflected in the cut crystal. The others followed his example, nodded to each other, and toasted.

When everyone had taken a sip von Beehn cleared his throat.

"Last year the three musketeers were on the scene. We've stayed together for more than forty years, Jan-Eric, Ola, and me. This year Ola is no longer with us." He turned to Volker. "To fill you in, he died in a car accident as he was driving home to Oslo after last year's moose hunt here at Dalsnäs. Our friend leaves behind a big hole that is impossible to fill. I want to make a toast to the memory of our friend and comrade Ola Forsnaess. To the memory of Ola!"

Everyone raised their glasses again, this time with serious expressions. They sipped the Champagne, and the conversation was subdued for a few minutes. Volker Heinz was the only one of the men on the terrace who had never met Ola Forsnaess. Obviously he, too, was moved by the emotional speech, but after a while he started talking with the others about things more near at hand, like the impending hunt. His enthusiasm and hopes were contagious, and an expectant mood spread on the terrace. When the last drop of Champagne was swallowed and the sun had long since disappeared behind the hills, they went in and sat down to dinner.

AFTER DINNER THE gentlemen moved to the library. The fire had started to die down but Anders fed it some sturdy logs, and soon a blaze was roaring in the open fireplace. The flickering light from the flames made the gold foil on the leather spines shine behind the glass doors of the bookshelves. Sated and content, they sat comfortably submerged in the English Chesterfield furniture. The whiskey they drank had been aged for eighteen years. Excellent, they were all in agreement about that, especially Jan-Eric Cahneborg, who enthusiastically requested refills several times.

When Anders went out into the kitchen to get another bottle, Jan-Eric followed him on unsteady legs.

"Anders . . . listen . . . we need to . . . talk." He spit out the words as he stumbled.

"Not now, Janne."

"It's im . . . important!"

The desperation in Jan-Eric's voice was clear. He swayed as he stood in the middle of the kitchen.

"A bandanna . . . a fucking ban . . . danna . . . who sent . . . who would send . . . such a thing?" he said, hiccoughing.

Anders almost sobered up when he heard what his friend was saying. "Did you get something in the mail?" He started to feel the burning pain in his stomach again. He recalled the key ring with the BMW logo and the little slip of paper that had floated out of the padded envelope.

"Of course you . . . understand. An envelope . . ."

With the new bottle in one hand Anders went up to his friend and took firm hold of his upper arm with his free hand and guided him toward the library. "We'll talk about this later," he hissed in his friend's ear.

• • •

THE GRAVEL SPRAYED around the tires of the Volvo 245 as Embla did a donut on the farmyard before coming to a stop, as she always did that when she pulled into Nisse's place. It was her way of signaling she had arrived. The move always made her uncle chuckle with delight, saying, "Here comes hot-rod girl" as she barged into his otherwise peaceful existence. The first time he had said that, Embla had been fifteen and had "borrowed" her brother's moped and driven all the way from Gothenburg. En route she had spent the night with a cousin and his family outside Vänersborg. She never would have made it otherwise. The soreness in her rear padding had persisted for several days. When she was going home again, her uncle had lowered the back seat in his Volvo 245, loaded the moped into the cargo space, and driven her home to Gothenburg.

Three years later he had given Embla that car when she got her driver's license.

She'd had the car for ten years, and at this point it had almost three hundred thousand kilometers on it. Even though the car was starting to show a few signs of old age, Embla loved it. The most serious complaints were that the speedometer was unreliable and the fuel gauge didn't work. After running out of gas a few times in the middle of nowhere she always had a full can of gas with her when she drove long distances.

As Embla got out of the car she heard Seppo's loud barking coming from the back of the house. Because he didn't come rushing around the corner she figured the Swedish elkhound must be in the dog run.

The front door opened wide and Nisse came out on the steps with a broad smile and outstretched arms.

"Hey there, hot-rod girl!"

He gave her a bear hug. She drilled her nose into his blue checked flannel shirt and took in the scent of barn and sweat. The smell of Nisse, her beloved uncle who was made of the same robust stuff as her mother, Sonja, and herself. Like his sister, he'd had a red, curly mop of hair in his youth. Nowadays only Embla and the youngest of her three brothers retained the family's striking hair color. Sonja's and Nisse's hair had turned gray, and as far as her uncle was concerned, there was almost nothing left on the top of his head. It hardly bothered him because he kept it cut short with his electric razor. It suited him and gave him a tough look.

"And the Veteran keeps on chugging," he said, giving the car a tender pat on the hood.

"You bet. Runs like a clock!"

That wasn't quite true but Embla knew that was what her uncle wanted to hear. The Volvo was the apple of his eye. He was also the one who had christened the car. At first she thought it sounded silly, but now she referred to it as the Veteran, too.

"Settle in while I take a shower and tidy up. As usual we're going to see Karin and Björn," he said.

Karin was the only one of her cousins who was still living in the village. She was the daughter of Nisse and Sonja's older sister. Her aunt and uncle had lived in Uddevalla for almost twenty years now. There they had worked in their one son's retail nursery, but now they were both retired. They felt at home on the coast and intended to stay there.

Even though Karin was five years older than Embla, the two cousins had spent quite a bit of time together on summer vacations. Karin also had older brothers—though only two—so over the years, they each became the sister the other had always wished for.

Nisse had been a widower for three years. He and Ann-Sofie had been happily married, but they never had any children, which had been a source of grief. During summer vacations Embla and her three brothers compensated for that properly. The boys got tired of rural life in their teens but she loved it. Maybe to some degree it was because she got to escape her brothers, but mostly it was because she felt at home with life in the countryside and on the farm.

For a while she had seriously considered becoming a farmer but hesitated because she knew what drudgery the job entailed. The farm could not even support Nisse and Ann-Sofie; he worked at the sawmill and she delivered newspapers.

It was Nisse who suggested that Embla start boxing. He himself had been district champion in his weight class before he got married and took over the farm. Perhaps he had seen that she needed an outlet for all the anxiety she harbored as a teenager, though she hadn't brought it up or told him where the racing thoughts came from.

She had never told anyone about Lollo.

It was also her uncle who had sparked her interest in hunting the summer she turned fifteen. He had asked her if she wanted to go still-hunting; a group planned to shoot some of the mangy foxes that had been seen in the area. Of course Embla thought that sounded really exciting and said yes at once. But it wasn't nearly as thrilling as she had hoped. Sometimes they all stood motionless before someone would suddenly start sneaking

carefully in a direction where he thought he saw a movement or heard some rustling. They never saw a trace of
any fox, with or without mange.

Despite that uneventful introduction, Embla had
become interested, and for the next three years she took
part in the drive during the moose hunt. When she
turned eighteen she took the hunting test. Since then
she and Nisse had hunted together several times a year.
Mostly they hunted in the fall, starting in early August
when deer and wild boar were in season.

Embla unpacked and hung up her clothes in the min-
imal wardrobe. There was a shower enclosure in the guest
bathroom, but she had showered before she left Gothenburg. A few dabs of deodorant, a couple sprays of perfume,
and a nice-looking sweater would have to do. Mascara
and lip gloss was more than enough makeup; she would
only be meeting with the hunting party.

Nisse was waiting down the hall. Dressed in a fresh
white shirt, light-blue knit sweater, light gray chinos, and
new light-gray leather shoes, he looked like he could be
on the cover of GQ. Around him was a light air of the
aftershave she had given him as a Christmas present the
year before.

"How stylish you are! What's her name?" Embla asked
happily.

His weathered face took on a shade of polished copper.
"Uh . . . or . . . Ingela," he stammered.

"How nice! Ingela Franzén?"

"The pastor's widow! Are you crazy? No, Ingela Gus-
tavsson at the Ica store. You know who she is, don't you?"

It took a moment for Embla to place her. "Light,
rather short, a bit younger than you . . ."

"Yes. She is. Although we . . . People talk. You know how it is . . ."

Here stood her retired uncle, hemming and hawing like a shy teenager trying to talk about his first serious infatuation. It was a bit moving but not that strange, considering that he and Ann-Sofie had been together since they were confirmed.

She gave him a big hug. "That's so great!" Smiling, she handed him one of the wine boxes she had brought with her. "Now let's go to the party and charge up before the hunt! Yee-haw!"

They put on their jackets and went out to the stable. There were Nisse's and Ann-Sofie's old bicycles, shining clean and ready to ride. Nisse always got the bicycles in order before the dinner that kicked off the year's moose hunt. He didn't want to have anything to do with drunk driving—not in a car, anyway. But the equivalent on something with handlebars he could overlook.

Leighton Gage
(Brazil)
Blood of the Wicked
Buried Strangers
Dying Gasp
Every Bitter Thing
A Vine in the Blood
Perfect Hatred
The Ways of Evil Men

Michael Genelin
(Slovakia)
Siren of the Waters
Dark Dreams
The Magician's Accomplice
Requiem for a Gypsy

Timothy Hallinan
(Thailand)
The Fear Artist
For the Dead
The Hot Countries
Fools' River

(Los Angeles)
Crashed
Little Elvises
The Fame Thief
Herbie's Game
King Maybe
Fields Where They Lay

Karo Hämäläinen
(Finland)
Cruel Is the Night

Mette Ivie Harrison
(Mormon Utah)
The Bishop's Wife
His Right Hand
For Time and All Eternities

Mick Herron
(England)
Down Cemetery Road
The Last Voice You Hear
Reconstruction
Smoke and Whispers
Why We Die
Slow Horses
Dead Lions

Mick Herron cont.
Nobody Walks
Real Tigers
Spook Street
This Is What Happened
London Rules

**Lene Kaaberbøl &
Agnete Friis**
(Denmark)
The Boy in the Suitcase
Invisible Murder
Death of a Nightingale
The Considerate Killer

Heda Margolius Kovály
(1950s Prague)
Innocence

Martin Limón
(South Korea)
Jade Lady Burning
Slicky Boys
Buddha's Money
The Door to Bitterness
The Wandering Ghost
G.I. Bones
Mr. Kill
The Joy Brigade
Nightmare Range
The Iron Sickle
The Ville Rat
Ping-Pong Heart
The Nine-Tailed Fox

Ed Lin
(Taiwan)
Ghost Month
Incensed

Peter Lovesey
(England)
The Circle
The Headhunters
False Inspector Dew
Rough Cider
On the Edge
The Reaper

(Bath, England)
The Last Detective

Peter Lovesey cont.
Diamond Solitaire
The Summons
Bloodhounds
Upon a Dark Night
The Vault
Diamond Dust
The House Sitter
The Secret Hangman
Skeleton Hill
Stagestruck
Cop to Corpse
The Tooth Tattoo
The Stone Wife
*Down Among
the Dead Men*
Another One Goes Tonight
Beau Death

(London, England)
Wobble to Death
*The Detective Wore
Silk Drawers*
Abracadaver
Mad Hatter's Holiday
The Tick of Death
A Case of Spirits
Swing, Swing Together
Waxwork

Jassy Mackenzie
(South Africa)
Random Violence
Stolen Lives
The Fallen
Pale Horses
Bad Seeds

Sujata Massey
(1920s Bombay)
*The Widows of
Malabar Hill*

Francine Mathews
(Nantucket)
Death in the Off-Season
Death in Rough Water
Death in a Mood Indigo
Death in a Cold Hard Light
Death on Nantucket

Seichō Matsumoto
(Japan)
Inspector Imanishi
Investigates

Magdalen Nabb
(Italy)
Death of an Englishman
Death of a Dutchman
Death in Springtime
Death in Autumn
The Marshal and
the Murderer
The Marshal and
the Madwoman
The Marshal's Own Case
The Marshal Makes
His Report
The Marshal
at the Villa Torrini
Property of Blood
Some Bitter Taste
The Innocent
Vita Nuova
The Monster of Florence

Fuminori Nakamura
(Japan)
The Thief
Evil and the Mask
Last Winter, We Parted
The Kingdom
The Boy in the Earth
Cult X

Stuart Neville
(Northern Ireland)
The Ghosts of Belfast
Collusion
Stolen Souls
The Final Silence
Those We Left Behind
So Say the Fallen

(Dublin)
Ratlines

Rebecca Pawel
(1930s Spain)
Death of a Nationalist
Law of Return
The Watcher in the Pine
The Summer Snow

Kwei Quartey
(Ghana)
Murder at Cape
Three Points
Gold of Our Fathers
Death by His Grace

Qiu Xiaolong
(China)
Death of a Red Heroine
A Loyal Character Dancer
When Red Is Black

John Straley
(Sitka, Alaska)

The Woman Who Married
a Bear
The Curious Eat Themselves
The Music of What Happens
Death and the Language of
Happiness
The Angels Will Not Care
Cold Water Burning
Baby's First Felony

(Cold Storage, Alaska)
The Big Both Ways
Cold Storage, Alaska

Akimitsu Takagi
(Japan)
The Tattoo Murder Case
Honeymoon to Nowhere
The Informer

Helene Tursten
(Sweden)
Detective Inspector Huss
The Torso
The Glass Devil
Night Rounds

Helene Tursten cont.
The Golden Calf
The Fire Dance
The Beige Man
The Treacherous Net
Who Watcheth
Protected by the Shadows

Janwillem van de
Wetering
(Holland)
Outsider in Amsterdam
Tumbleweed
The Corpse on the Dike
Death of a Hawker
The Japanese Corpse
The Blond Baboon
The Maine Massacre
The Mind-Murders
The Streetbird
The Rattle-Rat
Hard Rain
Just a Corpse at Twilight
Hollow-Eyed Angel
The Perfidious Parrot
The Sergeant's Cat:
Collected Stories

Timothy Williams
(Guadeloupe)
Another Sun
The Honest Folk
of Guadeloupe

(Italy)
Converging Parallels
The Puppeteer
Persona Non Grata
Black August
Big Italy
The Second Day
of the Renaissance

Jacqueline Winspear
(1920s England)
Maisie Dobbs
Birds of a Feather